POPULAR PUBLICATIONS · FACSIMILE EDITIONS

Dime Detective Magazine #14
(December 1932)

Dime Detective magazine was the flagship detective pulp in the Popular Publications stable, running for almost 300 issues over twenty years. The December 1932 issue contains stories by T.T. Flynn, Erle Stanley Gardner, and Frederick Nebel, and includes installments in the Cardigan, Dane Skarle, and Val Easton series.

Authors:

T.T. Flynn, Frederick Nebel, Erle Stanley Gardner, Richard J. Credicott, Joseph Mulvaney

Illustrators:

William Reusswig, John Fleming Gould

10¢ DIME DETECTIVE MAGAZINE

EVERY STORY COMPLETE   EVERY STORY NEW

Vol. 4   CONTENTS for DECEMBER, 1932   No. 2

Watch for the January Issue   On the Newsstands December 15th

---

Published every month by Popular Publications, Inc., 2256 Grove Street, Chicago Illinois. Editorial and executive offices 205 East Forty-second Street, New York City. Harry Steeger, President and Secretary, Harold S. Goldsmith, Vice President and Treasurer. Entered as second class matter Feb. 26, 1932, at the Post Office at Chicago, Ill., under the Act of March 3, 1879. Title registration pending at U. S. Patent Office. Copyrited 1932 by Popular Publications, Inc. Single copy price 10c. Yearly subscriptions in U. S. A. $1.00. For advertising rates address Sam J. Perry, 205 E. 42nd St., New York, N. Y. When submitting manuscripts, kindly enclose sufficient postage for their return if found unavailable. The publishers cannot accept responsibility for return of unsolicited manuscripts, although all care will be exercised in handling them.

This Amazing New
ROTARY SLICING MACHINE
is making Salesmen RICH

SLICES MEATS

Bologna, Tongue, and meats of most every description are sliced evenly, uniformly, and as quick as a flash. Cheese, too, is easy to slice with the General Slicer.

SLICES BREAD

Fresh Bread never crumbles when the "General" goes to work. Clean-cut, appetizing slices—thick or thin—drop off the whirling blade in rapid succession.

SLICES FRUITS & VEGETABLES

Oranges, apples, peaches, carrots, cabbage and potatoes—can be sliced in new and more tempting ways with the General Slicer.

POTATO CHIPS, NOODLES, ETC.

Potatoes cut so thin, the raw potato slice folds in half without breaking! That makes crispy, crunchy chips! And noodles—fine or coarse—and luscious Cole-Slaw!

Territories Now Open for Wide-Awake Me

Imagine a slicing machine that operates on the same rotary spinning principle used by $500.00 slicers—a machine that slices EVERYTHING—yet costs only $4.95! That's the new General Slicer! It's a storekeeper's dream come true.

The men who are selling this amazing miracle machine are reaping a harvest of cash profits. The minute it's demonstrated, the sale is clinched. Picture slicing a whole bread in 37 seconds; perfect, uniform slices. Or cutting an orange so thin you can actually see through each slice.

Up to now, rotary slicing machines cost from $200.00 to $500.00. Every storekeeper wanted one but few could afford it. But now the General—the miracle slicer at $4.95—is winning easy orders from coast to coast. Is it any wonder that General

salesmen are reaping $90.00 to $150. weekly? You can join this prospero group.

No house-to-house canvassing. No knocking doors. The General Slicing Machine sells STORES. Orders await you at every lunche ette, butcher, tea room, delicatessen, drug sto lunch wagon, restaurant, and road stand. Ambitious men who are anxious to get out the rut of a small pay job—men who are ti of worrying about "lay-offs" and wage cut men who are not afraid of big money—m who have the energy and spirit to profit w a real live organization that's sweeping nation with this new sensational specialty—invited to mail the coupon for full details. few spare time workers are needed, too. even if you are employed, you can double triple your income during spare hours. Wr at once. Territories are going fast. Gr yours now. Mail the coupon.

GENERAL
SLICING MACHINE CO.
635 West 158th St.
Dept. A   NEW YORK, N. Y.

4

5

Half a Million People
have learned music this easy way

You, too, Can Learn to Play Your Favorite Instrument Without a Teacher

Easy as A-B-C

YES, over half a million delighted men and women all over the world have learned music this quick, easy way.

Half a million—what a gigantic orchestra they would make! Some are playing on the stage, others in orchestras, and many thousands are daily enjoying the pleasure and popularity of being able to play some instrument.

Surely this is convincing proof of the success of the new, modern method perfected by the U. S. School of Music! And what these people have done, YOU, too, can do!

Many of this half million didn't know one note from another—others had never touched an instrument—yet in half the usual time they learned to play their favorite instrument. Best of all, they found learning music **amazingly** easy. No monotonous hours of exercises—no tedious scales—no expensive teachers. This simplified method made learning music as easy as A-B-C!

It is like a fascinating game. From the very start you are playing real tunes, perfectly, by note. You simply can't go wrong, for every step, from beginning to end, is right before your eyes in print and picture. First you are told how to do a thing, then a picture shows you how, then you do it yourself and hear it. And almost before you know it, you are playing your favorite pieces —jazz, ballads, classics. No private teacher could make it clearer. Little theory—plenty of accomplishment. That's why students of the U. S. School of Music get ahead twice as fast—three times as fast as those who study old-fashioned, plodding methods.

You don't need any special "talent." Many of the [h]alf million who have already become accomplished pla[yers] never dreamed they possessed musical ability. They [only] wanted to play some instrument—just like you—and [they] found they could quickly learn how this easy way. Ju[st a] little of your spare time each day is needed—and [you'll] enjoy every minute of it. The cost is surprisingly lo[w,] averaging only a few cents a day—and the price is [the] same for whatever instrument you choose. And remem[ber] you are studying right in your own home—without pa[ying] big fees to private teachers.

Don't miss any more good times! Learn now to [play] your favorite instrument and surprise all your frie[nds.] Change from a wallflower to the center of attracti[on.] Music is the best thing to offer at a party—music[ians] are invited everywhere. Enjoy the popularity you [have] been missing. Get your share of the musician's pleas[ure] and profit! Start now!

Free Booklet and Demonstration Lesson

If you are in earnest about wanting to join the crow[d of] entertainers and be a "big hit" at any party—if you re[ally] do want to play your favorite instrument, to becom[e a] performer whose services will be in demand—fill out [and] mail the convenient coupon asking for our Free Boo[k] and Free Demonstration Lesson. These explain our w[on]derful method fully and show you how easily and qui[ckly] you can learn to play at little expense. This booklet [will] also tell you all about the amazing new Automatic Fi[nger] Control. Instruments are supplied when needed—cas[h or] credit. U. S. School of Music, 36712 Brunswick B[ldg.,] New York City. Thirty-fourth year (Established 1[898).]

WHAT INSTRUMENT FOR YOU?

Piano	Piccolo
Organ	Hawaiian
Violin	Steel
Clarinet	Guitar
Flute	Drums and
Harp	Traps
Cornet	Mandolin
'Cello	Sight Singing
Guitar	Trombone
Ukulele	Piano
Saxophone	Accordion
Banjo (Plectrum, 5-String or Tenor)	
Voice and Speech Culture	
Harmony and Composition	
Automatic Finger Control	
Italian and German Accordion	
Juniors' Piano Course	

7

The Black Doctor

by

T. T. Flynn

Author of "The Red Venom," etc.

The needle was bending toward her wrist.

Across a world-wide chessboard of mystery and danger he moves his human pawns—this ghastly man-monster with the green-flecked eyes. And only Val Easton, crack Secret Service operative, knew the defense to check his ghoulish gambit—corner the Black Doctor in a murder mate.

CHAPTER ONE

S13

IT WAS the last evening on the *Laurentic*, the last dinner before quarantine, and the slow progress up the bay past the Statue of Liberty and into the river where snorting tugs would skilfully guide the big liner into her berth.

A COMPLETE NOVELETTE

Six days out from Southampton, the *Laurentic* had found five days of bad weather, of plunging seas and gale-swept decks. Four days in which fully half the passengers had remained below, shunning decks, games, amusements—and food.

But all that had passed magically. The skies had cleared. The sweeping seas had smoothed in the sunny calm that followed. And now the big dining saloon was crowded. Val Easton ate with only half an ear on the table conversation.

His mind was on other things. The mission that had taken him to London and Rome, by way of Paris, and then back to London again. The weeks of piecing together tiny bits of information to make the pattern which took shape in his final report. It had been good work too. The cable from his chief, calling him back to Washington, had said so.

A fragment of the conversation jerked his attention back to the table, without sign of it showing on his lean features.

The full-bosomed woman at the head of the table—a Mrs. Beamish—had said aggressively: "The whole thing was bosh! In wartime, perhaps. But not now. Spies are as old-fashioned as the dodo bird." And Mrs. Beamish glared around the table as if daring anyone to take issue with her over the matter.

They were, Val realized, talking about the picture that had been shown the evening before. One of the latest thrillers built around the adventures of a famous woman spy during the War.

Most of them had seen it. The discussion at once became heated. The most outspoken was the blond young Mr. Miller at Mrs. Beamish's left, who looked like a poet just out of college, and who stood by his convictions heatedly.

"Of course there are spies," he protested. "They're always working. You read about them all the time."

"And see silly pictures about them," Mrs. Beamish declared sarcastically.

"That picture was based on historical facts," he said with the positive assurance of youth. "Whether you liked it or not, it happened. Why—why, any of us here at the table might be a spy! I might be one, working for a foreign government." And visibly set up by the thought, he looked gallantly across the table at the pretty girl on Val's right.

VAL smiled inwardly. It seemed funny, this talk about spies. Almost like a fiction story. Something sinister and diabolical about it. He wondered if he looked the part. Wondered too, what would happen if this tableful of peaceful travelers were apprized of his identity, and could look for a moment into the roiling currents of international intrigue.

But Mrs. Beamish leaned forward with a glitter in her eye. "Young man," she asked sharply, "did you ever see a spy?"

"Er—well, no."

"Ahhh!" said Mrs. Beamish with a cutting smile, and leaned back in her chair as if that settled everything. And young Miller's weak retort of "How would I know one if I saw him? They don't go labeled," made no impression in her self-satisfied armor.

There was a chuckle from the slender, middle-aged Englishman who had sat at the end of the table every meal, beaming through rimless eyeglasses and talking books and authors to whomsoever would listen. Carmody was his name, a book salesman on a business trip to the States. Now he smiled and bobbed his head as he leaned forward and spoke.

"I fancy Mrs. Beamish is more than a little bit right. This is not wartime, nor is there the wide interest in such things that we had in the days of the old world-wide Imperial German spy service. My firm, by the way, has published two books on such things and I can—er—modestly claim to know something about it. Spies are practically as dead as the dodo. We have about as much chance of finding one here at the table as we have of missing our dinner in New York tomorrow evening." And Carmody beamed at them all.

The young man retorted sulkily: "Just the same, I'm still betting on spies. You might be one yourself."

"Ha ha, so I might," Carmody chortled. "And if you'll drop around to the nearest bookstore as soon as you land, at least I'll guarantee you a corking good book on the subject. Make your hair stand up no end if you believe everything that's in it."

"I don't have to read a book to have my mind made up," young Miller said darkly, and applied himself to his dessert with irritated jabs of his spoon.

Val said to Carmody good naturedly as he left the table: "I may get that book myself. I've always been curious about such things."

"Do," Carmody beamed. "At least it's jolly good reading. Almost made me wish I had been one myself back in the days when they were taken seriously."

A trim, blue-uniformed young man from the Marconi room came in, paging, "Mr. Easton. Mr. Easton."

Val lifted a finger; the blue uniform met him and an envelope was placed in his hands. "Radiogram, sir."

Val tore it open and deciphered the coded message with the ease of long practice.

V EASTON
ON BOARD SS LAURENTIC
CONTACT S13 BEAMISH ASSIST
IF NEEDED

        SIGNED GREGG

Sheer amazement almost made Val wheel around and glance back at the table. The signature "Gregg" was the code word for the chief, housed at the right elbow of the State Department in Washington. Its sense was plain. Its information stunning. And for the thou-

sandth time Val was swept with admiration for the perfection of the intricate and farflung web of which he was only one strand.

S13—Beamish.

Only one meaning to that. That full-bosomed, majestic woman, who had sat at the head of the table day after day on this crossing, was a part of the same web. That woman who looked like the stodgy, opinionated wife of some equally stodgy business man; that severe matron whose tall, slender daughter had appeared once briefly on deck with her, was—*must* be—a clever Intelligence operative.

Val smiled wryly at the thought of how he himself had swallowed her aggressive declaration that no longer did such people exist.

Why had she done it?

And Val paid her the compliment of believing that there had been a purpose behind it. He tucked the radiogram in his inside coat pocket and strolled out on deck.

HALF an hour later Val found Mrs. Beamish standing by the rail, peering pensively down at the endless ribbon of foam-flecked water that rushed astern. A blue coat was wrapped around her ample figure, a chiffon veil held her hair in place against the rush of the night breeze. Even now his critical scrutiny found it hard to believe she was the one Gregg referred to. He leaned against the rail beside her, said casually: "S13."

"What?" Mrs. Beamish demanded in a startled voice.

Val repeated it. She frowned at him. "Young man," she asked tartly, "is this a new way of flirting with an old woman like me?"

"Gregg suggested it," Val said idly.

"*Hmmmmp!*" said Mrs. Beamish shortly. She drew her coat closely around her shoulders, adjusted her veil slowly, turned and eyed him deliberately. A smile slowly broke over her angular face.

"So you're the one?" she said. "My, my—and to think we've been eating at the same table. Gregg radioed that one of his men would see us this evening. Come down and meet Nancy. She's been feeling bad the whole trip."

"Your daughter?"

Mrs. Beamish sniffed. "Bosh! It makes good atmosphere. Whoever would suspect an old fogy like me? I wish Nancy Fraser was my daughter. She's a girl in a million."

"Nancy Fraser? I've heard of her."

Val had indeed. Nancy Fraser, tales of whose daring ingenuity were already becoming classics of the Intelligence Service. An adept at disguise, a quick thinker, a beautiful girl, fearless, resourceful and blessed with uncanny luck was this Nancy Fraser.

MRS. BEAMISH, preceding him into the cabin on B Deck, said: "This is our man, Nance. Mr. Easton, Miss Fraser."

The girl who slid effortlessly to her feet from the bed almost took Val's breath away. She was softly feminine at first glance, a beauty with fine cleancut features, slightly sun-tanned. Her chin was firm and her mouth fairly wide, with a humorous quirk at the corners. She was a platinum blonde, and her silky hair, cut short, was waved close to her head in a style almost mannish.

He was to learn later that there was a reason for that. But at the moment he was conscious only of the calm, boring gaze of a pair of the bluest and deepest eyes he had ever seen. They took him apart in one swift look, examined the pieces—and approved. For she smiled and gave him a firm hand.

"I'm glad to see you, Mr. Easton. Sit down. This has been a rocky passage for me. I'm still a little wobbly."

"I was surprised to get Gregg's radiogram," Val told her as he seated himself. "I suppose something is up?"

Nancy Fraser's smile faded as she sank on the edge of the bed. She nodded. "Something is up. I coded Gregg a resumé of it, and he radioed back that he would have one of his men who was on the ship get in touch with me. I've been waiting for you."

"I would have guessed every other man on the ship," said Mrs. Beamish with a critical look at Val. "You're such a nice, harmless-looking young man. I thought you might be a college professor or a bond salesman."

The front of Nancy Fraser's silk negligée trembled as she laughed softly at Val's wry smile. "Don't mind Norah, Mr. Easton. She's apt to break out with some startling remarks."

"Hmmmp!" said Mrs. Beamish. "I say what I think, when it suits me."

Nancy Fraser became serious once more.

"Here's what we're up against, Mr. Easton. I'm working on a delicate matter. As near as I understand it, the stage is all set for some world-shaking moves that haven't even been hinted at in the newspapers. Anything may come out of it. The Shanghai business was only a move in a bigger game. Japan, Russia, England, France and Italy are all holding different hands in the Far East. Our government is vitally concerned. Treaties, agreements, protestations by statesmen are all for public consumption. Behind that the real moves are being made. The different foreign offices are the only ones who really know."

"And some of them don't know as much as they'd like to," Val commented.

"Exactly. None of them do. Each one is afraid of what the others may be doing. I doubt if the Intelligence Services have been half as busy since the War as they are now. Wires, cables and radio services are being tapped. Confidential codes being broken down and deciphered.

Mails are being watched. Intelligence operators planted where they can get at the contents of diplomatic pouches, and scores of men in high position are being watched day and night for some clue as to what their governments are driving at. It's a mess. World peace, or another war that will make the last look like a kindergarten exercise, are in the balance."

Val knew all that. But he liked the crisp way this Nancy Fraser went to the heart of the matter. He was seeing another side of the beautiful girl who had cordially greeted him. A woman, this, who was steely hard beneath her femininity; who thought straight and to the point.

"Where do you come in?" he questioned bluntly.

"At the moment I'm following a man who stands high in the British diplomatic service. A man who is coming to the States on a secret mission. He is traveling incognito as a Mr. Galbraith. I am confident he is carrying secret papers or instructions that can't be entrusted to the mails or cables."

"Who is he?"

"Sir Edward Lyne. A tall, thin man with a close-clipped black mustache."

"Haven't noticed him."

"Probably not. He has kept to his cabin most of the trip."

"That seems simple enough," Val said, offering his cigarettes to the two women, and holding a light for them.

Nancy Fraser leaned back on one arm and nodded. "It is simple enough. Only —we're being followed too."

Those last sharp, vibrant words brought a sudden tang of danger into the atmosphere of the cabin. Val snapped alert, eyed her keenly.

"Who is following you?"

Nancy Fraser shook her head. "That's the trouble," she confessed. "Neither Norah nor I have been able to find out.

But someone knows who we are, or suspects us. Our cabin was entered one of the few times we both were out of it. Entered, searched cleverly and left exactly as it had been."

"How did you discover it?"

Norah Beamish smiled proudly. "That girl is a wonder, Mr. Easton. She never leaves her room without fixing it so she knows at once whether it has been disturbed."

"A few little ends of silk thread that are never noticed when they are displaced," Nancy Fraser explained. "To make certain this time, I questioned the stewardess closely. She had not been in here."

She didn't have to say anything more. Too well Val understood why she was disturbed. It was bad enough to match wits with dangers one was aware of. But there was nothing more unnerving than to find that one's disguise had been penetrated, that unknown danger lurked close, and to be unable to discover it and take precautions. Until Nancy Fraser found out who had searched her cabin, she must suspect every one on the boat, must look for anything to happen at any hour of the day or night.

"Suspect anyone?" he prompted.

"No. We're up in the air."

The room had a narrow window opening on the promenade deck. A window halfway up, with the drawn curtains inside swaying slightly in the wind. And just as Nancy Fraser answered him, a harder gust than usual blew the right curtain aside. Val's eye caught a fleeting glimpse of a shoulder shifting hastily back to one side.

Someone was out there listening!

CHAPTER TWO

Death on B Deck

VAL made a catlike lunge to his feet, reached the window in a silent stride, and grabbed through it. As he expected, the shoulder was just outside. His fingers dug hard into the rough woolen cloth, and he jerked hard to bring the lurking figure over where he could see the face.

The other made no sound. But the hard edge of a taut palm struck the bone just above his wrist a terrific blow. It was *jiu-jitsu* skilfully, savagely and instantly applied. His hand went numb and useless, and the blinding pain shot above his elbow.

With a twist the shoulder tore away and was gone.

Val jerked his arm in, biting his lower lip against the gasp of agony that rushed to his teeth. Nancy Fraser had come to her feet alertly and was staring wide-eyed as Val whirled toward the door.

"Someone listening out there!" he threw at her, and jerked the door open with his good hand and rushed out on deck.

The promenade was brightly lighted. At least a score of people were visible from the back of the long sweep of deck. But most of them were leaning over the rail; the others were strolling astern. No one at the moment had his eyes fixed on the spot. And the deck was empty!

A deck bay was a few yards away. His man must have gone there. But when Val reached it he found the bay empty and none of the chairs occupied. The companion door at the back was closed. He opened it looked into the passage beyond, and swore under his breath. His man had moved fast and surely. Had gotten away. Val was forced to admit that fact after a few moments' search.

He met a steward in the passage, asked the man sharply: "Did you see a man come through here a few moments ago?"

His tense manner drew a curious look from the white-jacketed little Cockney.

"Ayn't seen a soul, sir."

"Sure?"

"H'I don't myke mistakes, sir. A man carn't afford to w'en 'e's holdin' down a nick on a top'oler like the *Laurentic*, sir. Is there something wrong?"

"Nothing," said Val, turning back. "Thank you."

NANCY FRASER had put on pumps and a coat that covered her negligée. She was standing near her door when Val returned. She met him with a questioning look.

"He got away," Val admitted unwillingly. "I was a fool to grab at him through the window like that. But I wanted a quick look at his face. He gave my wrist a crack that paralyzed it, and was gone."

"You didn't see him at all?"

"No."

"Let's take a turn around the deck," she said abruptly. "We've made a mess of things. Whoever it is knows you're with us now. I wish we had thought of that."

"I shouldn't have gone to your cabin," Val admitted. "Wouldn't have if I'd known what was up. But I didn't suspect it was this bad."

"Norah knew. She should have stopped you. And I should have closed that window. But we all make mistakes. I wonder how much he overheard."

"We weren't talking loud."

"Loud enough, I'm afraid," she said gloomily. "Darn it, the cat's out of the bag now. I'm much worse off than I was when I radioed Gregg. It's terrible! We've got to find out who it was."

"Line up a few hundred first-class passengers and look them in the eye, I suppose?" Val suggested.

"Your ideas are about as good as mine."

"This is the last night. On shore we may be able to do something about it."

"And maybe not. Don't you see we're

both practically useless now until we get at the truth of this?"

They made the circuit of the deck twice, and finally. Val suggested: "You might as well turn in. I'll stay up later and keep my eyes open. I'll let you know if I see anything."

Her handclasp was cool and firm, her "good night" brief, but her smile warm. Val walked away thinking about her.

AT MIDNIGHT the deck lights were dimmed. The strollers began to thin out. Val stayed out, for he was not sleepy. For hours he had been thinking about Nancy Fraser and this new bit of business. Who was so interested in her? What did it mean?

In other professions one might have shrugged the whole matter aside until something else happened. But not in his and Nancy Fraser's. If they didn't think at least two jumps ahead of the other party the results might be disastrous.

A steward passed with a tray holding a pot of coffee.

"Bring me a pot of coffee," Val told him.

And the steward touched his cap. "Yes, sir. Soon as I get back, sir."

Val leaned on the rail and stared out at the vast expanse of sea heaving slowly under the moonlight. Light steps came to his side. It was Nancy Fraser.

"I couldn't sleep," she said under her breath. "I wondered if I would find you out here."

"I'm having coffee in a few minutes. Care for some?"

"Sounds good. It might help my memory. I've been lying in bed trying to think of any suspicious move I've seen since I came aboard. I'm stymied."

"Ditto," Val admitted.

They waited there at the rail, talking low. Nancy said finally: "I thought you had ordered coffee."

Val looked at his wrist watch and saw that twenty-five minutes had passed as they lingered at the rail. "That steward must have forgotten it," he said irritably. "Let's look him up."

They walked slowly back along the deck. And suddenly, without warning, a woman screamed with shrill hysterical fear!

Nancy Fraser stopped short, her hand gripping Val's arm convulsively. "What's wrong?" she gasped.

The scream had come from ahead of them. Near the rear of the dimly lighted promenade Val saw two feminine figures backing toward the rail.

"I'll see," he jerked out under his breath, and leaving Nancy Fraser to follow, he ran toward the spot. He met the two women hurrying toward him. Two middle-aged spinsters. He had noticed them before during the trip. And now they were badly frightened. One was near hysteria as she turned and pointed back to the spot where Val had first seen them.

"There's something wrong there!" she cried shrilly. "I s-stumbled over an arm sticking out of the doorway! I—I think someone is d-dead!"

"Wait here!" Val ordered sharply. "If anyone's dead you can't be hurt!"

He found the door a moment later, and as he came up to it saw an arm thrust out at the bottom. A white-clad arm, sticking straight and motionless into the dim light of the deck. An arm that lay on the floor, its rigid fingers grasping talonlike at the empty air.

Val swore softly under his breath. It was a ghastly sight. For that arm seemed to be reaching, groping with desperate futility for something that had withdrawn beyond reach.

He stooped and lifted the hand. The flesh was clammy and cooling already. It was flaccid, limp, with that slackness which comes only from one thing. Whatever the arm had been reaching for, it had found only—death.

The door was ajar. The cabin inside was dark, silent.

Doors were opening along the deck; passengers were looking out. Nancy Fraser joined him.

"What is it?" she asked breathlessly.

Val reached inside for the light switch. "You'd better not look," he advised. "This won't be nice."

"I've probably seen worse sights," she retorted coolly, and looked in past his shoulder as the light flashed on inside.

WHATEVER sights Nancy had witnessed before, they had not hardened her enough to stop the gasp of horhor which burst from her. Even Val himself could not take it coolly. The steward whom he had accosted half an hour before was lying there on the floor before them. Lying, twisted on his side, knees pulled half up, one hand clutching the front of his white jacket and the other reaching out through the door in that frantic, gruesome gesture. And on the doorsill his face was turned up to them drawn and crimsoned with congested blood, mouth open, tongue protruding, and bulging eyes set in a horrible sightless stare.

"He's dead!" Nancy said huskily.

Val nodded. "Yes. Dead all right. This is the man I ordered coffee from. No wonder he didn't bring it!"

Looking beyond the body, he saw on the floor the tray the steward had been carrying. It had been dropped. Cup and saucer were shattered into bits. The pot lay on its side, the dark brown contents making a long stain on the rug, surrounded by a snowy sprinkling of sugar.

"He died almost as soon as he entered," Val muttered. "Didn't even have a chance to put his tray down. Dropped it cold."

His eyes ran over the body as he said

that. There was no sign of blood. And no marks of a struggle either. Except for the spot in front where the starched white cloth was caught in convulsive fingers, the coat was neat and trim. Even the man's carefully combed black hair was in place. It had been smoothed down with hair dressing, and was as sleek as it had been when he had walked along the deck.

Nancy noticed all that too, for she said: "It must have been heart failure."

"Looks that way," Val agreed.

A deck officer came running up in the van of half a dozen passengers closing in on the spot. "What is it?" he panted.

"One of your stewards must have had a heart attack," Val said, standing aside so that the officer could get a good look.

The bronze-cheeked, broad-shouldered young man pushed the door open all the way and stepped inside.

"Here's what's this?" he uttered in a startled voice. "Wake up, sir!" And over his shoulder: "The man must be a sound sleeper!"

Stepping in too, Val saw what he had missed with the door partly closed and his attention centered around the doorway. The bed was occupied by a man clad in blue silk pajamas.

"That man's not sleeping!" Val said sharply.

The young deck officer swore softly. "He—he's dead too!" he said shakily.

In fact, it was hard to see how the officer had been mistaken in the first place. No man would be sleeping that way. For the occupant of the bed lay in a twisted, contorted position also. One hand clutched his throat. The other had hooked around a pillow drawing it tightly against his side as if he had grabbed wildly at the nearest thing. The covers had been kicked down. One more roll would have taken the body off on the floor. And the mouth was open, the tongue protruding, the features congested with blood exactly as the steward's were.

Both men had died the same way.

All that Val got in a glance. And in the same moment he recognized the man on the bed with dumbfounded surprise. It was Carmody, the cheerful British book salesman!

CARMODY'S body bore no marks of violence either. No wounds. No blood. The death that had come to him as he lay in bed was the more ghastly and mysterious because of it.

"I'll get the captain and the ship's doctor here!" said the deck officer hoarsely. "Watch the cabin will you, please? Keep these people out." And as he stepped out, the young man closed the door as far as he could and said appealingly to the passengers gathering outside: "Please return to your cabins."

But by the excited remarks that drifted in, none of them paid any attention to the request. Val bent over the bed and touched the arm clutching the pillow. It was rigid. Frowning, he tested one of the legs. *Rigor mortis* had already set in. The flesh was cold.

It was not logical. He turned to the steward. That body was still flaccid, and the flesh was warm in comparison with the body on the bed.

Val fumbled for a cigarette, and then thought better of it and stood staring from one to the other. Both men had died in the same manner. One body was cold and set with *rigor mortis* and the other was warm and limp. It did not make sense.

There were cases, Val knew, where *rigor mortis* set in quickly. But this death that had come in the same manner to both men would not react so differently. There was only one conclusion to draw. The steward had been dead for half an hour—Carmody had been dead for hours.

And yet both had died in the same manner! Both had died horribly, yet without marks of violence! The door opened and Nancy slipped in and closed it behind her. "They're gabbling out there like a flock of excited chickens and roosters," she whispered. "What's the explanation of all this?"

Val shrugged helplessly. "I'm wondering." He told her what he had discovered. "D'you know this man?" he asked, jerking a thumb toward Carmody.

"No."

Carmody's coat and trousers were neatly hung up; his shoes were together on the floor, his shirt and tie and underwear on a chair as he had taken them off and arranged them. Under the bed was a gladstone bag, apparently undisturbed. Everything else in the cabin was in order.

The window was closed. A fragment of memory sent Val to the door. In the outside of the lock was a key with a small wooden handle to it—the steward's master key which he had apparently used to open the locked door.

Val shook his head in answer to the questions that were thrown at him by the people outside, and closed the door again.

"It's got me stumped" he confessed to Nancy. "There's a gruesome mystery here."

And when, a few moments later, the captain and the ship's surgeon entered, Val explained how he and Nancy happened to be in there, and pointed out what he had found.

Captain MacCreagh was a burly, weather-beaten man who still carried the dogged gruff manner of old sailing days. Doctor Simms, the ship's doctor, was short and slender, with a neat Vandyke and shell-rimmed glasses. He made a swift examination of the bodies, and then pulled the steward's outstretched arm in enough to let the door close tightly.

Captain MacCreagh had been watching

impatiently. Now he demanded: "What do you think of it, doctor?"

The doctor polished his glasses with the middle of a handkerchief. "Mr. Easton is right," he said slowly. "These men did not die at the same time. That one on the bed has been dead for hours. And this steward died very recently."

"What killed them?"

THE doctor fitted his glasses precisely on his nose, glanced at the bodies, and then at the captain. "I would suggest an autopsy, captain. Neither of them has been wounded in any manner, as far as I can see. They have all the appearance of dying from suffocation, yet there are no marks about their throats to indicate any violence which would cause that."

"In other words," the captain snorted, "you don't know anything about it."

The doctor was unruffled. "Precisely," he answered calmly. "I have never seen anything quite like it. The window is closed. The door was apparently locked, or the steward would not have used his key from the outside."

"That means," Val pointed out quickly, "that the steward was delivering an order to a man who had been dead in his locked cabin for hours."

The captain glared at him. "Then who ordered it?" he snapped.

"Perhaps the autopsy will show that," Val smiled.

"*Hmmmmph!*"

The captain stepped to the door, opened it, beckoned the deck officer, and growled: "Check up on the order that was brought here by this steward. Find what time it was given and who ordered it." And when he closed the door again, the captain said: "I wonder who this chap is."

Val mentioned what he knew of Carmody which was little enough.

"We'll search his effects and see if there's anything more," the captain decided. "He ought to have his passport and some papers. His people will have to be notified by radio, and asked what to do with the body. Blast it, I hate a business like this! It's bad for a ship's reputation."

Val suggested: "Right now it's more to the point to find out what killed them."

"You talk like a detective."

"I'm not," said Val calmly, and let the matter rest there. But he and Nancy Fraser stayed as the captain and the doctor hurriedly searched the cabin.

They found a billfold and some small change, a pocketknife, a fountain-pen flashlight clipped inside the coat, passport book and several letters, a key that opened the locked gladstone.

The captain's thick fingers fumbled through the clothes inside. With a grunt he drew out an English army-model automatic pistol and two extra clips filled with cartridges.

"*Hmmmph,*" he said, tossing them on the bed. "What does he want to carry these for? Army model too. I guess that's all. No—what's this?"

The captain drew out a small thin black leather wallet. As he opened it a little silver badge dropped to the floor. He let it lie as he looked inside. The wallet was empty and he tossed it and the silver badge on the bed also.

"That's all," he said. "And not much. His address is on the passport. That will be enough for my purpose, I guess."

Val hardly heard him. His glance had riveted in startled surprise on the badge the captain had picked up. And Nancy Fraser's had done the same thing. Their eyes met for a moment and it would have taken many words to interpret the meaning that flashed between them.

For Carmody, the smiling book salesman, had been proved by that badge to be a Secret Service agent of the British government!

CHAPTER THREE

Cold Steel—Well Done

THERE are times when terror can be quiet, insidious, hidden. So it was now. Murder had been done. Cold-blooded murder, unbelievably clever in its execution. How it had been done Val Easton did not pretend to know at the moment. Why, he might never know. But from the instant he was aware of Carmody's real mission, he knew it hooked up with Nancy Fraser. The man who had been lurking outside her cabin window was the one to explain this.

And if Carmody had been removed so skilfully and ruthlessly, why not Nancy Fraser and her companion? Why not himself, now that he was identified with them?

The deck officer returned.

"The coffee's easy to explain, sir," he told Captain MacCreagh. "This chap Carmody left an order with the steward to bring him coffee around midnight every night. Seems he was troubled with insomnia, or something like that. Couldn't sleep if he didn't have his coffee in the middle of the night."

"He'll have no trouble sleeping now," the captain remarked grimly. Doctor Simms fingered his Vandyke thoughtfully. "Queer. Mighty queer," he murmured, glancing at the bodies.

"What?" the captain rasped.

"This steward's death. Carmody had been dead for hours when the man arrived with the tray. The cabin was dark and the door was locked. It isn't reasonable to suppose that the killer remained in here all that time."

"No," admitted the captain testily. "He'd be a fool to do it."

"Exactly. The steward arrived, unlocked the door, stepped in—and died almost instantly. There was no struggle. There could not have been any noise, or someone out on the deck would have heard it. He simply died on the spot as Carmody had done. From the position of the body I would say he died as he was trying to back out the door."

"Dammit, man, something happened to him!" the captain snorted impatiently.

"I can't suggest what it was," Doctor Simms remarked coolly.

And there the matter rested.

While preparations were being made to put the bodies in the morgue, Val casually glanced at the papers which had been taken from Carmody's coat. He found nothing that might help him, and left the cabin a few moments later with Nancy Fraser.

They walked half the length of the deck before either spoke. Then Val said soberly: "It looks pretty bad."

"I think I'll stay up tonight," Nancy said calmly. "I don't want to be found that way in the morning."

Val shot her a quick look. "You think it touches you?"

"Don't you?" she countered.

"Perhaps. . . . . ."

Nancy said with conviction: "I'm not timid, but I have a hunch this is far worse than anything I've been up against before. This isn't wartime. Murder isn't on the cards now. An ordinary espionage agent wouldn't try a thing like that. It's creepy, ghastly."

"American and British agents are out," Val said soberly. "Carmody didn't seem especially dangerous to me. I think you're right. You've walked into something bigger than you think."

"Big enough for—murder," said Nancy slowly. She chuckled softly in a way that showed her nerve was unshaken, and laid a steady hand on Val's arm. "At least, my friend, we should be thankful we know as much as we do. We might have gone ahead blindly—and drawn the same thing. Tomorrow is another day. We'll see. . . ."

TOMORROW was another day, of bright sunshine over the fantastic, serrated skyline of New York, as the big liner plowed slowly up the bay.

During the night the ship had been in the grip of suppressed excitement. The bodies had been removed to the ship's morgue. The room had been locked and sealed. Wireless messages had crackled forth to shore. Passengers had been questioned, scrutinized. And at quarantine detectives hastily summoned from shore had come over the side with the ship reporters. Flashlight pictures of the cabin were taken; thumbprints were photographed. Passengers were diplomatically interrupted at their packing and last-minute preparations for going ashore, and questioned suavely. The newspapermen probed like hawks.

Val and Nancy were questioned by newspapermen and detectives. Their stories were brief and of little help. Of their business, or the man who had been lurking outside Nancy Fraser's cabin window nothing was said.

Carmody, it appeared, was a man who had little to do with anyone, outside of those he met at his meals. He had had no trouble with anyone, had no intimates.

Val himself had radioed Washington in code before daylight, giving such details as he knew. And Washington had replied in code. Val took the message to Nancy Fraser.

V EASTON
ON BOARD SS LAURENTIC
LONDON DISCLAIMS KNOWLEDGE OF CARMODY OR INTEREST IN HIM SAVE AS BRITISH SUBJECT YOUR IDENTIFICATION AS INTELLIGENCE AGENT ERRONEOUS ON NO ACCOUNT LET IT INTERFERE WITH MATTER IN HAND WORK TOGETHER UNTIL FURTHER INSTRUCTIONS
                    SIGNED GREGG

When Nancy had read the decoded words, Val tore the message into bits and dribbled them over the rail.

"Chalk up another puzzle on your list," he said drily. "If Carmody isn't a British agent, what is he? What was he doing with that badge? And why was he killed? It's more tangled than ever if we take that honor away from him."

"Could it be possible," Nancy suggested "that London is pulling Gregg's leg? Won't admit Carmody's their man, for fear it might tip their hand on something they're anxious to keep hidden?"

"Quite possible. It's been done plenty of times before. Carmody's dead. They can't help him now. And again, they may have told the truth."

"The badge?"

"He might have found it."

Nancy tossed her head. "Badges like that aren't left lying around for people to find. What about his gun?"

"People carry guns."

"It's an official issue."

"Might have found it too," Val grinned.

"Your suggestions grow worse," Nancy told him.

Val lit a cigarette. "We're cleared on it, anyhow. Gregg seems a trifle annoyed. Suppose I pick your man up when he leaves the Customs and get in touch with you at your hotel? Give you a little leisure that way. I don't think we'll be held on board. They won't detain a shipload of people without evidence."

"That would be nice," Nancy nodded. "We'll go to the Blockman."

No one had shown any interest in them that morning. And yet Val could not shake off the feeling that he was being watched. He tried every trick he knew to prove it, and got nowhere. The feeling persisted, irritating him finally. Nerves, he told himself. And yet he knew it wasn't. They were both under silent, insidious scrutiny, and there was nothing worse.

And the thought of Carmody horribly dead behind a locked door made things no better.

VAL had been right about the ship's passengers. Among them were many influential people who could not even be considered as suspects. The men from shore were as baffled as the ship's company had been. They had no clues, no concrete suspicions. Names and addresses were taken, and other data, but nothing else was done. The debarkation was under way in full force shortly after the ship was moored in her berth.

Val had looked up Galbraith, studied the man from a distance. He was typically British in a quiet, unassuming way. A sparse, medium-built man in tweeds, with a long, pale, unsmiling face, a neatly trimmed mustache, an indifference to his surroundings that bespoke much travel. He conversed with no one, kept to himself. Carmody's death, of which Galbraith evidently knew, aroused no visible interest in the man. Val, following him that morning on a stroll around the deck, noticed that Galbraith did not even glance at the door of Carmody's cabin.

And Galbraith's manner when he left the ship was leisurely and indifferent. He went to the "G" section in the Customs line-up, stood by indifferently while his kit bags were examined, and then followed a porter and the bags to a taxi.

Val had managed to have a few words with the man in charge of his own luggage. His bags were mysteriously passed and whisked out of line. Val caught a taxi-ahead of Galbraith. Outside the pier shed he ordered the driver to wait. A few moments later they were following Galbraith's cab.

Galbraith did not look back, seemed not to suspect he might be followed.

Val kept watch behind to see if any cab was noticeably following him. But in the crowded traffic it was almost a hopeless gesture.

Galbraith went directly to the Rosecrans, one of the big hotels overlooking Central Park from Fifty-ninth Street.

He entered the lobby behind his luggage in time to see Galbraith step into an elevator. The card registration system was in use at this hotel. There was no way of telling what room Galbraith had been given. Val smiled disarmingly at the clerk, and tried a random shot.

"My friend, Mr. Galbraith from London, told me on the boat he was going to register here. I'd like a room near him, if possible."

"Mr. Galbraith has just registered," the clerk replied. "Let's see—I can give you Room 717. That's just across the corridor from him. Mr. Galbraith is in 716."

"Excellent," Val nodded.

As soon as he was settled in his room he telephoned Nancy.

"Norah and I will come over there and register," Nancy said. "If he goes out, follow him. We must know whom he sees."

But Galbraith did not go out at first. He had a caller. Through his door, which had been left ajar an inch or so, Val saw a gray-clad back as the visitor was admitted to Galbraith's room. Just a glimpse, and then the door closed on them as Galbraith said formally: "How do you do, Mr. Ramey?"

The two were closeted in Galbraith's room for half an hour. In that time Nancy Fraser and her companion registered and Nancy telephoned from their room on the third floor. Val told her of Galbraith's visitor, suggested she be ready to tail him when he left.

Val was sitting inside his door when Galbraith's visitor stepped out into the hall once more. He heard the man say unctuously: "Tomorrow right at Oakridge then. Follow those directions after you reach Washington and you can't miss it."

And the fleeting glimpse through the cracked door showed a stocky, pasty-faced fellow, whose downsnapped hat brim shaded features that were as unctuous and oily as his voice had sounded. Before he was a dozen paces down the hall Val had closed the door and was at the telephone, calling Nancy's room. "All right—catch the next elevator," he rapped to her. "Blue suit, pudgy, pasty face, brim of gray hat snapped down."

"Right," said Nancy briefly and her receiver clicked.

Val was smiling thinly with satisfaction as he lighted a cigarette and resumed his watch at the door again. Galbraith's visitor would have a hard time shaking her. But as he conned over his one hasty glimpse of the fellow his smile faded to a thoughtful scowl. Ramey was a queer person to be calling on Sir Edward Lyne, to give Galbraith his right name. If long experience in judging people at a glance held good, Ramey was a shyster, tricky, smooth, untrustworthy.

Tomorrow night at Oakridge—near Washington.

What was behind that rendezvous which had been arranged?

GALBRAITH left his room shortly. He walked down Fifth Avenue and over to Times Square, slowly window shopping. He went to two of the Times Square newsreel theaters, window-shopped some more, dined leisurely and walked back to the hotel, with a leg-weary Val Easton still within sight of him.

Val called Nancy Fraser's room when he got in. Norah Beamish answered instantly, and her voice was sharp with worry.

"You haven't seen Nancy?" she queried anxiously.

"No. Isn't she in?"

"I haven't heard from her since she went out this afternoon," Norah informed him. "Do you think something could have happened?"

"I doubt it," Val reassured her. "She'll show up in a little while. Have you eaten?"

"I had some food sent up," Norah told him. "I won't leave the room until I hear from her. She may telephone."

"If she does, let me know. And if she comes back have her telephone my room at once. I'll leave word at the desk if I go out."

Galbraith seemed set for the time being. Val hastily stripped, took a hot shower and dressed again. He found himself wondering about Nancy Fraser. Had something happened to her? She was the kind of girl who would take chances. Val found it impossible to forget those two still forms on the *Laurentic*, grim warning of the price of carelessness.

He had barely finished dressing when knuckles rapped sharply on the door. Val answered it with a feeling of relief. It must be Nancy, returned finally and come up for a word with him. He opened the door with a grin on his face.

And. . . . .

The grin faded to astonishment. A black-coated waiter confronted him, bearing a cloth-covered tray.

"You've made a mistake," Val told him. "I didn't order anything."

The waiter looked doubtful. "Mr. Easton, isn't it?"

"Yes."

"This is right then. A young lady telephoned down and said to bring this order to your room. It's for two. I believe she is supposed to share it also."

"Oh," said Val blankly. "All right, bring it in."

His reaction was pleasure. This was such a thing as Nancy Fraser would do.

Thoughtful of her. Eat while they talked. She was back then, and everything was all right. And he wondered what news she was bringing.

The waiter had a small folding rack under his arm. Opening it, he set the tray carefully down. He was a swarthy, poker-faced man with powerful shoulders bulging inside his black jacket and wrists which protruded out of sleeves that were too short.

"The young lady said to cook the steak well done," he declared. "Will you see it now, sir?"

From the moment the fellow had entered the room, closing the door behind him, Val had been struggling with a feeling of bafflement. Something was out of place in this picture. Wouldn't Nancy have telephoned him, after all, as soon as she got in? And he hadn't been under the shower more than a few minutes. Hardly long enough to have a steak well cooked and a full meal sent up to the room after she returned.

And there was something else. . . .

Suddenly he got it. How the devil did the waiter know that the woman who ordered the dinner over the telephone was a young woman? He couldn't know.

And the man's coat was too small, his face was tanned where a man used to working indoors would be pale. And a degree of insolence had come into his manner. He leered at Val across the tray as he whisked the cloth away.

One look was enough to tell Val that his suspicions had been right. For the dishes that had obviously contained food a short while before were empty now, and in the midst of them lay a large flat automatic.

Val jumped for that gun instantly.

It was a long chance—and it failed. A muscular hand closed over the gun and its muzzle jerked up and met him.

Val stopped short, arms tensed at his sides. For a moment silence held the room, while Val's eyes locked with a pair of dead slate eyes which stared at him with a cold unwinking gaze. Politeness, mockery, pretense were gone now.

"Lift your hands!" the other ordered across the littered tray.

"What's the idea?" Val countered.

"Shut up! Don't argue! Put your hands up!" As he spoke the other stepped around to Val's side. The gun was steady in his hand and his manner was venomous. A slight foreign accent tinged his words.

Slowly Val raised his arms.

"Turn around!"

Val did that too. And a second later steel crashed against the side of his head brutally. Everything went blank, black. He pitched forward to the floor.

CHAPTER FOUR

The Hollow Needle

THE light overhead was still burning brightly when Val's eyes opened again. He was stupid for a moment, senses whirling, pain roiling in his head. He couldn't think what it was all about.

And then he remembered. The waiter —the cloth-covered tray—the gun—the stunning blow against his head. . . . .

The tray was still sitting on the rack in the center of the floor before him, the white cloth tossed on the floor and the soiled dishes mocking him.

The waiter and his gun were gone. The room was silent, deserted.

And there by the side of the bed Val sat in the straight-backed chair, tied hand and foot with lengths of fine silk cord.

His ankles were fastened to the legs of the chair and his arms were tied behind it. Silk cord was lashed about his wrists so tightly the circulation had been cut off. His hands were numb. Cloth had been stuffed into his mouth and tied in place by a towel, making an extremely uncomfortable but highly efficient gag.

He was helpless, miserable and impotent.

As his predicament burst over him, Val's first reaction was a struggle to free himself. He quickly saw it was impossible. He couldn't rub the gag out of his mouth and call for help. Over his shoulder he saw that the window had been closed and the shade pulled down.

THE phone was on the other side of the bed. By the side of the door was the bell button that would quickly bring help. Only a few feet away—and yet it might have been as many miles.

Val raged at himself for a moment. He had been a fool to be caught off guard that way. And yet it had been smooth work, well planned and executed. Whoever had done it had known about his connection with Nancy Fraser; had known that Nancy was out and might be back any time.

Only one man could have known that —the one who had been watching them on the *Laurentic*.

What was the reason for it? Not Nancy. She was out of the hotel. Hardly Norah Beamish, on a lower floor. Galbraith then! Galbraith across the hall, where Val's door commanded his, where no move could have been made without danger of interruption.

He didn't know how long he had been tied here in the chair before regaining consciousness. It might have been minutes, or an hour or more.

In that time what had happened to Galbraith?

Val eyed the telephone narrowly. If he could inch the chair around to it he might tip the phone over. Using his toes and throwing the weight of his body at the same time he managed to shift the chair inch by inch. But it was slow, hard work. Perspiration broke out on his forehead.

And in the midst of that the telephone suddenly buzzed.

Val cursed behind his gag. That was Nancy or Norah. And he couldn't answer. It was maddening to know help was so near and be unable to summon it.

The telephone buzzed again and again and then stopped. He hadn't covered a quarter of the distance to the instrument. Stubbornly Val kept on.

And then a few minutes later a key grated suddenly in the door. A bareheaded, broad-shouldered stranger stepped into the room, took one look and uttered in a startled voice: "Hey—what's this?"

From behind his back Nancy Fraser darted into the room. Relief broke over her face as she saw Val staring mutely at her. With a swift little rush she reached his side, snatched the towel down and pulled the wadded cloth out of his mouth.

"Thanks," Val mumbled through cramped lips.

"Who did this?" Nancy asked tensely.

"Fellow disguised as a waiter. Get across hall and see if Galbraith's all right. I think they got me out of the way because of him."

"This looks mighty funny to me," the broad-shouldered stranger said ponderously. "You hurt, buddy?"

Val had him placed by now. A hotel detective, already muddled and uncertain about everything.

"I telephoned as soon as I got in," Nancy said swiftly. "When you didn't answer I queried the desk and they said you hadn't left any word there. I suspected something was wrong, so I got the hotel detective to come up here with me and unlock your door."

Nancy whirled around on the detective. "Cut him loose from there!" she snapped. "Where's your master key?"

THE master key was produced with a puzzled frown. Nancy snatched it and made for the door. "Hey, where you going with that?" the detective protested.

But Nancy whirled out of the room without answering either of them. The detective turned after her in indecision. "Is that dame gone nutty?" he uttered plaintively.

"Cut these damn ropes!" Val snarled. "Don't stand there like a lunkhead! Get me out of this chair!"

The fierce command in his voice brought the desired result. The detective's thick fingers fumbled open a small pocketknife, and he hacked at the cords. Val was chafing his wrists and wringing circulation back in them as the detective stooped over and slashed at the cords around his ankles.

Val staggered to his feet.

From across the hall keened a cry of distress that broke off sharply in a choked gasp. Nancy's voice!

Val plunged for the doorway without stopping for the gun in his bag. Galbraith's door was standing ajar. He crashed it open with his shoulder and plunged into the room—into a scene of confusion and violence.

The place had been looted hurriedly. Bureau drawers were out and their contents tossed heedlessly on the floor. Bags had been slit open with a sharp knife and searched hastily. The closet door was open, the bed turned down. And Galbraith's body lay huddled in the center of the floor.

All that went unheeded. For before him Nancy was fighting off a tall, stooped, black-caped figure which clutched her throat with one long talon-like hand as it tried to wrench its other hand from Nancy's desperate grip.

They staggered around as Val entered the room.

A pale, ghastly, cadaverous face turned toward Val. He was aware of a parted,

writhing mouth, of blazing, green-flecked eyes, of teeth that showed momentarily like fangs.

It was the face of a monster, a fiend, lashed by murderous fury, indescribably venomous, vicious, dangerous. Some horrible fate had been in store for Nancy. The hand she clutched so desperately held no gun, no knife, no club. Its talon-like fingers were tensed about the small, gleaming barrel of a doctor's hypodermic. And the long sharp needle was bending in toward her wrist with all the shuddery menace of a deadly serpent's fang.

As the door slammed shut behind Val he threw himself at that sinister black-caped figure. A swift turn brought Nancy between them. She was hurled violently back, her grip tearing away.

Val's arm saved her from a bad fall.

Behind him the house detective hammered violently on the door, bawling: "Open up, inside there!"

"Look out!" Nancy gasped warningly. "He'll kill you!"

Her words were too late. A hand plunged under the black cape as its wearer backed toward the open window. It came out with something that looked like a small, shiny metal fountain pen. But the instant he saw it leveling at them Val knew better.

He tried to shove Nancy behind him, and was too late. There was a dull *pop*. A whitish ball of vapor leaped at them, expanded rapidly, enveloped them. . . .

And suddenly they were blinded with tears, coughing, choking, sneezing and fighting for breath. Helpless, Val backed toward the door, sweeping Nancy with him when his arm touched hers. He was thinking of that vicious hypodermic needle and the man who wielded it. They were at his mercy now.

It had been long since Val Easton had known such fear. And it was for Nancy Fraser, not himself. When the tear gas cleared out of the room, would she be stretched out there on the floor also?

The door was shaking before the assault of the house detective. The commands to open up were growing loud and furious. The tumult guided Val to the door. That dick had a gun. His hand found the knob. And still nothing had happened to him as he turned that knob. For some reason the black-caped attacker was holding back.

The door was shoved in violently against him, knocking him off balance.

"By God, what's the idea of all—" the house man bawled as he charged in, breaking off into a fit of sneezing and choking before he could finish the question.

VAL was mopping at his streaming eyes with his handkerchief, trying to see. The dick blundered into him. The hard muzzle of a gun poked roughly into his ribs.

"Watch that gun, you big ox!" Val yelled. "You'll shoot the wrong person!"

The gun was pulled away. "Come out in the hall!" Nancy choked. Val stumbled out after her. And there, away from the insidious gas, they gained a measure of control and sight.

The house dick was standing in the doorway, mopping at his eyes and swearing under his breath. Peering blearily at Val, he raved: "Did you shoot that stuff off?"

"Do I look like it?" Val retorted. "Is that fellow in the room yet?"

"What fellow?"

"Tall chap with a black cape."

Peering through the doorway, the dick said angrily: "There ain't no one in there! Hell—is that him on the floor?"

But it was Galbraith's body he spoke of. It had not moved since Val first saw it. Air was pouring through the doorway, driving the last of the gas out the window. Wiping his eyes and peering as best he could, Val edged into the room.

The tall, black-caped figure had vanished!

From nearby rooms other guests had poured out into the corridor, gathering around the door now. A woman caught sight of Galbraith's body on the floor and gave a stifled cry.

"Get back, you folks!" the house man ordered through his teeth.

Val looked out at them. "Did anyone escape from this room?" he demanded.

One of the men said flatly: "I was looking when the door was opened. You two men and the young lady were the only ones who came out. What happened?"

Val hurried over to the window without answering. It was open, and when he looked out he saw four stories below the dark roof of an adjoining building.

It was to this window that Nancy Fraser's assailant had been backing when Val last saw him. He hadn't gone out into the hall. He wasn't here in the room. He must have gone out of the window.

But the sheer side of the tall building offered no refuge. There was no ledge by which he could have gained an adjoining window. No fire escape near. No ladder of any kind, up or down. And yet it was the only way he could have left the room. Val whirled on the house man, jerking a thumb at Galbraith's body as he did so.

"The man who did that went out the window!" he rapped out. "He may have fallen. I can't see the roof down there very well. Better search it and the building underneath. And the hotel here. He was tall, thin, wore a black cape and dark suit."

So fast and furious had everything happened that this was the first chance for more than a fleeting look at Galbraith. Val dropped to his knees beside the motionless body as he spoke.

Galbraith lay on his face, one arm under his head, the other thrown out awkwardly. He was dreadfully still and limp. Had no pulse in neck or wrist. And as Val lowered the lifeless wrist, his gaze was caught by a tiny smear of blood just below the coat sleeve.

Taking care not to disarrange the body before the medical examiner viewed it, he bent over and scrutinized the spot closely. Skin and flesh had been punctured by a needlelike instrument. A drop or two of blood had welled out before the wound closed. An area of flesh around the spot, no larger than a dime, was discolored slightly. That was all. And yet Val shivered as he rose to his feet, rubbing his hands slowly together. He was thinking of that glistening hypodermic needle in those talonlike hands . . .

The hotel dick was staring at him with wide eyes. "Is he dead?" he queried, nodding at the body.

"Very," Val answered drily. "Better call the police. And then get down after that man!"

The detective had closed the door against the curious in the hall. He stepped to the telephone, called headquarters and reported the matter. And then swung around and glowered at Val and Nancy.

"I didn't see anyone else in here," he said deliberately. "I'll just wait here with you two until the coppers come."

CHAPTER FIVE

The Black Doctor

IT took Val a moment to realize that he and Nancy Fraser were under suspicion. And when he did a wave of anger rushed through him.

"You fool!" he said crisply. "Can't you see we didn't have anything to do with this? I was tied up in the other room, and Miss Fraser was only in here a few seconds. You heard her cry out,

didn't you? And you got a dose of the gas that chap left!"

"No one could have got out of here," was the stubborn answer. "If there was a guy, he jumped, and he's down there on the roof dead. And if there wasn't, you two can explain it to the cops. Better sit down there on the bed an' make yourselves comfortable."

Nancy Fraser met Val's angry glance with a philosophical shrug. "He's gone by now, anyway," she said. "We might as well make the best of it. I've got something to tell you."

While talking with the detective, Val had been conning over something else in the back of his mind. That pale, furious face with the blazing, green-flecked eyes had been strangely familiar. He was certain he had not seen the man before, and equally certain he knew something about him.

Nancy's face was pale from the shock she had just experienced, but her voice was steady. "That man," she said under her breath. "Did you ever see him before?"

"No. But I've a feeling that I should have," Val confessed.

"I saw him once in Switzerland," Nancy declared. "He was pointed out to me in Geneva. That was Carl Zaken, better known as the Black Doctor."

"Good God—the Black Doctor?"

"Yes!"

And neither of them needed to say any more.

Through the shady, secret channels of international espionage, tales of Carl Zaken, the Black Doctor, seeped like fantastic nightmares. He was in the way of becoming a legend to those who dealt in such matters. There were men willing to swear that no such person existed, but they did not know the facts.

No country claimed the Black Doctor, and he served none more than momentarily. Master spy, incredibly clever, cold-blooded, ruthless, a wizard at disguise, the Black Doctor gave orders to a wide-flung web of desperate characters. That much was definitely known. How many people received those sinister orders, only the Black Doctor himself knew.

At times he worked alone, and at others as many as a score had helped him. His influence was like an evil miasma. When murder suited his ends, he killed with technical skill. If torture would help, he used torture with all the fiendishness of expert medical training. He was an adept at languages and disguise. And his favorite role was that of a doctor, friend of man and trusted by everyone. For, so rumor had it, Carl Zaken had once been a doctor.

He dealt in information for the most part, stopping at nothing to get what he wanted, and selling the results to the highest bidder if he could not use them better himself.

"Are you certain he was the Black Doctor?" Val urged in amazement.

"The man who pointed him out had been caught by the Black Doctor once. He'd never forget him, and warned me never to. We only caught a glimpse of him, but I marked that face for good. This was the man." Nancy smiled wryly. "And I had to meet him without a gun."

"What happened?"

NANCY gave a little shudder. "He jumped at me just as soon as I slipped through the door. I caught one glimpse of his face and that hypodermic in his hand, and knew what I was up against. I tried to scream for you, and he caught me by the throat. All I could do was try and keep that needle away. There was murder in his face. It—it was ghastly."

"And a good thing you dodged it," Val said soberly. "Galbraith evidently didn't."

"Was that what killed him?"

"Needle puncture in the wrist. If he'd had time, he'd probably have cleaned the smear of blood away, and there would have been another mystery for the police to solve."

"You think he was on the ship?"

"Who else?"

"But why kill that poor devil, Carmody?" Nancy asked.

"Ask the Black Doctor. He must have a good reason. He's after something."

"What?"

"God knows. Galbraith here knew—and he's dead."

"Do you think he got it?"

"He tried hard enough," Val said, looking around the looted room. "I don't know. Evidently he was still busy when you walked in on him." Val's jaw set. "He killed that chap on the boat and Galbraith here in cold blood. It wasn't a question of putting him out of the way while he searched the room. He simply slaughtered him and then went about his business. Evidently came all ready to kill."

"Was he the man who tied you up?"

"No. Must have been one of his men. And clever work it was. The fellow came to the door disguised as a waiter, saying he had brought a meal you had ordered for us. I let him in without thinking, and when I did tumble that something was wrong it was too late. He had a gun on me then. Knocked me out and trussed me up."

"I can't understand why they didn't kill you," Nancy said. "It would have been easy enough."

Val rubbed his forehead and shook his head. "Lord knows," he admitted. "It would have been easy enough all right."

They were silent for a moment.

"That pseudo waiter must have left a trail around the hotel here some place," Nancy muttered.

"I'm not worrying about him," Val

shrugged. "I'm wondering what this is all about. Why kill Galbraith and search his room here? He could have done it just as easily on the boat. Even the Black Doctor doesn't go around killing people for the fun of it. He could have left Galbraith alive just as well as he did me, if he had only wanted to look through his things. What about that chap you followed? He had evidently made a date to see Galbraith somewhere near Washington tomorrow. He was an oily-looking bird."

"Wasn't he?" Nancy agreed. "And a suspicious one, too. I think he was afraid someone might be following him. He tried all the tricks to shake anyone off."

"D'you think he saw you?"

Nancy rubbed the side of her nose carelessly and shrugged. "I've cut my teeth at that sort of thing. I'm pretty sure he didn't see me. After riding around town, taking the subway, ducking into a movie and out a side exit right away, he finally went into a telegraph office and sent a wire."

"Who to?"

"I didn't have a chance to find out. I wanted to see what else he did."

"The little bloodhound," Val grinned. "Did you?"

"I did. He popped into a telephone booth in a cigar store, and then took the elevated to Battery Park and went through the Aquarium."

"What?"

"'Pon honor. He looked at all the little fishes like he was going into his second childhood. And then met a man and woman back in one of the dark corners and talked at least fifteen minutes with them."

"What did they look like?"

"It was shadowy where they were standing," Nancy said. "I couldn't see them well. And my man left first. I had to tag him. He chivvied back uptown on the 'El' again, got off at Forty-second

Street, hailed a taxi—and I lost him there. I couldn't get another cab quick enough. Any other time there would have been a dozen on hand."

"It doesn't matter. He's going to Washington."

Nancy arched a delicate eyebrow. "How do you know?"

BEFORE Val could reply the door burst open and admitted the hotel manager, patrolmen and detectives. The law took charge of the situation; and the ponderous house detective stated his case flatly.

"That lady there," waving his hand at Nancy, "comes down and says will I come up and open a door for her. She thinks maybe there's trouble. And when I do that gentleman is tied up in a chair. While I'm cuttin' him loose she takes my key an' runs into this room. He follows her an' they slam the door in my face. I don't know what happened in here, but when they opened the door the room was full of tear gas an' that body was on the floor. They tried to tell me there was another guy in here who knocked him off, but I didn't see no one. There wasn't no way he could have gotten out. So when they tried to run me off the scene after this guy they claim was in here, I call headquarters an' sit on the lid."

Though no direct charge was made, the house detective's story was damning as he told it.

A brusk, lantern-jawed detective seemed to be in charge of things. He had examined the body and made a quick survey of the room while the house man talked. Now he stepped to the window, looked out, and turned on Val and Nancy.

"No one could have gotten out that window!" he rasped at them. "What's the straight of this?"

"What's your name?" Val asked coolly.

"I'm Lieutenant Ives of the homicide squad. And since this is murder I warn you to make your statements correct."

"Step into the bathroom with me, Lieutenant Ives," Val requested curtly.

Ives hesitated, fingered his lantern jaw, and then said gruffly: "All right, if it'll make you feel any better."

Val closed the door behind them and met Ives' scowl with an icy stare.

"I didn't bother to reason with that addle-pated fool who suspected us" he said icily. "I'm going to tell you what happened; and then I want to get away as quickly as possible. You can check us at Washington, of course."

Val palmed a small badge for Ives to see. The detective took one look at it and whistled softly. His manner changed abruptly to fraternal courtesy.

"I couldn't know," he apologized. "What's the lowdown on all this?"

Val told him what had happened.

"What's your interest in this fellow who got bumped off?" Ives asked when he finished.

"That doesn't matter," Val refused him. "A lot of things don't matter right now. The man who killed him went out the window. May have gone up a rope ladder to a window above, or slid down a rope to that roof below."

"Where's the rope then?" Ives demanded skeptically.

"A hard flip from below on the rope would have loosened the hook over the window. You may find marks on the sill made by a hook. I'd suggest you try and trace him, and look over this hotel for a check on the pseudo waiter who took me in."

"I don't need to," Ives commented. "Coming up in the elevator the manager told me they had just found a waiter who had taken a meal up to Room 701 and hadn't returned. They found him tied up and minus his coat. The tray and dishes he had brought up were gone also.

The fellow who had occupied the room had checked out ten minutes before. All the waiter could say was that as soon as he brought the tray into the room he was knocked out, and when he came to, stuffed under the bed, two men were eating the meal as if he wasn't there. He didn't get a look at them."

Val thought with unwilling admiration that the Black Doctor would have the nerve to stop and eat part of the meal, which had evidently been ordered to get the waiter and tray where they could be used. But he said nothing of that. Too much information might throw obstructions in their way. For there was small doubt in Val's mind now that this murder of Galbraith was only a move in another, bigger game that the Black Doctor was playing. And it was that game in which he was most concerned. Time enough when it was uncovered to think about bringing the Black Doctor to book for murder.

Ives took out a little black book and wrote down the description of the Black Doctor and the man who had impersonated the waiter. He asked for more information. Val referred him to Washington. Ives gave up with a shrug.

"I don't know what it's all about," he confessed. "You evidently know what you're doing. I'll call headquarters and they can let the commissioner decide what to do."

"Tell him to get in touch with Washington at once," Val ordered. "We've got work to do. Later on we can return for testimony."

"It's unusual," Ives warned.

"Washington will settle it."

AND Washington did settle it in a bit less than an hour, such was the power of that secret arm of the government which Nancy Fraser and Val Easton represented.

Neither of them knew exactly what

had flashed back and forth over the wires; but Ives himself, still at the hotel, answered a telephone call, and told Val with a wry grin: "I guess you two have got something on the ball all right. Orders from the commissioner himself are to let you go and forget about you for the time being. So long—and luck to you."

"We'll probably need it," Val said.

VAL regarded the penciled message which he had obtained from the manager of the telegraph office. It had taken pressure to get a look at it against all rules of the company. But it told him what he wanted to know.

J. B. Tillson,
Oakridge Manor,
Hartsville, Virginia.
Party arriving tomorrow.

Signed, Ramey.

So Galbraith had intended to meet Ramey at Oakridge. Hartsville, Virginia, was close to Washington. The answer to everything must center there.

He returned to the hotel and looked in at Nancy Fraser's room on the way to his own.

"Pack up," he said with a grin. "There's just time to catch the next plane to Washington."

Norah Beamish shifted her ample form on the edge of the bed and said tartly: "Nancy needs a good night's rest. She's been through an ordeal, young man."

"That's right," Val said contritely. "Get your rest then and I'll run along."

Nancy had just been powdering her nose when Val stepped in, and a nice nose it was too, he noted. She tossed the powder puff on the dresser and stretched slender arms over her head, yawning luxuriously like a lazy cat.

"Nonsense," she said cheerfully. "I'm just getting warmed up. You must stay here and get the rest and we'll run on."

Norah Beamish charged to her feet like a formidable battle cruiser getting under way.

"Leave me here?" she snorted. "My great aunt's transformation you will! Do I look like an old grandma who needs to be parked in the corner? The idea! I won't have it! Where're those bags, Nancy? Get packed, young man! We'll be ready!"

Though Nancy had disavowed fatigue, when the wide-winged monoplane swept off the lighted landing field with a roaring rush, climbed high, and swiftly dropped the blazing panorama of lights that were New York back over the horizon, she promptly closed her eyes.

Norah Beamish sat behind her with a defiant tilt to her chin. When Val looked at her he received a visible sniff. Plainly Norah held him responsible for the suggestion that she be left behind to take her ease.

Val grinned, and then glanced across the aisle at the smooth curve of Nancy's throat. Her eyelids lifted and she smiled lazily at him, and then they closed and she seemed to doze.

What a girl, Val thought. Nerves like steel, inexhaustible energy, ready to tackle anything. She had come through an ordeal that would have reduced most women to nervous hysteria. And now, knowing that they were pitting their wits against Carl Zaken, the dreaded Black Doctor, she was dozing as peacefully as an untroubled child.

He felt a slight tightening of his throat as he remembered again that heart-stopping moment when death had grazed her wrist. And hard on the heels of that Val felt a cold chill as he wondered what lay ahead for her before this business was done.

The Black Doctor had not earned his reputation without cause; and somewhere at this very moment he was moving craft.

ily through the mystifying web he was spinning about them.

CHAPTER SIX

Mystery at Oakridge Manor

BY fast passenger plane the service from New York to Washington is a matter of less than two hours air time. Considerably less. And if a long-distance telephone call has been made from the New York airport, resulting in a speedy automobile waiting at the Washington airport, the time elapsed from Central Park to upper Pennsylvania Avenue is phenomenally low.

It lacked five minutes to midnight when Val, Nancy Fraser and Nora Beamish stepped into that sedan and were gruffly greeted by the heavy-set, saturine man behind the wheel. It was Gregg himself, as unknown and overlooked by the world as were the actions of that subtle force which he controlled.

"You people are playing hob with my sleep!" Gregg snarled as he sent the car through the gears with a rush and they whirled off the air field. "One would think I had nothing to do but stay up nights and nurse a lot of agents joyriding around the world. Let's have the straight of all this. I couldn't make heads or tails of your gabble over long distance a while ago, Easton."

That was Gregg's way, and no one who took his orders paid any attention to it for very long. Behind it Gregg was fanatically on the job, as witness his presence here tonight, when he could have remained in bed and sent any of a score of men in his place. His presence too, was testimony of the importance he placed on the curt reference to the Black Doctor that Val had made over long distance.

Val sketched what had happened as they rolled swiftly toward the heart of the city, with the slim white-lighted shaft of the Washington Monument spearing the heavens to their left, and the flood-lighted dome of the capitol ballooning toward the sky off to their right.

Gregg sucked a cigar and listened closely, grunting to himself now and then. At the end he blew his horn viciously at another car that seemed about to pass in front of them, flicked cigar ash out the car window, and spoke.

"Carl Zaken, eh? I'd give my liver to get him. He's caused me trouble before. Get this—there'll be hell and furies over this business. Two English citizens murdered, one on a ship flying the United States flag, and the other in New York. We can't pretend to know much about it, or the fact that we've been watching one of their men will be known. Can't have that. If they catch on we're suspicious of this chap who called himself Galbraith, they'll start hunting for the source of our information. It'll be embarrassing. Blast it!"

"What was Galbraith after?" Val asked bluntly.

"Don't know," Gregg said equally bluntly. "We got a tip that something unusual was in the air, and a man was being sent over here *sub rosa* empowered to spend as high as a million pounds for something. That's a hell of a lot of money, if you'll excuse my English, ladies."

"*Hmmmph!*" Norah snapped from the back seat beside Nancy. "I can do better than that, Jim Gregg, as you well know. Go right ahead."

Val grinned in the darkness, remembering that Nancy had said Norah Beamish had once been Gregg's private secretary.

"Huh? Er—all right," said Gregg, thrown off his stride for a moment. "As I was saying, I cabled Miss Fraser to pick this man up and see what he did. And all this other has broken out of a clear sky. It's hard to tell what to make of it."

"I'd do a lot for a million pounds," Norah observed acidly. "Doubtless this Zaken would do the same. Has that occurred to you?"

"Galbraith didn't have a million pounds on him!" Gregg snapped. "He was only empowered to offer it."

"If you were to offer me a million pounds—" Norah said, undaunted.

"I wouldn't," Gregg growled. "But I'll offer you a suggestion. Let Easton give me his views on the matter."

"Well, I like that!" Norah commented indignantly. "Ouch, Nancy, stop poking me with your elbow."

The silence was thick for a moment as Gregg restrained himself with an effort. "Norah Beamish," he said ominously, "pipe down."

"Oh, all, right," Norah said sulkily.

A MATCH flare lighted Val's red face as he held the flame to a cigarette. "Zaken is after that money," he stated, tossing the match out the window. "If it's worth that to someone else, it's worth it to him. He can cash in on it."

"If he gets it you're all fired," Gregg said calmly. "This thing is getting out of hand. I want Zaken in custody before he gets a chance to do any more harm, and I want to know what Galbraith was after over here. Those two murders will go unsolved until we have all that. There'll be complications. You say you haven't the slightest idea what happened to Zaken?"

"He vanished out of the room," Val said slowly. "His man had the room directly above that. By the time I could do anything it was too late. Both were gone."

Val paused and looked out of the window.

"Yes?" Gregg urged.

"I don't know what Zaken was after in Galbraith's room," Val admitted, looking at him. "Or why he killed Galbraith. But I've got a good hunch that wherever Galbraith was heading for, we can expect Zaken to appear, sooner or later. He gained no money immediately by killing Galbraith. And, from everything I've ever heard about the fellow, he never kills unless there's a good reason for it."

"Where does that get you?" Gregg countered impatiently.

"I know where Galbraith was going."

"Ahhhh—you do?" Gregg suddenly chuckled and laid an approving hand on Val's arm. "I knew you wouldn't let them run you out on the end of a limb and saw it off. Now, let's have the rest of it."

Val remembered Norah Beamish sitting quietly in the back seat and letting him talk. "This isn't really my case," he reminded. "Miss Fraser may like to handle it her own way."

"Ridiculous!" Nancy jeered. "The thing had gotten out of my hands. Where would I be if you hadn't barged into Galbraith's room just in time? I'm helping you now, and bother all the modesty."

"She's right. Let's have it," Gregg agreed.

"I don't know where this Ramey comes in, with his dodging around New York, or what to think of the couple he talked to," Val admitted. "But the next move seems to be at Oakridge Manor. I came down here tonight as quick as possible to do that. If Zaken shows up there we'll collar him and get the truth."

"Why all the rush, if you're going out there tomorrow?" Gregg queried irritably. "You could have let me sleep."

"Going out tonight," Val told him. "It's only about an hour's drive. We'll stage an auto breakdown and go up to the house in search of a telephone. Or I'll say that Galbraith was found dead in New York with that address in his pocket, and pass as a newspaperman asking for information. And in the morning you can post men around the place, working with the information I get tonight."

Gregg considered. "Good enough," he decided. "But don't mention Galbraith. Let them expect him. Just look around the place and play dumb. It ought to work. They'll know nothing about what happened in New York tonight, of course."

They had traversed the long length of Pennsylvania Avenue as they talked. Gregg turned in to the curb at Fourteenth and the Avenue, opened the door and stepped out.

"You might as well take this car" he said. "I'll taxi home and get some sleep. I'll take you with me, Norah. You're probably tired out."

"You will not, Jim Gregg," Norah said defiantly. "Don't think because you O. K. my pay check you can order me around all the time. I'm going out there with Nancy. If there're any car breakdowns and shenanigans I'll fit right into the picture as the helpless mother—what are you laughing at?"

"At the idea of anyone thinking of you as helpless!" Gregg choked. "God. help the people at the Manor! They don't know what's landing on their doorstep. And I warn you, Norah, if you bungle anything you'll come back in the office and take dictation. Good night." And Gregg departed hastily, still shaking with laughter.

"The old hyena!" Norah said heatedly, glaring out the window. "I'll make him sweat for that."

HARTSVILLE was a small suburban town south of Washington, some thirty minutes of fast driving. Houses were dark and wanly lighted streets deserted. But a gas station and a drugstore were still open for business. In the drugstore Val asked casually as he bought

a package of cigarettes: "Know of a place around here called Oakridge Manor?"

"Sure," was the prompt reply. "That's the old Mason place out on the river road. Fellow by the name of Long bought it a few years back and tacked that name on it."

"What's he like?"

"Don't see much of him," said the druggist as he rang up the sale. "Queer sort of man, I hear. Don't welcome visitors. And when people want to be let alone around here, folks most generally let 'em alone."

"How do you get there?"

"Six miles out on the highway, and you turn to the left. It's about three miles down the river road, I reckon. Kind of lonesome country back in there, although the road is used a heap. Long's land backs up clear to the Potomac. You'll see a sign over his gate."

Val thanked the man and went back to the car. As soon as they got away from the little village it became apparent that the druggist had not been wrong when he had described the country as lonesome.

Mist was rising off the river, swirling across the stabbing headlight beams in ghostly streamers. The damp smell of the river bottoms off to the left of the road poured in through the car windows. Great oaks and poplars grew alongside the road, and they passed many stretches of scrub-pine woodland. Now and then a small house was visible behind a whitewashed picket fence, but for the most part the country seemed deserted.

Norah Beamish said flatly: "I don't like this country. It gives me the creeps. I didn't know you could get this wild so close to Washington."

"You should have stayed in the city and gone to sleep," said Val.

It was the wrong thing to say. "Young man, I know my business!" Norah crushed him. "I may have the creeps, but I'm as good as any man we'll find in this section. Nancy, give me a cigarette."

A match flared; and Norah Beamish had taken perhaps half a dozen puffs from her cigarette when a stout wire fence on the left of the road suddenly gave way to massive stone gate posts with a wooden arch between them. A lettered sign hanging from the arch said: OAKRIDGE MANOR.

Val cut the ignition and brought the car to a stop at the side of the road.

"Here we are," he said. In the sudden silence which wrapped them his voice sounded with startling clarity.

Nancy chuckled softly. "Broken down and everything. And where is the house?"

The fog was thicker, if anything, rolling its damp breath through the open car window at Val's side, swirling through the yellow glare of the headlights like endless tenuous tentacles. The distant boom of frogs pulsed dismally on the night. It was a lonely, deserted spot.

Norah Beamish said with conviction: "Anyone who would park himself out in a place like this for very long must be a trifle addled. If anybody had told me this morning on the ship that I'd be here tonight, I'd have hooted them down."

Nevertheless she followed Nancy with alacrity when Val stepped out and opened the rear door.

"You can wait in the car," Val told her.

"Young man," Norah answered majestically, "if Jim Gregg can't tell me what to do, it's useless for you to try. I came here to play a helpless old mother and I'm going to hobble up to that house and play her. Save your breath."

"Hobble on," Val surrendered. "Let's go. I can't see the house, but it must be back there somewhere."

"Are you taking a gun?" Nancy questioned.

"Hardly need one," Val assured her. "After all, we can't possibly be suspected.

And with—er—a helpless mother along, we'll fit the part perfectly."

"Nancy shan't stir one step from this car without a gun in the party," Norah said firmly. "She's a helpless girl—and I don't like the looks of this place. It gives me the creeps."

"A gun it'll be then," Val agreed cheerfully. He leaned in the car, pulled his bag out from their luggage, and slipped his automatic in his pocket. On second thought he added the flashlight he always carried somewhere in his effects.

THEY walked back to the gate and headed along the driveway into the fog. The hoarse booming of the frogs gradually grew louder, and by that Val knew they were approaching the river. Huge old trees lined the driveway, stretching heavy branches out over their heads. Once the fog parted briefly and he caught sight of a gibbous moon hanging high in the sky. But for the most part they walked blindly in the mist, which blotted and enfeebled the beam of his flashlight.

And the walk seemed endless.

"I don't believe there's a house around here," Norah panted finally. And then said something not entirely ladylike as her heel turned on a stone and she lurched against Val. "Drat it!" she grumbled. "I should have put on hunting boots!"

Val himself was beginning to wonder how much farther they would have to walk. This estate of Oakridge Manor seemed to be endless. The drive made several turns, seeming to run almost in the shape of a sprawling "S". He judged the house was invisible from the road. And then without warning a dark automobile appeared before them; and beyond it the lighted windows of a large house emitted a sickly glow through the mist.

"Thank heavens we won't have to wake

them up," Norah remarked with relief.

Val turned the flash into the machine. It was empty; and bore D. C. license plates. Oakridge Manor, he judged, was having visitors this night. All the better.

The drive widened into a big circle in front of the house, with a flower bed in the center, and they could make out dimly the looming bulk of a large Colonial mansion, with a wing at each end. They started around the flower bed; and suddenly Norah stumbled again, and gasped sharply as she jumped quickly aside.

"What is this?"

Val's light was on it a moment later— a huge Great Dane dog lying dead on the driveway with a trickle of blood staining the ground in front of its chest. It had been shot, and had not been dead long as Val discovered when he touched it with his foot.

The sight shocked them out of their calm. "I don't like this!" Nancy whispered sharply.

"I'd like to get my hands on the man who killed that beautiful animal!" Norah exclaimed indignantly under her breath. "Look at him—poor thing!"

Val looked at the house instead. Looked warily. Of a sudden the drear silence had taken on an ominous quality. He couldn't say why. After all, there were a score of reasons why the dog might have been killed. It might have been a strange dog, for instance, trespassing in some way. But nevertheless the feeling persisted.

"Perhaps you two had better go back to the car," he suggested under his breath.

"We'll stick together," Nancy told him quietly.

"I'm not afraid!" Norah Beamish insisted defiantly. "It takes more than a dead dog to upset me. Go on."

Val hesitated, and then against his better judgment led the way to the front door. It was made of heavy planks, with small diamond-shaped panes of leaded glass at the top. Curtains inside cut off the view beyond. He found a big wrought-iron knocker breast high, and used it. The clanging sounds seemed to echo back through the house, which despite the lights was strangely silent.

The knocking was not answered. He repeated it. And while he waited, he roved the beam of the flash around the big dark front porch. Not ten feet away the bottoms of a pair of shoes caught his eye.

It was a man, lying there on his face, with the bone handle of a knife sticking up grotesquely from under one shoulder blade!

CHAPTER SEVEN

The Woman Upstairs

NANCY Fraser saw that sight past Val's shoulder an instant later. Her fingers bit into his arm as she pressed close to him. "Is—is he dead?" she asked unsteadily.

"Looks that way," Val muttered, stepping forward to the side of the motionless body.

He stooped, caught a shoulder and turned the face up. The flashlight showed a dapper, well-dressed young man with a sharp face, prominent nose and tousled black hair. It was no one he had ever seen before.

Norah had moved to the spot also. She did not cry out. She was calm as usual. "Nancy—I think we had better go back to the machine."

"What do you think is happening here?" Nancy asked Val swiftly.

"Haven't the slightest idea," he confessed. "But it looks bad."

Just then the front door opened, letting a bright swath of light out across the front porch.

Val whirled around, sliding his hand into his pocket.

A broad-shouldered, heavy-set man stepped out into the light and peered at them. He had a gun in his hand, and as he stared at them the weapon slowly lowered to his side and he asked gruffly: "What's this?"

"I think you're the one to do the explaining," Val countered, walking toward him. "Who killed that man?"

"You aren't the sheriff?" the stranger mumbled, looking at the two women.

"No. I'm not the sheriff."

"Then who the devil are you?"

Norah Beamish ranged alongside Val, and there was not the slightest trace of a quaver in her voice as she said firmly: "Our car ran out of gasoline down there on the road, and we came in here looking for a telephone or enough gasoline to take us on."

The man who stood there in the light had a wide flat face, with lumpy, muscular jowls, blue-black with a close-shaven beard. His eyes were narrowed, his mouth was a tight line and his manner suspicious as Norah Beamish spoke to him. But the suspicion gradually left.

"Out of gasoline, eh?" he said.

"Yes," Norah answered clamly. "Have you any to spare? And while we're asking questions, what is that dead man doing there? It's—it's horrible."

VAL kept his hand on the automatic in his pocket. He was aware of the narrowed eyes resting on the pocket for a moment, and suspected that the fellow knew what was in it. But the fact seemed to make no difference. They couldn't look very suspicious with Norah Beamish standing there very much the *grande dame,* asking imperious questions.

"I guess it does look pretty funny to find a thing like that on a front porch, doesn't it, madam?" the man chuckled. "The fact is, I'm waiting for the sheriff now. I thought when you knocked it was he. You see, this fellow, whoever he is,"

with a jerk of his head at the body, "was prowling around here tonight with at least one other man. The dog ran out barking at them, and they shot him."

"They should have been shot themselves for that!" Norah sniffed.

"My sentiments exactly, madam," she was assured. "I heard the disturbance and ran out to see what was the matter. One of them took a shot at me in the dark. I made a good target against the light, I imagine. The bullet just missed me. See where it hit the side of the door?"

He turned and pointed to a small round hole in the wood at the side of the door which Val had not noticed when he knocked.

"And so you stabbed him?" Norah queried, wide-eyed.

That drew another chuckle. "No, madam, I did not stab him. I had stepped out without my gun, and I ran back inside and slammed the door. It was 'Big Buck', the nigger yard man, who threw that knife. He's quite handy with one, and he had dodged out at the side of the house when he heard the noise. Standing there, he saw one of the men run up on the porch and take a stand at the side of the door with a gun in his hand. Evidently waiting for me to show myself again, madam. Buck didn't know what it was all about. But he knew I was in danger, and when I started to open the door again, having gotten my gun, Buck threw his knife. Unfortunately with fatal effect. The man fell. And his companions must have gone one way while Buck went the other. When I stepped out on the porch with this revolver, I found the fellow breathing his last, and it took me ten minutes or so to get the straight of the matter. I've telephoned the sheriff, and he said he would get out here as soon as he could.

"And that," said the man drily, "explains the gory scene, madam. If you people will step inside you may use the telephone, and save yourselves the unpleasantness of being out here with him."

With a polite inclination of his head he indicated the doorway hospitably.

"Thank you. We will do that," said Norah firmly, and she sailed inside before Val could say anything to her. Nancy looked at him inquiringly.

Val swiftly conned the facts. "You say there were two of them?" he asked.

"At least that many."

"And the others ran?"

"I haven't seen anything more of them. I guess they didn't know how many men were out there in the darkness throwing knives, so they left while the leaving was good," the man chuckled again.

GALBRAITH had been intending to come here. He had been killed. Now violence had appeared at this house a few hours later. Was it the work of the Black Doctor, Val wondered. Was this house unaware of the danger threatening it? Had the Black Doctor, or some of his men, been closing in on it and been checked by an unexpected knife thrown out of the darkness?

It looked that way.

The mystery was growing thicker at every move, but this was the chance he had wanted to get inside the house. Val nodded slightly at Nancy and followed her into a wide, spacious hall.

"My name is Easton," he said clamly as their host joined them, closing the door behind him.

"Tillson is my name, sir," the other answered promptly.

This was the man, then, to whom Ramey's wire had been sent. But what about Long, the city man who had bought the place several years before, according to the owner of the drugstore back in Hartsville? Val had been wondering about that all the way out. Long owned Oakridge Manor, yet Ramey had wired a J. B. Tillson. Did they live here together? Were they partners, friends? Those were questions he wanted to ask, but didn't dare to, under the circumstances.

"You are the owner, I presume?" he suggested.

And received a negative shake of the head.

"No. Mr. Long is the owner here. He's upstairs in bed with a broken leg."

Norah Beamish had been looking around as they talked. "You have a nice place here," she complimented.

"Thank you, madam," Tillson bowed. "I think it is myself."

He was a curious combination of hardboiled sophistication and ultra-polite civility. The fact that a man lay dead on the front porch did not seem to disturb him in the slightest. In fact he seemed amused, if anything. Val surprised a quirk at the corner of his mouth that was suppressed almost instantly. And since the telephone was not pressed on them at once, he talked casually.

"Do you have a farm here?"

Tillson shook his head. "Only a vegetable garden. I guess there isn't enough money in farming these days to tempt John. And since he has enough money to live on he lets the place lie as it is."

"I imagine the women folks are upset by this business tonight," Norah Beamish observed shrewdly.

"There are no women in the house," Tillson told her. "John is a bachelor, and my wife is in California."

"Where all wives should be," said Norah.

Tillson was the perfect host as he smiled at her sadly. "There are different opinions about that, of course, madam. I miss Mrs. Tillson a great deal. Won't you ladies sit down? Mr. Easton, the telephone is in the back of the house. I'll take you there. Better get the call in before the sheriff gets here."

Talking to this man, looking about the spacious hall, listening to the peaceful quiet of the old house, Val had felt increasingly that something was wrong.

All this did not hook up with Galbraith's errand to this country; with Gregg's declaration that the man had been empowered to spend a million pounds; with the British agent that had evidently been tagging Galbraith; and the cold-blooded way both men had died. What could one of the great powers find interesting in this spot? In this man Tillson or his friend who lay upstairs with a broken leg? What did New York have to do with this peaceful lonely spot on the banks of the Potomac?

And while those thoughts had flashed through Val's mind, he was wondering about Tillson also. For despite the ultra politeness, the soft, almost genial manner of the man, the effect fell flat. He didn't look like a country gentleman, or a man who would be satisfied to hibernate in a quiet spot like this. He looked hard, cold, clever. And every once in a while there was a glint in his eyes, a catlike scrutiny of his surroundings, a cold, quickly caught inflection of his voice, that bore out that impression.

NO, THE man didn't ring true. The situation didn't ring true. There was peace in the air. But it was a taut, quivering peace, a quiet that seemed charged with electric tension.

Instead of quieting the nerves it put them on edge. Val had a very definite feeling that all this pleasantry might change instantly to tragedy.

And against all the facts he had marshaled there was the evidence of the dead dog and the lifeless corpse out there on the front porch. That dead man belonged to the cities. He wasn't a casual country prowler. He didn't belong out here in the mist-filled night, far from houses or people—unless the facts were

right. Unless there were more to all this than appeared on the surface. Unless Galbraith had been intending to come here, and the Black Doctor was also interested in the place.

That was evidence that could not be disputed. Val wished the women were back in the machine, heading toward Washington. He was, he told himself, a fool for bringing them out there. He could have done the job just as well himself.

"I'll use your telephone," he agreed briskly. "And then we'll go out to our car and cause you no further trouble."

"It is a pleasure," Tillson assured him. "It does this house good to have women in it once in a while."

And the words were barely out of the man's mouth as he turned to the door on his right when the quiet of the house was rudely shattered by a rush of feet upstairs. And following that came the high, shrill, terror-stricken cry of a woman . . .

They all froze in their tracks, staring toward the top of the wide sweeping stairs that led up to the second floor, whence that scream had come.

Val's eyes dropped to Tillson, whose head had hunched forward and whose face had darkened with an ugly scowl.

That was all the proof Val needed of his suspicions. Tillson had lied flatly when he said there were no women in the house. And that woman who had screamed was in mortal terror or great pain. It drove a shiver down his back.

"What's wrong up there?" Norah Beamish uttered explosively, swinging around on Tillson.

It all happened in seconds. Later on Val was to wonder why he hadn't moved fast enough. But he didn't have a chance, couldn't guess what was going to happen.

After the scream cut off sharp, the running feet still pounded upstairs. They reached the head of the stairs and started down.

The four of them standing below in the hall saw the feet, the legs, the whole figure of a man dashing down the stairs. He was hatless, coatless, shirtless—a sleek, pudgy form half running, half falling down the stairs in his mad haste.

His hair was rumpled wildly; blood was streaming from the corner of his mouth, spattering the white front of his under shirt and his arms. And one hand brandished a gleaming revolver.

With a shock Val recognized Galbraith's New York visitor—Ramey!

Only now the sleek unctuousness of the man had given away to wild, uncontrollable fright and desperation. His face was twisted in a mask of terror as he catapulted to the turn of the stairs.

"Get back!" Val cried at Nancy Fraser. His arm swept her roughly back against the wall.

And an instant later, as Ramey reached the turn in the stairs, their ears were deafened by the report of a gun. It was Tillson shooting. Standing there calmly, jaws clenched until the bunching muscles ridged out. His gun spat once—twice—three times . . . .

Ramey's legs gave way under him. The terror-stricken mask of his face suddenly looked horrible as it was struck by a bullet. His body raced forward, the gun flying from his fingers.

And as Norah Beamish lost her poise and screamed aloud, Ramey's limp body tumbled and bounced and slid to the floor of the hall at their feet.

CHAPTER EIGHT

The £1,000,000 Secret

THE odor of burnt powder was strong on the air. Their ears were ringing from the shattering explosions in the confined space of the hall. And ghastly

death there before them was stark evidence that they were not dreaming.

Val turned on Tillson, tugging at the automatic in his pocket—and met the steady muzzle of Tillson's revolver. Behind it he saw a new Tillson. A man no longer smiling, polite. The narrowed eyes were cold and hard. The flat face was a mask that was not good to see.

"Put your arms up!" Tillson ordered through his teeth.

Val hesitated only a fraction of a second. Proof of what might happen if he did not was too close at hand. He jerked his hands from his coat pocket and lifted his arms in the air.

"You—you cold-blooded killer!" Norah Beamish gasped.

"Shut up!" Tillson ordered her roughly. "You talk too much, old lady!"

"Old?" Norah choked. "Why—why—"

"Do I have to shut your mouth for you?" Tillson asked coldly.

"Norah, be quiet," Nancy ordered clearly. She stepped to Norah's side and laid slender fingers on Norah's arm.

Tillson gave her a cold grin. "You have some sense, young lady," he remarked.

"You haven't acted as if you had," Nancy told him in the same cool voice. Her deep blue eyes were boring at the man as if she were trying to look behind his face and see things that had not become visible heretofore.

Tillson sneered at them. "Gas!" he said. "Ran out of it right by the front gate. It was convenient, wasn't it? And too bad."

"Your name isn't Tillson," Nancy said coolly.

"No? What is it?"

That was what Val was wondering. The whole picture had changed. He was trying to get his bearings again, linking up the facts to make a new picture. And while he was doing that someone else came to the top of the stairs and descended leisurely.

Val saw black-clad legs, a white shirt, with sleeves rolled up—and a tall, stooped figure descended into view. A pale, cadaverous face looked down at them as the newcomer halted at the turn of the stairs and surveyed the scene for a moment with an inscrutable smile on his lips. The bony arms below the rolled-up sleeves were covered thickly with dark matted hair. And the long talonlike fingers of the right hand held a keen, gleaming surgeon's scalpel.

Nancy uttered a choked cry. Val swore under his breath, and a chill crawled down his back. For that stooped figure holding the little gleaming knife was Carl Zaken, the Black Doctor.

"So?" said Zaken mildly, gesturing with the scalpel. "These are our visitors. This is a surprise."

And the very mildness of his voice made the words sound worse. For Val and Nancy had seen what the man could do, and had heard tales of what he was capable of. Standing there holding the surgeon's scalpel he looked like a smiling fiend.

Norah Beamish's harsh whisper to Nancy was audible to all of them. "Who —who is that man?"

Nancy's face was pale. Val saw the fingers of her free hand curling tightly into her pink palm, and guessed the terrific effort she was making to keep a grip on herself. But her voice was steady as she spoke.

"That is the man who attacked me in the hotel this evening. His name is Carl Zaken."

"Oh!" said Norah weakly, and for once she seemed at a loss for words as she stared up at Zaken.

Zaken leaned against the railing, toying with the scalpel. He betrayed no surprise at Nancy's knowledge of his identity. His greenish eyes seemed to blaze and glow as the light from the hall fixture struck into them.

"What were you doing to that fellow?" Val asked harshly, nodding at Ramey.

"We were having a little confidential talk," the Black Doctor said smoothly, and his lips parted in a ghastly grimace and he slowly tapped the back of the scalpel against a thumb.

"You mean," asked Val thickly, "you were torturing him?"

"Persuading," Zaken corrected. "Unfortunately he knocked my man down, seized his gun and tried to leave us, forgetting entirely his woman friend. But then, cheap criminals of his type think only of their own skins."

ALL the tales Val had ever heard about the Black Doctor flashed before him now. He understood the terrible fright and agony on Ramey's face as he had plunged down the stairs. This lonely house was being given over to things too horrible to contemplate. And Nancy was thinking the same, for he saw her smooth white throat flutter as she swallowed convulsively.

"He was in New York this afternoon," Val said mechanically.

"Yes. He and his friends should have stayed there instead of hurrying here as soon as he was through with Sir Edward Lyne," Zaken said contemptuously.

"You came quick enough. How did you get out of that room and down here in Virginia so fast?"

Zaken grimaced again with amusement. "I have found that he who moves fastest moves safest, Mr. Easton. Leaving the room was a small matter. My man, who had tied you up so I would not be interrupted, had lowered a thin silk rope from his room just over Sir Edward's, to call our late friend by his right name. I left you via the rope, the fire escape from the roof below, and a taxicab that I hailed at the mouth of the alley. I picked my man up at the hotel entrance a few minutes later. We passed the police car as we turned into Fifth Avenue. A fast ride out to a chartered plane. A faster trip to Washington and out here. *Voila*—and the thing was done. I presume you came by plane also?"

Val nodded. "I didn't expect to find you here," he confessed bluntly.

"*Touché*—the surprise is mutual. I did not believe you had been able to find out where Galbraith was going. I killed him for that reason—so the matter would end there for you—and him. Had I suspected otherwise I would have used lethal gas."

"Like you used on those poor devils aboard ship," Val charged swiftly.

Zaken gestured delicately with the scalpel. "The steward was an accident. The gas lingered in that closed room longer than I thought it would. He walked into it. The wind must have blown in through the door he left open and aired the cabin thoroughly before he was discovered. You found no trace of it?"

"No," said Val shortly.

"Just as well," Zaken murmured. "It is very deadly. It had to be because of the small amount I was able to inject through the keyhole."

"Why do it?"

"He was a member of the British Secret Service, dispatched as an unofficial guard over Sir Edward Lyne. We bumped into each other on deck that evening, and I think he recognized me. I couldn't take chances. You understand how it is in delicate matters like this, Mr. Easton?"

"In a small way," Val agreed sarcastically. "I suppose you found out what Lyne was after when you searched his hotel room. And then put him out of the way because you needed him no longer."

"But I knew what he was after," Za-

ken declared humorously, showing his fanglike incisor teeth as he smiled. "But I did not know where it was. You are quite right about the rest. I simply—ah—eliminated competition which might have proved embarrassing. He would have come here at once, of course. You would have followed—and my plans might have been upset. I have only three men with me. The whole matter broke so suddenly I barely had time to get passage on the same boat with Lyne. No matter what I pay for information, my sources are not always infallible."

Zaken's casual manner changed abruptly. "Bring them upstairs," he commanded. "Shoot the first one who makes a wrong move. Are you sure they're alone?"

"Yes. I was waiting near the gate when they stopped their car."

Zaken nodded, waited until they were almost up to him and then preceded them. He turned to the left at the top of the stairs and led the way to the back of the house, to a long, high-ceilinged room with a great bay window, curtained now, opening out into the night.

Standing beside the door and furtively fingering a swelling eye was the man who had posed as a waiter only a few hours earlier. "Did you get him?" he asked Zaken uncertainly.

"Yes," returned Zaken coldly. "And the next time you grow careless, Stubbs, it will be the end. I stand for blundering no more than once."

"Yes, sir," Stubbs replied uneasily, his eyes dropping before the greenish glare that transfixed him. And pallor swept over his face as Zaken led the way into the room.

IT WAS an upstairs library, with bookcases along the walls, comfortable chairs, and a large brick fireplace against the end wall. Over the fireplace hung a large copy of the Stuart painting of

George Washington, and the inscrutable eyes of the stately figure seemed to look down and ponder this strange scene that was taking place.

Six people were seated in that room, as strange and heterogeneous a collection as Val had ever seen. Every one of them was marked with the sickly brand of fright and terror.

Sitting in the bay window were two; a pretty, slinky, tawdry young woman dressed in flashy clothes, who was slowly rubbing an angry red wrist; and a hard, sophisticated man of about thirty, wise, worldly, and at this moment pale and haggard as he wet his lips and stared at them.

On a bench beside the fireplace were a lanky negro in overalls and a fat negress, the whites of their eyes rolling.

Two chairs near the end of the library table held a stiff, severe, waspish woman of about forty-five, and a small, slight man with a bulging forehead and shrewd eyes, a strange mixture of intelligence and pomposity. He was haggard also, with sunken, feverish eyes and a limp appearance, as if worry and fear had crushed him.

STANDING near the doorway, a gun in his hand, was a cool, self-possessed man in his early thirties, his face cast in a shrewd cold mold, with a cruel mouth under a small black mustache. He looked foreign—was foreign Val found out a moment later.

For Carl Zaken, continuing with the same mocking politeness, gestured at them with a scalpel. "The people you came to see, Mr. Easton. Study them at your leisure. In the window there we have Miss Dolly Mae Hall, as perfect a sample of your shopworn New York night-club siren as one could wish to find. Her specialty is understanding love, and she seems to be good at it."

Val saw the pompous little man with the bulging forehead wriggle uneasily in his chair, and glance fearfully at the severe woman at his side, who pursed her mouth and glared at him.

Zaken flashed them a humorous glance and went on.

"With her is 'Badger Bill' Marcus, a sterling partner, I understand. Those two negroes work about the place. And in these chairs by the table we have Professor Henry Long and his gentle wife. This man guarding them is Vollonoff, who has been with me for some years, under one name and another. You recognize these three, Vollonoff? Easton, Miss Fraser, and a Mrs. Beamish, of the American Secret Service. They worked faster than we thought possible. Don't underestimate Easton and the girl, Fyodor. They are dangerous."

Vollonoff flashed a cold smile under his black mustache. Val judged him to be almost as dangerous as Carl Zaken himself.

"The man you saw on the front porch," continued Zaken, "is Sammy McGee, alias Tillson, a partner of Ramey and Marcus. The story, as I gather it to date, is that Professor Long, to celebrate the successful culmination of several years' work, and the undoubtedly trying company of his wife in this isolated spot, went to New York to taste the bright lights. Or, as I have heard your countrymen say, 'to throw a bust.' He drank not wisely but too well, talked indiscreetly about what he had been working on and had accomplished, and in that alcoholic daze found himself in the grip of an undying passion for Dolly Mae. They progressed to her apartment—control yourself, Mrs. Long—the flesh is weak at times.

"The play that was staged must have been masterly, Easton. When it was over Professor Long found himself apparently laboring under the onus of having shot his new love's husband, with

Ramey, one of her men friends in the role of rescuer, who hustled him away from the police net to safety. It developed that the price of continued safety and silence was a share in the fortune that Professor Long stood to gain from his invention.

"Under duress Professor Long was constrained to turn the marketing of his invention over to the gang controlled by Ramey, which had him in its grip. They sent Sammy McGee down here under the name of Tillson to keep an eye on the professor and make certain he did not forget that at any moment he might be hauled back to New York for murder. And Ramey took up the marketing of the invention, not with his own country as any patriotic citizen would do, but with the British government, who could be counted on to pay almost any price for it. The upshot of the negotiations was the hurried dispatch of Sir Edward Lyne, with instructions to look into the matter and offer anything up to a million pounds on the spot if he considered the claims correct."

Carl Zaken shrugged.

"And that's where we came in, Easton. Ramey had evidently stipulated a secret rendezvous in New York with the man sent over, with more directions there. His intention was to bring Lyne down here, convince him, wait until the money was paid over, and probably decamp with all of it. After giving Lyne directions, he and his confederates hurried down here instantly. We found them here when we arrived. The dog barked as we came up and had to be put out of the way. McGee rushed out, and Vollonoff dispatched him with his usual skill. And so we came in and went to work. I had just finished a little session with Ramey in the other room, finding out that Professor Long has been canny enough to keep the final drawings of his invention hidden. And now I am ready to take that little matter up with him."

ZAKEN smiled without mirth as he stood there in his shirt sleeves, drawing the gleaming little knife through his fingers. Professor Long's face went grayish as he met the grimacing smile the Black Doctor gave him.

Mrs. Long sprang to her feet and cried shrilly: "You'd better leave Henry alone! You—you'll suffer for this outrage, whoever you are!"

Vollonoff stepped forward and shoved her roughly back in her chair.

Val hardly saw the play. His mind was on the astounding revelations Zaken had made apparently under the impression that he knew almost as much about it. What could that shrinking, pompous little man with the bulging forehead control that would be worth almost any price to a foreign government?

He said casually: "I doubt if Lyne would have offered much for it. And you probably won't get anything for your trouble, either."

"No?" Zaken mocked. "Not for the answer to the problem that every general staff in the world has been seeking for fifteen years? An infallible range finder that will locate and bring correctly to bear anti-aircraft guns by day or night, or in fog? Your own army engineers have been working on it for years. And according to Ramey, the professor here has solved the problem with a sensitive finder that picks up the spark emanations from the motor timer, calibrates their distance and height and speed by instant triangulation, and brings the guns hooked up to the system to bear instantly. With it a fleet of bombing planes can be located whether seen or not, and shot down at once. It will make the country that controls it safe from aerial invasion. Think what that will mean to England—to know that she is safe from attack by air! Millions saved in defensive air fleets, and probably the winning or losing of the next war.

Japan, with her great cities near her island coasts, will pay any price for it. The general staffs of every great power will be bidding wildly for it, once the information gets out that Carl Zaken can turn that invention over to them."

And Val knew with a sickening feeling that the man was right. If this Professor Long had perfected an invention like that and it looked as if he had —no price was too much to pay for it. And Carl Zaken, master spy would offer it to the highest bidder. The chances were that some other country would get it, possibly a future enemy of the United States.. In this lonely house tonight a world issue was being decided. And in the balance were only himself, Nancy Fraser and Norah Beamish.

Zaken's mocking glance was on him. "You don't agree?" Zaken questioned.

Val shrugged. "Perhaps. D'you think Long will tell you? He doesn't look like the type of man who would give as important a secret as that into the wrong hands."

Professor Henry Long sat up and spoke for the first time. "I'm not!" he burst out passionately. "I didn't know what Ramey was going to do! He said he was dealing with our government! I won't turn it over to another country! I won't . . . ."

Zaken showed his fanglike incisors in another grimace. "Your sentiments do you credit, professor. We will see what a short consultation will do. I have been very successful in the past as a persuader. Kroner, bring him in. We won't embarrass the ladies by doing it in here."

The powerful fellow who had posed as Tillson pushed to the professor's chair without a word, seized his arm and hauled him up. When the little man tried to struggle, he received a blow in the face that knocked him limp and mumbling. And in that state, while his wife wailed shrilly and the others looked on with horrified helplessness, the professor was half dragged, half carried out of the room.

The Black Doctor slowly scraped the edge of his scalpel across the matted hairs of his left arm. The gesture was casual, but the effect was ghastly as he grimaced ,and turned to follow.

"I shall write Gregg tomorrow and compliment him on his agents," he said to Val and Nancy. "A pity I can't let you live to tell him about this. But a million pounds is too much to risk . . ."

CHAPTER NINE

Gas Trap

NORAH BEAMISH cast a venomous glance at Vollonoff and went over and tried to comfort the nearly hysterical Mrs. Long. Twin spots of color were vivid on Nancy's face as she looked at Val silently. Stubbs stood outside the door, fingering his gun. Vollonoff lounged inside, his eyes watching every move they made. The couple in the window seat huddled together miserably. And the fat negress began to mumble, "Oh, Lawd—Oh, Lawd—Oh, Lawd..."

A piercing shriek suddenly rang through the house, the cry of a man in torment and agony.

Professor Long's wife gasped and fainted, which was perhaps best, for more shrieks followed.

Norah Beamish whirled on Val, her eyes blazing. "Can't you do something about it?" she cried.

Vollonoff smirked expectantly.

And Val stood there with his shoulders slumped, the picture of dejection. "And get shot for trying?" he answered Norah helplessly. "You saw what happened to that chap downstairs."

Norah glared at him. "I thought you were a man!"

"Val—" said Nancy helplessly.

"It's no use," Val said wretchedly.

"We're going to die anyway," she reminded through stiff lips.

"Perhaps they'll let us go if we promise to let them get away. They could tie us up—"

"Oh!" Norah blazed contemptuously.

Even Vollonoff was affected by this show of helplessness. "Sit down," he advised, with a curl of contempt on his lips. "Not so dangerous, after all."

Val shrugged helplessly and turned toward the nearest chair. And as he passed slowly in front of Nancy, with his back to Vollonoff, words slid almost inaudibly from the corner of his mouth. He didn't even look at her to see what their effect was.

Nancy's face suddenly twisted in helpless grief. She fished for a handkerchief and dabbed at her eyes as she turned toward the other end of the room.

"He c-can't help us," she wept. "Come over here with me, Norah."

Norah stared at her in amazement and then swiftly followed her. "Don't you cry, honey," she begged bruskly "There's a way out of this."

"No, there's not!" Nancy wailed.

Val could see them as he pulled the chair around to sit down. But an instant later he heard Nancy gasp: "Catch me! I'm—I'm . . . ."

And Val snapped the chair off the floor, whirled around and hurled it with every ounce of strength in his body. As he had planned, Nancy's gasp had drawn Vollonoff's attention for a second. Vollonoff sensed what was happening—too late. As he jerked his head back the edge of the chair seat caught him squarely in the face. The gun in his hand roared deafeningly, missing. And an instant later Val was on him, smashing his fist over the top of the falling chair.

The jar of the blow rocked Val's arm clear to the shoulder. And it drove Vollonoff reeling backward, knocked out cold, the gun falling from his hand.

Val ducked into the protection of his body, caught Vollonoff under the arms and heaved him at the doorway. Stubbs, leaping into the room in confused surprise, caught the full impact of Vollonoff's weight, and for an instant was tied up in confusion there in the doorway.

"Here!" Nancy cried at Val's side. She thrust Vollonoff's gun into his hand. She had seized it off the floor. Her eyes were shining, her voice thrilling in its disregard for danger.

"Get down on the floor!" Val rapped at her as his fingers closed over the revolver. A wave of confidence swept through him. No longer were his hands tied by futile helplessness. The very thought of the odds against them, and the consequences if he failed, brought strength.

The revolver leveled just as Stubbs hurled Vollonoff's falling body back into the room and raised the automatic in his hand. Both guns spat at once. A cold, searing sensation raked Val's side. He knew he had been shot there. But Stubbs reeled around, clasping a shattered elbow. And then dodged out of sight beside the door before Val could fire again.

A LEAP, a kick, and the door crashed shut. An instant later Stubbs poured a fusillade of shots through the door. But they all went wide, hitting no one.

Everyone had come to their feet. The negress began to shriek in terror.

"Shut up!" Val yelled at her, and when that had no effect he ignored her.

He heard Carl Zaken's voice shout in the hallway. "What happened in there?"

And Stubbs replying shakily: "He knocked Vollonoff out with a chair, got his gun, and shot me in the elbow! I'll bleed to death!"

"And good enough for you!" Zaken snarled. He broke off into French, cursing Vollonoff and Stubbs for ignorant fools. "Clumsy pig! Son of a goat!" Zaken shouted. "Watch that door! Don't let them get out! They can't get away! I'll fix them! With gas!"

Nancy and Val both understood the words. The rest did not. Marcus asked uncertainly: "What'll we do?"

"Gas!" Nancy whispered to Val. "It won't be tear gas this time!"

"No," Val agreed bruskly. "He's gambling high tonight. He'll slaughter the lot of us as quick as he can now."

Nancy looked at him desperately. "What will we do? We can't get out that door."

"Here! Watch the door! Don't waste the bullets! We'll need them!"

Val grabbed up a chair, stepped to the great bay window and began to swing the chair vigorously. Glass crashed and fell away before it. A few seconds of that and the windows were cleared away.

WRAITHS of fog swirled in. The croaking of the riverside frogs sounded very close. He judged the house sat almost on the river bank. He turned around and snapped at the others:

"Get out on that roof! Quick! Your lives may depend on it!"

Professor Long's wife was still unconscious in her chair. Val picked her up and strode to the window. He had to wait a moment as Marcus and his girl friend and the two negroes scrambled through, ignoring the jagged edges of glass. None of them waited to help him. Val hadn't expected it. Their nerves were too shattered by terror. He heaved his burden through and lowered her roughly to the roof below. She would have a measure of safety out there.

Norah Beamish and Nancy were at his side, waiting for orders. Norah's eyes were shining too. "Young man," she cried, "I apologize!"

Outside the door Carl Zaken's voice snapped in French: "One side, pig!"

"Give me that gun!" Val husked to Nancy. He fired two shots at the door. Couldn't see whether he had hit anything or not.

Vollonoff stirred on the floor just before he fired. The sound of the shots seemed to bring him out of his daze. He sat up groggily. And an instant later Nancy caught Val's arm and pointed to the doorway.

"Look!"

Through one of the bullet holes in the door thrust the glistening point of a sharp needle. From its end a tiny spray of liquid spurted into the room. And that spray dissolved into a bluish vapor as they stared at it.

"Out that window quick!" Val urged. He whirled Nancy around himself, and started her with a shove.

And as he waited for them to get through to safety, Val saw a sight he never forgot. Vollonoff was staggering to his feet just in front of the door, his eyes on them with dazed surprise.

"Look out!" Val shouted at him. "Come over here, quick!"

Instead Vollonoff turned around to the door, obviously intending to escape. And the first dissolving wave of gas closed about him. Vollonoff's hand shot to his throat. He strangled. Too late he realized what was happening and turned toward the window.

The gas cloaked him like an evil halo now. He staggered, his face turning purple and his eyes starting from their sockets. His mouth opened to cry out— and only a horrible strangling issued from it. Vollonoff took one lurching step toward the window, and then tumbled forward on his face, kicked and lay still.

Val ducked out the window, white-faced and shaken.

"God!" he husked to Nancy. "No wonder that steward couldn't get out the door! Get down off this roof before it starts to drift out the window. One good whiff of it seems to be all that's needed."

HE DRAGGED Long's wife to the end of the roof. She recovered consciousness as he did that. The negro was down on the ground. The negress slid off, hung by her hands a moment, blubbering, and then dropped the short distance to the ground and was caught by her companion.

"Pass her down to me," Val ordered Nancy.

He dropped the same way. Nancy and Norah Beamish lowered the protesting woman and he caught her. Nancy and Norah followed. And while they did that Marcus and his girl companion made the drop successfully. They were all safe.

"Get back out of sight and stay there!" Val said to Nancy and Norah. "No more foolishness! I'll see what I can do."

He raced through the damp mist to the front of the house, gun in one hand and his flash in the other. The front porch was still and quiet. A wink of the flash showed the dead body lying where he had left it. The front door was closed.

But as he looked, it was jerked open from inside and the man who had opened it once before stepped out. Val shot at him and missed. The man jumped back inside, slamming the door.

Val waited tensely, wondering what what would happen next.

It came from behind; running feet poked out of the fog and closed in on him. Val faced them crouching, wondering with a sick feeling if Carl Zaken had lied, and had more men out here in the night.

But a voice shouted: "That you Easton?"

It was Gregg. And as Val relaxed and lowered the gun, Gregg came running up with half a dozen men. "We heard the shouts," he panted. "Having trouble?"

And all Val could think of at that instant was to say foolishly: "I thought you were going home to sleep."

"Got to thinking that this was too important to leave up in the air till morning," Gregg told him. "I called some of the men and started out here to get the lay of the land myself, and station them. We saw your car back there by the gate and had started to look the ground over when we heard something that sounded like shots. And then we heard you shoot here again. What happened?"

"Two of you go around and watch there!" Val ordered before he replied. "Shoot anyone you see trying to leave. Anyone outside is all right."

"Do that!" Gregg ordered hastily.

And as two of the men ran, Val hurriedly gave Gregg the highlights.

"Surround this house!" Gregg snapped to the rest of his men. "And shoot to kill. We've got one of the most dangerous men in the world cornered."

The words were hardly out of his mouth when three quick shots barked at the back of the house.

Val sprinted for the front door, and Gregg pounded after him, gun in hand also. Val opened the front door and peered in cautiously. The hall was empty. Ramey's body sprawled at the foot of the stairs. The interior of the house was still. Ominously still. Deathly still. But as he and Gregg stared in, the door at the back swung silently open. Carl Zaken leaped into the hall with a catlike movement, holding a gun in each hand.

He saw them at the same instant and jerked the two weapons up.

Val shot him first. Emptied the revolver in a tearing burst as fast as he could pull the trigger. Zaken went down, shooting wildly and futilely. He tried to rise on his two hands, dragging his guns with him. And slumped forward again. And then with a sudden movement he threw them weakly from him.

"*Touché*, Easton," he called weakly, turning a ghastly, pain-racked face toward the doorway. "I told Vollonoff you were a dangerous man."

And so it ended. Zaken's other two men had been trapped at the rear of the house, where they thought no one was watching, shot seriously and captured. They found Professor Long upstairs in one of the bedrooms, half dead from fear rather than pain. A few moments later, downstairs, he thrust a roll of drawings in Val's hand.

"Here," he said weakly. "Keep these. I—I never want to see them again. I'll take whatever the government offers for them."

Gregg's men, after performing hurried first aid, were already loading the wounded into their car, which they had brought up to the house and the body of Carl Zaken went with them.

Gregg was saying to Norah Beamish: "Want to ride back with us?"

"Nonsense!" Norah snapped. "I'll go with Nancy and Mr. Easton. Nancy needs me."

There was a slight inscrutable smile on Nancy's face as she said: "I think I'll be taken care of all right, if you want to go, Norah."

For a moment the older woman looked at Nancy shrewdly. And then she, too, smiled, and sighed. "I'll go with you, Jim Gregg," she said. "I think I'm getting old after all. Nancy doesn't need a mother tonight. Do you, Nancy?"

But Nancy was smiling at Val and didn't hear her.

A Truck - Load

A Cardigan Story

by

Frederick Nebel

Author of "The Candy Killer," etc.

Cardigan knew that fifty-grand diamond necklace hadn't just melted away—even if it was hot ice. Someone had the loot and he was going to find out who—if he had to fill the morgue and a couple of hospitals to do it.

Of Diamonds

He smiled innocently. Cardigan said: "What the hell?"

CHAPTER ONE

The Hesitant Mr. Micah

IT WAS something about a jewel theft in Thirty-seventh Street, over near Fifth Avenue . . .

Pat Seaward pronged the telephone receiver, sat back, killed a cigarette against the side of a corroded ashtray and read quickly the notes she had taken down.

Meantime she fooled with a lock of hair, near her left ear. It was late noon. She was the only one in the agency office—a trim, neat symphony of clothes, hairdress, good looks. She glanced up, reflected. Sunlight winked on the distant Chrysler spire.

Opening a desk drawer, she withdrew a dog-eared notebook, flipped the indexed pages to "C." At the head of the "C's" was the name Cardigan; beneath it, in parenthesis, an explanatory line: "Addresses at which he might be found." There were twenty-one addresses. Alongside one of them was the word "home"; alongside eight, the word "girl"; to the other twelve addresses was appended the one word—"speakeasy." And there was also a footnote: "If not at any of the above, try police stations, jails, hospitals, or the city morgue."

She began using the telephone. The sixth call, ending in "Foggy Joe" Pomano's place, brought results; and Pat said: "Well, you vanishing American, it's about time."

His voice said: "You old nagger, you."

"Listen," she said. "Now listen. Traum and Fleer, the jewel people, just called up. Listen now, because they're one of our best clients. They've just had a sixty-thousand-dollar diamond bracelet snatched from their man Harold Micah, in East Thirty-seventh Street. They want you to look after their interests. The crowd's at the Twenty-fifth Precinct house. Are you able to ambulate?"

"Ever see me when I wasn't?"

"Well, I shan't go into that. Will you go over?"

"O. K., precious. Soon as I finish this stud hand I'll take a tramp over?"

She said: "Why take a tramp along?"

"You bring back my childhood," Cardigan said. "Haven't heard that one since I was six. Goom-by, chicken."

SO IT was something about a jewel theft in broad daylight, some minutes shy of high noon, four blocks from the Traum & Fleer establishment.

Cardigan entering a large room of the precinct house, saw Captain Garrity, an H. Q. dick, sitting on a desk and spinning a coin in the air. Two precinct dicks leaned against the wall. Harold Micah, the jewel firm's man, sat in a swivel

chair; he was small, plain, commonplace in looks and dress—and about fifty years of age. On another chair sat a tall, wiry, waspy man—cool, collected, with dark pool-like eyes. There was a blue bruise on the olive skin near his left cheekbone.

Garrity—hard, bluff, clean-boned and straight as a ruled line—Garrity said: "Did I hear you knock, Jack?"

"How come you're up in a white man's neighborhood, Pete?"

"Well, I guess that makes us even. I'll tell you, you gorilla. I just happened to be Johnny-on-the-spot . . . This man is Mr. Micah. He was carrying the bracelet."

"We've met," Cardigan said.

"How do you do, Mr. Cardigan," said Micah. "I'm relieved to find you on the case."

Cardigan grinned at Garrity. "I guess that puts you in your place, Pete."

Garrity could take it. He grinned back with his hard bony face, then jerked a thumb, said: "This man says his name's Paul Kinnard. Have you met?"

"Havn't had the pleasure," Cardigan said.

Garrity said: "He was supposed to have snatched the bracelet."

"Yeah," said Kinnard. "I was supposed to have."

"Suppose now," Cardigan said, "instead of all this nice bright repartee—suppose I get some details."

Garrity flipped the coin, caught it, pocketed it. His voice was blunt, clipped. "At eleven-forty Mr. Micah left the establishment carrying the bracelet in a small case. The case was in his pocket. A man named Fitchman had telephoned them to send over the bracelet. Said he'd seen it in the window. The address was an office building on Broadway near Thirty-sixth. You've heard of Reuben Fitchman—the big silk man. The establishment was glad to send the bracelet over. We just checked up. Fitchman never phoned at all. It was a stall.

"Mr. Micah was jostled in a crowd in Thirty-seventh Street. He was tripped—accidentally maybe he fell; he says he was tripped. A man helped him up. He says this looks like the man. This man hurried off, west. Mr. Micah missed the case from his pocket and yelled. I was watching a safe being hoisted at the time. I got to him when he was running west. We saw Kinnard hiking it up the Thirty-eighth Street "El" station. A northbound train was pulling in. It pulled out with Kinnard on board. We hustled into a cab.

"Traffic was at a standstill on Sixth Avenue. Some company was making a movie of a wild auto ride. We passed the outfit like a bat out of hell and reached the Forty-second Street station. We beat it up the stairs and got to the platform just as the train was stopping. I told a brakeman to keep the train stopped. We watched the people get off. Kinnard didn't get off. Then I gave orders to close all the doors. Mr. Micah and I went through the train We found Kinnard on the rear end platform. I nailed him. He started to argue and I took a poke at him—"

"How the hell did I know you were a cop?" Kinnard said.

"I dragged him off the train," Garrity went on, "but he didn't have the bracelet. He claims he wasn't the guy helped Mr. Micah up. He claims he never swiped the bracelet."

Cardigan looked at Micah. "You're sure this is the man?"'

"I'm pretty sure."

"You ought to be absolutely sure."

Micah looked uncomfortable. "I—I was a little upset when I fell. I didn't look squarely at the man who helped me up. But when I missed the bracelet, my instinct chose this man. There was something about his clothes—his walk. And

when I yelled I thought I saw him walk faster. He didn't look around. And he ran toward the station—"

"Naturally," said Kinnard. "I saw the train coming. I wanted to catch it. Why shouldn't I run?" He scowled at Micah. "This guy's lying. He had to pick someone out. So he picked me. I'm the goat." He returned his dark gaze to Garrity. "You've got to get a little more to hold me, mister. I'll be no goat."

MICAH grimaced painfully. He wasn't sure, and this embarrassed him. Perspiration stood out on his face. Kinnard remained cool, dark, a little resentful, but unruffled. Garrity sighed. He motioned to Cardigan and they stepped outside the room.

"Jack . . ." Garrity paused, made a face, knuckled the hard slab of his jaw; then he looked up, puzzled but keen-eyed. "Jack, this case is punk. Either Micah's scared to come right out and say this bird robbed him, or he's not sure the bird did rob him. Maybe he just picked him at random. Hell, he had to save his face to some extent, didn't he? If he couldn't name anybody—if he said he just lost the ice, it'd look suspicious. Hey—" his voice dropped—"what do you know about Micah?"

"Been with the firm ten years. Lost his wife two years ago and collected ten thousand insurance. All alone now. Far as we know—steady, reliable, short on the brains side but that helps. A guy that messengers jewels around shouldn't have too much imagination. Think it's a frame?"

Garrity growled: "Hell, I was just thinking. Forget it. The guy seems kind of goofy. Why the hell didn't he come right out and say Kinnard was the guy? It'd make it easier."

"What about Kinnard?"

Garrity looked at a slip of paper in his

hand. "He's living at the Hotel Gold on Lexington. I checked that up. He's played in a couple of movies—minor parts. Used to play a piano on the vaudeville stage for a while. Now he's a piano player and wit that hires out for swell parties, banquets, things like that. You see, Jack, things don't reason out. This bird has an address, a business. There's a fluke somewhere. If Micah don't come right out and identify him for sure, we can't hold him."

"If you let him go right away," Cardigan said, "you'll have the insurance people on your neck. You'd better stall around. Take him down to H. Q. See if he's got a record. If he swiped the ice, he could have passed it to a pal and steered you wrong."

"He's no sap. He'll want a lawyer and I wouldn't blame him."

Cardigan said: "Get Micah out here."

THEY took Micah to another room and Cardigan eyed him for a long minute. Micah's face looked pasty and he kept at it with his handkerchief.

"It's like this," Cardigan said. "You've got to know if this is the man. You've got to be pretty sure about it. You can't guess. You see, you work for a house that's got piles of dough. If you had this man arrested and filed the charge formally against him—and if it turned out he wasn't the guy, your firm might have a lawsuit on its hands."

Micah was troubled. "I—I should not like to have an innocent man arrested. I said I thought this was the man. I tell you I didn't look squarely at him—I was so shaken after the fall. I just said, 'Thanks,' brushed myself off and by that time he was gone. I suppose I just saw him, so to speak, out of the corner of my eye."

"Look here," Garrity chopped in, a little impatient. "I want to help you all

I can. I've got a reputation I'm kind of proud of: I never pinch a guy just because I need a pinch. I won't do it now. I'll give you a break. If you swear outright that Kinnard's the man, I'll pinch him. Will you do that?"

"I—I—you see, an innocent man—I—"

"Oh, nuts!" Garrity growled. "Is this the guy or isn't he? Yes or no? Do you want to arrest him? I'm just a cop. This is up to you. You may not be certain, but if you just say you are, I'll arrest him. That plain?"

Micah inhaled deeply, stared at the floor. "I—I can't say for sure he's the man. I—I couldn't swear to it. There was, really, quite a crowd around me at the time. It might have been—I might have just thought . . ." He slumped, sighed hopelessly. "I don't know. I'm all —all upset."

Garrity snorted. "O. K. So I'll let this guy go." He made a decisive gesture, swiveled, stalked to the door. His hand on the knob, he paused, turned around, then returned to face Micah. "Listen, Mr. Micah. I hate to do this. Can't you for cripes' sake know if this was the guy? Can't you say it was? Just so we can hold him. Huh?"

"No-o . . . I can't. I—I'm sorry—"

Garrity barked: "Now you should be sorry! After I clown all over the street and bop a guy—now you're sorry! What the hell kind of a cop do you think I am?"

Micah made vague gestures.

"For crying out loud," Cardigan said, "don't be an old woman, Pete. Let the guy go. Be noble. But—listen, Pete— like an old pal, hold him for about fifteen minutes longer."

"Why should I?" crabbed Garrity.

"Now you wouldn't go cutting corners on a pal, would you?"

Garrity leveled an arm. "No longer, Jack—no longer than fifteen!" He jerked his chin toward Micah. "Come with me, Mr. Micah."

Micah and Garrity left the room. Cardigan scooped up a phone, leaned comfortably back on his heels, called the agency. George Hammerhorn answered.

Cardigan said: "This is Jack, George. Pat there? . . . No, I don't want to talk to her. Tell her to shoot right down to Thirty-fifth Street, near the Twenty-fifth Precinct house. . . . No, not in the house; near it. I'll walk out with a guy. She's to follow this guy and see if he meets anyone after I leave him. . . . Well, George, there's just something screwy here. . . . The guy's name is Kinnard."

CHAPTER TWO

The Girl in the Gold

THE house was in the respectable West Eighties. Cardigan found the hall door open. The foyer was clean; an expensive but worn carpet padded the staircase. Once this house must have been the stronghold of the rich, but wealth had since migrated eastward, ramparted itself east of the Park, hard by the river. Renovations had not entirely wiped out the Georgian influence. The third floor was dim, cool; doors shone darkly. The door marked "33" was in the rear. It took Cardigan three minutes to find the proper master key.

The room was small. One window overlooked a courtyard. It was the modest room of a man of small means—neat, a little shabby, comfortable. Cardigan went to work. Clothes were hung orderly on hangers; two pairs of shoes, polished, stood side by side and rigid with shoe-trees. Linen lay neatly in bureau drawers. Paper, writing materials, lay on a small desk. The desk drawer was locked, but Cardigan opened it. A packet of letters was held in shape by rubber bands. There

was a checkbook showing a balance of $248.50. There was a savings-account book from which, over a period of fifteen months, a total of $8,000 had been withdrawn; the balance was for $100. Cardigan read the letters, frowned, shook his head. He hunted around for canceled checks, found none. Finally he replaced everything in order, stood for a moment immersed in thought, then left the room, locked the door.

He took a cab to the Traum & Fleer establishment on Fifth Avenue. Carl Traum, the senior partner, was a pale, distant man behind a tremendous mahogany desk. He did not rise when Cardigan entered. He did not stop writing. The office was silent but for the scratching of his pen. He did not look up.

"News?" he said in a dry, flat voice.

Cardigan said: "You satisfied as to the integrity of your man Micah?"

The pen scratched on. "Why do you ask?"

"Naturally I want to take all angles into consideration. I know that in two months he'll have been with you ten years."

"Not quite. That is, Micah finishes here the end of this month."

"Firing him?"

"Not because of this. He received notice the first of the month. Times are hard. We've had to cut down. I have utmost faith in Micah. This was indeed unfortunate. There has never been an irregularity in the house of Traum and Fleer. We could, you understand, hardly afford it. This was plainly a ruse, a daring daylight robbery. I can't understand why the police let that fellow go."

"You can't arrest a man when the victim can't identify him. I'm interested in Micah."

Traum laid down his pen, sat back, laid his fragile hands on the desk. Rimless spectacles glittered coldly beneath frosty white eyebrows; the thin, hueless face was bare of expression.

He said: "We have retained your agency for twelve years, Mr. Cardigan. It's your duty to keep, at all times, an eye on our men. Men do not turn thieves over night. Your regular reports on Micah have been such as to cause us no qualms. It is your business to warn us of any irregularity before an unpleasantness occurs. The house of Traum and Fleer can't afford a scandal. It has paid you well for protection against the unexpected."

Cardigan regarded him for a long moment in silence. "Do I understand I'm to drop this case?"

"Did I say so? No. You're to recover this bracelet, if possible, but you're not to choose a man at random merely because other channels might call for more work. Insurance companies are becoming pretty careful. I don't want rumors to get around that this was an inside job. Rumors are dangerous things. Only the facts must be used, my dear Mr. Cardigan. I value, you understand, the reputation of my firm. I believe—have I said this before?—that Micah is thoroughly honest."

He picked up his pen, returned to writing. Cardigan knew that the interview was over. His "Good-by" was hardly more than a husky whisper. He went out, nursing a peculiar feeling of frustration. The insurance company, he realized, would have to pay through the nose if the bracelet were not recovered. It was plain that Traum was more interested in the reputation of his firm than in the recovery of the bracelet. He wanted the bracelet but it would not please him if Micah turned out to be a thief.

CARDIGAN phoned the agency from a drugstore booth. He was told that Pat had called up from a booth in the lobby of the Hotel Gold. She had tailed Kinnard there and was waiting further instructions. Cardigan grabbed a cab and dropped off five minutes later in front of the Gold. He found Pat sitting in the lobby.

"So what?" he said.

"I picked him up when you left him at the corner of Fifth Avenue and Thirty-fifth Street. He took a cab and I took one and he came right here. He didn't stop to make any calls. I didn't hesitate about walking right in after him. He went to the desk for mail. There was none. See that big leather chair over there? There was a girl sitting in it. Nice. Did she know how to wear clothes! Kinnard spied her and went over to her. They talked for a few minutes. Then he went up in the elevator. The girl powdered her nose, watched the elevator door. When the elevator came down, she got up and went over and took it up. It stopped—I could tell by the indicator—it stopped at the ninth floor." Pat smiled. "That was the floor Kinnard stopped at."

"Two and two," mused Cardigan.

"Make four. Chief, she was a honey—and those clothes—"

"You women, you women! Forget clothes for a minute. Did she come down again?"

"No."

"Know what room he's in?"

"No."

Cardigan said: "Wait here. Stay right here and watch if she comes out—or if he comes out. I'll find the house dick."

He asked a bellhop. The house officer was in a small office beyond the desk. His name was Riordan and he was an old-timer. Cardigan showed credentials. "I want to do things right," he said.

"What do you call right?" asked Riordan.

"Well, how about ten dollars?"

"I couldn't think of it."

Cardigan said: "You don't have to think," and dropped a ten-dollar bill on the desk.

Riordan pocketed it. "This hurts me." He got up, left the office and reappeared in a couple of minutes. "It's an apartment—Number 909—one of those bed-living-rooms, with an in-a-door bed."

"What do you know about him?"

"Nothing. Never causes any trouble—quiet, apparently O. K. Has lady friends, but his apartment's on the residential side and so it's none of my business. If it's a pinch you want, you better get a cop."

"No pinch yet. Listen, Riordan. How far will you go if I need you?"

"It depends."

Cardigan stood up. "O. K. You can put yourself in the way of some dough if you want to."

"It depends."

"Sure. I get you."

Cardigan returned to the lobby and Pat said: "No come down."

"Swell. Stay here." He dropped his voice. "I think the house dick's all right, so long as there's dough in it."

He took the elevator to the ninth floor, made his way slowly down the pale gray corridor. He used a bronze knocker on the door of 909. There was no response, and after a moment he knocked again. This time there was the sound of movement inside. The latch clicked, the door opened. Kinnard, immaculate in dark clothes, peered through a lazy column of cigarette smoke.

"You remember me?" Cardigan said.

Kinnard said: "Of course."

"I'd like to have a few words with you."

"Have them."

Cardigan made a wry face. "Kind of—well—you know—in the corridor . . ."

"Seems to me I've been subjected to enough nonsense for one day, Cardigan. I don't think I can help you. Mind if I ask you to go?"

Cardigan shrugged. "I won't take much of your time—"

"I'm sorry."

KINNARD stepped back, closed the door. But the door didn't quite close; it rebounded against Cardigan's foot and Cardigan walked in as it swung back. Kinnard tried to grab it, to close it, but by the time he had the knob in his hand Cardigan was in the room, his hands tranquilly in his pockets and his battered fedora shadowing his eyes. He looked about the room. The room was large, cozy, with two windows, a bath, and double doors of the kind that conceal an in-a-door bed.

Kinnard kicked the door. It banged shut. Color rose to his smooth olive skin and he said, irritably: "It's damned funny when a man can't have any privacy in his own home!"

Cardigan was softly whistling the refrain of a Broadway musical show. He took off his hat, sat down in a large armchair, hooked a leg over a knee. He was calm, unhurried. He kept looking around the room, tilting his head from side to side, whistling softly.

Kinnard seemed to have grown taller; he did grow darker, tightening his lips, bending his brows. He was a handsome man, with his well-cut clothes, his smooth black hair, his slightly arrogant air. Cigarette smoke spurted from his nostrils. "Well?" he snapped.

Cardigan stopped whistling. "You know, Mr. Kinnard, that diamond bracelet didn't vanish in thin air. It went somewhere. Micah's a fool—one of those men who doubt his own convictions. Micah wound up by being pretty certain you weren't the man who robbed him. That happens. If you tell a guy enough times that he killed a man, and if the guy's got a bum head, he'll wind up by believing that. I'm inclined to believe Micah's first impulse was sound. He picked the man who robbed him. When he began to think about it, when he tried to be rational about it, he got all balled up."

Kinnard did not become indignant. He chuckled drily. "Maybe if you work on me that way, I'll wind up by believing I robbed him. That would be swell. Why don't you try telling me I'm the man who built the Public Library?"

"Who cares about the Public Library? Suppose for the time being we leave the Public Library out of it. Let's stick to a diamond bracelet worth approximately sixty thousand dollars. You happened to fall into the hands of one of the whitest cops in New York. Garrity will never make a pinch unless he has a sound reason. As a matter of fact, he's so white that sometimes he's a fool."

Kinnard smiled ironically. "You—I suppose you are just brimming over with brains."

"It's not that. You see, Mr. Kinnard, you were shadowed from the moment you stepped out of the police station."

"Leading up to what?"

"A woman."

Kinnard's eyes narrowed but his ironic smile did not fade. He said: "Things I never knew till now."

"I think that crack's copyrighted by a famous columnist. Will you ask the woman to come out?"

Kinnard sighed heavily. "You're getting tiresome."

Cardigan stood up. "Get her out."

Kinnard's jaw set. He crossed the room, picked up the phone and said to the house operator: "Will you send up the house officer? . . . Yes, this is Mr. Kinnard." He hung up.

Cardigan was grinning.

"We'll see," Kinnard said, "what right you have to pull a song and dance in my apartment."

"We'll see," Cardigan said.

They waited ten minutes. Impatient, angry now, Kinnard returned to the telephone.

Cardigan said: "Don't waste your time. I saw the house officer before I came up here."

Kinnard pivoted from the telephone. "You've got a hell of a nerve!" He took four hard steps toward Cardigan. "You get the hell out of here before you get thrown out."

"Get hot," Cardigan said. "I like it."

"Get out!"

Cardigan was cool, hard. "Tell the woman to come out."

"Get out!"

Cardigan ducked, caught Kinnard's fist in his open right hand; gripped hard, twisted. Then he heaved. Kinnard hurtled backward, struck a chair, crashed down with it.

THE closet door opened. A woman stood there for a brief moment, then took a few steps into the room. She was tall, white-faced, exquisitely dressed. She was breathing rapidly, and her large, dark eyes kept darting from Kinnard to Cardigan. Kinnard got to his feet, brushed his clothes. His breath came hoarsely.

Cardigan said to the woman: "What's your name?"

"I—I don't care to tell."

"Oh, you don't!"

Kinnard rasped: "Don't pay any attention to him! By God, I'll see I get some justice in this town!"

Cardigan had not taken his eyes from the woman. "Where were you at noon today?"

"I was—I was downstairs—in the lobby."

"You can prove that, I suppose?"

She bit her lip and looked helplessly at Kinnard. "Paul, what is this, what is this?"

"I'd like to know," Kinnard said. "I'd

certainly like to know about it myself."

"Never mind, you," Cardigan cut in; and then to the woman: "I suppose you can prove you were in the lobby?"

She held her breath. "I can—if I have to. I tell you I came in at a quarter to twelve."

"That's not proof."

"But why do I have to prove it?" she cried.

Kinnard said: "He's just a very smart person. I told you what happened. Some fool said I robbed him. This intelligent gentleman here has an idea, I suppose, that you were in the street at the time and that I passed the bracelet to you."

"To me?"

Kinnard laughed harshly. "He would think of something like that, you know"

"Can you," Cardigan hammered at the woman, "prove you were in the lobby?"

She nodded. "If I have to—yes. The little bookshop off the lobby—I was in there for at least half an hour—from a little before twelve until half-past. Looking at books. In fact, I discussed books with the girl who works there."

"What's your name?"

She colored. "If you don't mind, I'd rather not—" She looked confused. "This—this was a totally innocent visit, but if—if my name—" Her lip quivered.

Cardigan nodded. "Maybe I get you. O. K. Come downstairs with me and we'll see about the girl in the bookshop."

Cardigan and the woman went down in the elevator, crossed the lobby and entered the bookshop. The girl there smiled when she saw the woman. Cardigan's questions confused her, but she replied promptly. A moment later Cardigan and the woman went out into the lobby.

He said: "I'm sorry."

Her head was lowered. She walked away across the lobby, passed through the revolving doors into the street. Pat drifted up alongside Cardigan.

"Isn't she a knockout, chief?"

He said: "Listen, chicken. Tail her. Find out where she lives. Snap on it."

"What's the matter now?"

"Everything. This case gets nuttier and nuttier. Come on—shoo—get after her."

"I'm just crazy about the way she wears clothes—"

"Shoo, I tell you! Shoo! Scram! Get going!"

CHAPTER THREE

Cardigan Crashes the Gate

GEORGE HAMMERHORN, the agency head, was deep in the throes of a crossword puzzle when Cardigan entered the office. Hammerhorn did not look up. Cardigan unlocked a desk drawer, drew out a bottle of Scotch and poured himself a generous jolt.

"Say, Jack," Hammerhorn said, "what's an eight-letter word beginning with 'E,' that means greedy?"

"Who swiped the Traum-and-Fleer bracelet?"

Hammerhorn sat back. " Who did?"

"It occurred to me a little while ago that in all the hue and cry nobody searched Micah. The cops took his word for it that it had been stolen.

"I don't like to think he did. I like to think Kinnard did. I was just up to Kinnard's apartment and I let myself in for a nice lot of razzberry. Before I went there I frisked Micah's room. According to his books, he's almost broke. He's been doing things for a sick sister in California. I read some letters. In the past fifteen months he's spent about eight thousand on her. First of the month he loses his job. There's your motive. And yet, George, I can't forget Kinnard. I can't help feeling that Micah's instinct was right—that Kinnard was the man. I thought I had Kinnard where I wanted him. Pat tailed a woman to his apartment. I thought she'd be the pal Kinnard passed the ice to after he'd swiped it. But no. She was nowhere near the scene of the robbery."

The telephone rang and Cardigan picked it up. "Oh, hello, Pat. . . . I see. Good work, kid." He hung up, scribbled on a pad of paper. "That was Pat," he said. "She tailed the woman I was talking about. Woman lives at the Saborin, a swank apartment house in East Sixty-second Street."

"That's funny," Hammerhorn said. "You remember that when Micah left with the bracelet he was headed for Fitchman's office on Broadway."

"Sure. Fitchman was supposed to have called up. He didn't. That was a stall. The guy's got millions."

"I know. What's funny is this: Fitchman lives at the Saborin. I met him and his wife at a party once."

"What's she look like?"

"Tall—about five feet eight. A lulu to look at. A blonde. About twenty-eight or so. The kind you'd climb the highest mountain for. Fitchman's a little fat, a little old. He'd—you know—have a hard time climbing mountains."

Cardigan pointed. "It was puzzling me why the guy who phoned for that bracelet used Fitchman's name. Garrity had an idea he used it because it was a big name, one easily recognized. Fact is, I thought that too. It gets clearer now. Fitchman's bought several articles at Traum and Fleer's. There's your answer."

"Hell, Mrs. Fitchman wouldn't be mixed up in a robbery."

"Who's saying she would? But if she's the woman I saw in Kinnard's apartment, it would have been easy for Kinnard to have found out where Fitchman bought his jewelry. George, this guy's a heel."

He corked the bottle, jammed it tight with the palm of his hand. "Untie that!"

CARDIGAN sailed out of the office, got in a taxicab and was driven to Times Square. He still had his doubts, still felt that he was stopped at the fork in the road. One way led toward Micah; the other led toward Kinnard. The razzing he had taken in Kinnard's apartment rankled, but did not impel him to run blindly. Swiftly he went, but with a narrowed eye.

He was known in several theatrical booking offices. Men there had good memories, and if these failed they had old books, old records. Here and there Cardigan gathered morsel on morsel of information, putting each down on paper, building up gradually a kind of composite picture of Kinnard's past. Kinnard had once been a gigolo in a Broadway cabaret. He had played bits in three motion pictures. He had been on the vaudeville stage as a piano player. Once he had taken the part of a footpad in a play. He had also been assistant, for two months, to a magician named Fogoro—a man famed for sleight-of-hand.

An old time theatrical man said to Cardigan: "After that, Kinnard studied magic and tried to put on an act of his own. He was pretty good—but not good enough. He became obsessed with magic, however. But the business was on the wane and there was no room for him. As the footpad in that play, he was good. I saw it. I could have sworn he never touched the fellow who was supposed to have been robbed—in the play. But he did. It was neat work."

It was half-past four when Cardigan climbed into a cab. He settled back, lit a cigarette, inhaled deeply and with relish. He gave the address of the Hotel Gold. As his cab was rolling up to the hotel entrance, he saw Kinnard swing out and get into a taxi that was waiting there.

"Follow that one," Cardigan told the driver.

He sat on the edge of the seat. The possibility of Micah being guilty was outbalanced now by the information Cardigan had gathered concerning Kinnard. There was, Cardigan reasoned, another man, perhaps a woman. The police had searched Kinnard and found no bracelet. He must have passed it on to a confederate in the street.

Kinnard's taxi turned west at Fortysecond Street. Traffic was heavy, loud with the hoots of auto horns, the clanging of crosstown trolleys. They passed beneath the Park Avenue ramp and continued west past the Public Library and Bryant Park. At Eighth Avenue Kinnard alighted and stood on the windy corner. Cardigan's cab crossed Eighth Avenue to the northwest corner. He got out here and saw Kinnard walking north on the east side of the street. He followed, but on the west sidewalk.

Farther north a corner had been razed. Here a new hotel was to rise. A board fence enclosed the now vacant lot on the west and north sides; below the level of the street the earth was raw; steam shovels were at work and trucks were being loaded with broken rock, earth, débris.

Kinnard was strolling. He paused at this corner, leaned on the wooden fence, watched the men and shovels at work. Cardigan leaned in the doorway of a cigar store He looked at his watch. It was almost five o'clock. He saw Kinnard move on a few feet, then pause again. There was a crowd watching the business of excavating, but in a few minutes the steam shovels stopped, the day's work was done. The crowd moved off, and Kinnard, lighting a cigarette, continued to stroll north. Four blocks farther north he climbed into a taxi. Cardigan followed in another. Kinnard's cab moved slowly west on Fifty-third Street, stopped at the corner of Tenth Avenue. But Kinnard did not get out.

A minute later, however, the cab moved off, turned north into Tenth Avenue. The street was crowded and there were three trolley cars in a row, taxis hooting and speeding, trucks rumbling. At Sixty-second Street Kinnard alighted, stood on the corner, tapping a foot, drawing absently at a cigarette. Presently he turned and entered Sixty-second Street, heading east. The way was choked with traffic; children played and yelled in the street; women leaned from the windows of shabby tenement houses and shouted back and forth. Hard-looking men leaned in doorways, sat on stone stoops.

Cardigan followed his man with difficulty, and he began to feel a sensation of futility; for Kinnard had not the manner of a man destined for any definite objective. He strolled easily, casually. Finally, however, he stopped in front of a house, looked up at the doorway. Cardigan stopped, shifted behind a parked car. Several persons entered the house in front of which Kinnard lingered. The last of these was a roughly dressed man. Cardigan saw Kinnard's lips move. The last man paused halfway up the stoop, turned, scowled. Kinnard climbed the steps easily, stood gesturing casually; and presently the two entered the house.

AFTER a moment Cardigan moved past the house. A sign said "Rooms To Let." Cardigan went on, crossed the street, waited. In five minutes Kinnard reappeared. This time he walked rapidly toward Ninth Avenue. Cardigan followed him to Eighth Avenue, and here Kinnard boarded a taxi. Cardigan followed south. At Fortieth Street Kinnard dropped off, crossed Eighth Avenue and entered Fortieth. He walked a few yards, turned into a vestibule flush with the street, disappeared.

Cardigan knew the place: Cousino's, a speakeasy specializing in ravioli and steaks. He returned to the corner and waited, his eyes never leaving the dark vestibule. Half an hour passed. Several times Cardigan was on the point of entering the speakeasy, but each time he changed his mind. He had been on the corner for an hour when he saw a man get out of a cab at the corner and make his way into Fortieth Street. The man wore a blue overcoat and a derby. He was the man Cardigan had seen in rough clothing in front of the house in Sixty-second Street. The man entered the speak.

IN a few minutes Kinnard and the man came out of the speakeasy. Cardigan ducked around the corner. The two entered a cab and headed south and Cardigan followed. He was becoming impatient, puzzled. Kinnard's cab turned east at Thirty-sixth Street, south into Seventh Avenue, went past the Penn Station and continued south; sped into Varick Street and then turned east into Canal and crossed the town to East Broadway. Street lights were glowing here. A surface car clanged and rattled south. Kinnard and the burly man got out of the cab and walked down East Broadway.

Cardigan went along in the shadow of house fronts, past blatant radio stores, cheap novelty shops, across iron gratings that rang beneath his feet. He saw Kinnard and the burly man pass into a narrow doorway hard by a dusty-windowed pawnshop. He heard the door slam shut. Stopping, he looked through the window of the pawnshop. A man was standing behind the counter, reading a newspaper, smoking a cigar. A rear door opened and a youth beckoned. The man laid down his paper and disappeared through the rear door, and the youth took his place behind

the counter. Cardigan looked at the name on the window—S. Goldfarb.

He moved on, stopped, eyed the narrow doorway beside the store, put his hand on the knob. The door opened. He entered a dark hallway, closed the door, stood for a moment listening, blinded by the impenetrable darkness. After a moment he shook his head, turned, groped and found the doorknob, opened the door and returned to the street. He stood for a moment deliberating, flexing his lips. He had no wish to blunder in that dark hallway. His jaw tightened. He swung on his heel and walked into the pawnshop.

The pasty-faced youth looked up from the newspaper. Cardigan was in a hurry and inclined to be blunt and to the point. He reached over and plucked a handkerchief from the youth's breast pocket. "This," he said, "you'll stuff into your mouth."

The youth was sleepy. "Huh?"

"Cram it in your mouth." Cardigan leaned on the counter and hefted his gun absently in his right hand "The handkerchief, little one—in the mouth"

The youth's eyes popped at sight of the gun. He grabbed the handkerchief and pushed it into his mouth. His cheeks, his eyes, bulged.

Cardigan said: "Say 'ah', son."

The youth couldn't say anything.

"That's swell," Cardigan nodded. He drew out a pair of handcuffs, went behind the counter, made the youth bend down. He then manacled his hands to the leg of a work bench, took off the youth's tie and fastened it around his mouth so that the handkerchief could not be worked out. He knotted the tie at the back of the youth's neck.

Going to the door, he threw home the bolt. The youth on the floor behind the counter made no sound. Cardigan's gun was in his overcoat pocket; so was his hand, warming the butt. He opened the rear door and entered a small, cluttered stockroom. There was a door at the left, open, and a boxed-in staircase that rose abruptly toward regions above. Cardigan looked up. A door at the top was partway open and there was light beyond. He started up, placing his feet at the extreme sides of the steps to prevent them from creaking. There was no platform at the top; the staircase ended at the threshold of the upper room and Cardigan pushed the door wide open and stepped in.

He said: "Pardon my French."

CHAPTER FOUR

Diamond Truck-Load

IT WAS a cozy, comfortable scene— three men sitting around a table, a bottle of wine in the center, cigar smoke drifting slowly before their faces, clouding the shaded droplight that hung from the ceiling. Cheese and crackers in a convenient bowl. Mr. Goldfarb, putty-faced, fat and soft-bodied, with spectacles pushed up on his forehead. Kinnard with a glass of wine in his hand. His burly friend, shiny-faced from a recent shave, spreading cheese on a cracker.

"Ahem," said Mr. Goldfarb.

Kinnard's eyes narrowed for a brief instant. It seemed that he was about to rise, but he did not; he calmly took a drink of wine, set the glass down, reached for a cracker and nibbled off a small piece.

Cardigan said dully: "You've been doing an awful lot of chasing around, Kinnard."

"Any law against it?"

"I suppose Mr. Goldfarb is just a sick friend you're sitting up with. My, my— what a swell, domestic picture!"

The burly man's forehead was wrinkled. "Say, who's this here now mug?"

"A kind of busybody," Kinnard said.

Cardigan said: "You know what I've come for, Kinnard. You'll save yourself a great big headache by coming across."

Kinnard laughed, explained to the others: "You see, this busybody thinks I have a diamond bracelet."

The burly man sat back and looked stupidly at Kinnard. Mr. Goldfarb wiggled his eyebrows and his spectacles dropped neatly to his nose. He looked shrewdly at Kinnard, at the burly man, at Cardigan. "A bracelet yet?" he said to Cardigan.

The burly man slapped the table and laughed roughly, good-humoredly. "Ain't that the nuts now!"

"I ask you!" Kinnard chuckled.

Cardigan's dark brows drew together, his lip lifted. "I'm being given the razz, huh?"

Kinnard tipped his chair back, put his tongue in his cheek. He looked very immaculate, very smooth and brown and self-contained, and very droll.

"You begin to get really funny, Cardigan. Honest, I get a great kick out of you."

Goldfarb said: "What about a bracelet? Who's got a bracelet yet? What's all this talk about a bracelet? Hey, Kinnard—you got a bracelet?"

Kinnard winked broadly. "Yeah. Want to buy it?"

"Sure. Where is it?"

"Ask—" Kinnard pointed— "ask Mr. Cardigan. He knows. He knows everything. Is he smart? Well, just ask him— just ask him!"

Cardigan looked somber. "I know, baby—I know."

"What did I tell you, Goldfarb? What did I tell you?"

Goldfarb looked peeved. "Go way, go way; you're only kidding yet, Kinnard, you old kidder, you!"

Kinnard chuckled with an air. The burly man laughed and slapped the table again. Goldfarb blinked, smiled, shook his head, said: "Yeah, you old kidder, you!" And the tobacco smoke moved sinuously around the droplight.

Cardigan looked from one to the other. His face was not pleasant. He towered in the room, his hair shaggy beneath his hat, sprouting alongside his ears.

His voice was low. "So I'm a monkey, huh?"

The men shook their heads, chuckled.

Then Cardigan's gun was in his hand. "I'm this kind of a monkey, sweethearts."

THEY stopped laughing. Goldfarb sat back in his chair and turned his head away but kept his eyes sidewise on the gun. The burly man looked suddenly stupid, and his big, gnarled, calloused hands plopped to the table, remained motionless there. Kinnard lifted his chin; a shadow passed across his face; his mouth warped.

"Put that gun down, you idiot!"

"So on top of being a monkey I'm an idiot. Open your ears, Kinnard—and you, Goldfarb—and you, roughneck: you know what I'm here for, all of you. You've jazzed too much, Kinnard. This roughneck is the guy you passed the bracelet to. That's the guy I've been looking for."

"Nobody passed no bracelet to me!" rumbled the burly man. "I ain't seen no bracelet."

"Of course he's seen no bracelet," Kinnard said.

"And this," Cardigan said, nodding to Goldfarb, "is your fence."

"And where," said Kinnard, "is the bracelet?"

"One of you three men has it."

Kinnard stood up, scowled. "I told you once before, Cardigan, that I'm getting tired of this clowning around. It's about time you found out you're up a wrong tree. There's no bracelet here. I never saw the bracelet you're beefing about. Damn it, search us if you want to!"

He held up his arms.

"Go ahead, begin with me. Stand up, boys. Once and for all, we'll get this thing over with. Come on, Cardigan, search me." He set his glass on the table and stepped back from it. "Come on, get it over with."

Cardigan eyed him for a long minute. He shrugged, but his gaze remained fixed on Kinnard. "Never mind, Kinnard. You're pretty smart, pretty smart. You've trumped an Irish dick's every move, but I still think you're a heel. See? Listen, baby—I've been in this business long enough to know a rat when I see one. You're a rat. I know who that woman in your apartment was. It was through her you found out the name of the jewel house Fitchman did business with. You're a sleight-of-hand artist. I know all about you. Your piano playing is not only a good blind—it's a good in. You get into swell homes and play for parties— and you find out things. It's a new racket, Kinnard, and a neat one. I know when I'm licked. Thing is, I'm not licked yet. You fooled a square cop named Garrity— you haven't fooled me."

Kinnard snapped: "You dumb Hibernian, you haven't got a thing on me—you haven't got a thing on anybody! I told you to search me. To search these two men here. No—you wouldn't! You know damned well you'd find nothing. There's not a thing you can do."

"No?"

"No!"

"How would you like me to tell the cops that the guy's name you used when you phoned for that bracelet was the husband of the woman I saw in your apartment?"

"I never phoned for any bracelet."

"It would," Cardigan said, viciously, "be a nice puzzle to explain how it happened the woman was in your apartment, how it happened her husband's name was used."

Kinnard snarled: "Like all dicks, you've got a big nose for tabloid scandal."

"Have I? If I had, you wisecracking lounge lizard, I'd have turned her up when I found her. I didn't. O. K.—but I can turn her up now. You think you're making a jackass out of me, don't you? I'll show you that when any guy tries to do that I can be dirty. I don't care what or who the woman is—if I've got to use her to get you pinched, I'll use her."

Kinnard's eyes glittered. "It won't get you any bracelet, Cardigan. Not a bit of it. Because I haven't got it and I never did have it. Turn her up, if you want to. Can I help it if she went soft on me? I'm leaving, Cardigan. Come on, Babe," he added to the burly man.

"You wait," Cardigan said.

"I'll wait my eye! If you want me to wait, call a cop. Make a jackass out of yourself. I don't have to try to make one out of you. I'm clean, Irish. Get the whole police department. Why, you big fathead," he laughed, "you're a swift pain in the neck. You're last year's prize joke. There's a phone. Why don't you call the cops?"

CARDIGAN walked across the room and without stopping hung his left fist on Kinnard's jaw. Kinnard went down like a felled tree. Cardigan swiveled and aimed his gun at the burly man.

"Watch yourself, big boy." Cardigan's face was dull red; there was reddish color in his eyes. He said tautly: "I hate like hell to be razzed. This pal of yours thinks he's tough, but he's never been around."

Goldfarb flapped his arms. "Now, now, all this yet—all this fighting business yet! *Ach*, don't!"

Kinnard was coughing. He sat on the floor, shaking his head from side to side.

He grabbed the edge of the table and got slowly to his feet. His eyes looked bloated. He stood leaning on the table, coughing, making faces. Then he straightened, his eyes shuttered.

"Thanks," he said, catching his breath.

"Please, now—please, now," Goldfarb said. "Don't fight. Like good guys, go out."

There was a moment of silence, broken only by the hoarse breathing of Kinnard. Then there were stumbling footfalls on a stairway. Cardigan's eyes jumped to a closed door across the room. He reasoned that beyond the door a stairway went down to the hall door. Next minute there was a knock on the door.

Goldfarb rolled his eyes. The burly man looked stupidly at the door and Kinnard's lips tightened.

"Open it," Cardigan said. "You Goldfarb!"

Goldfarb shivered and stumbled to the door. He unlocked it and hurried back to his place at the table. A short fat man stood in the doorway. He wore a loud gray suit, a wild tie the color of burnt orange and a funny hat that sat on the very top of his head. His cheeks were like red apples. His grin was cherubic. He waved a hand.

"Ah, dere you are, Babe!! Watcha t'ink—I damn near busta da head on de stairway, shoo! Dark as-a hell, shoo!" His grin faded and he looked puzzled, "Hey, Babe, whassa da mat'?"

The burly man was beginning to perspire. The little Italian came into the room, ducked his head comically, took off his quaint hat and rubbed it against the underside of his sleeve. Goldfarb rolled his eyes, picked up his glass, sipped it, patted the side of his head.

The Italian looked embarrassed. "Geez-a, Babe, dis-a no way to treat a pal, huh? What da hell—you call me on de telephono, tell-a me to come to dis watcha call him number on East-a Broadway."

The burly man made a sound something like "*Ahk*" and looked sickly, stupidly at Kinnard. Kinnard's eyes were glazed, his tightened mouth warped.

"You," Cardigan said to the Italian. "What are you doing here, huh?"

"I joosta say! Ain't I joosta say Babe call me on de telephono? What's all dis-a monkey-beezness?"

Cardigan said "What did you come here for?"

The little Italian's hand went into his pocket. He withdrew a black leather case, snapped it open. A diamond bracelet glittered. He smiled, innocently.

Cardigan, said: "What the hell?" He took a step, took the case and bracelet. He snapped the case shut, dropped it into his pocket. The little Italian looked mystified.

"Thank you very much," said Cardigan. "Where did you get this bracelet?"

The Italian laughed good-naturedly. "Was watcha call good joke on Babe! Ho-ho! Ask-a da Babe." He held his stomach and shook with honest mirth.

"Well, you?" Cardigan shot at the burly man.

Babe's face was mottled. His lip shook. "Geez, guy, I didn't steal it. I'm a truck driver. I come up from the East Side today with an empty truck except for some picks—a half a dozen picks I had. We're on a job on Eight' Avenue—where the new Hotel Morris is goin' to go up. Well, I get there. Tony jumps up to the truck to chuck the picks out. When he jumps down that thing drops from his overalls and I ask him what it is. He says it's a gadget he got for his wife at dinnertime. There's a funny look on his mug, but I don't think much about it. Well, it turns out the thing was in my truck, just layin' there. Tony found it."

"How'd it get there?"

Babe looked uneasy. "Listen, mister—

I ain't a crook, see. Neither is Tony. But, hell, when a thing like that drops out o' the sky—a thing worth a thousand bucks and a guy wants to give me and Tony two hundred a piece—gosh!"

Cardigan chuckled drily. "Two hundred, eh? You know how much it's worth, Babe?"

"Huh?"

"Fifty thousand dollars."

"Fifty thou—"

'Exactly."

THE burly man's face flamed. His eyes settled on Kinnard, then swung back to Cardigan. He said: "This guy said it was a thousand. I thought he was on the up-and-up because he said we'd all meet here at a jeweler's and the jeweler'd buy it for a thousand."

"He'd fixed it up with Goldfarb. How did the thing get in your truck?"

"I don't know. This guy follered me home from work and nailed me on the doorstep. I told him I didn't have it. He said he knew it was in my truck. Then I remembered Tony and I said maybe I could get it. I said I'd have to call a guy. I said I'd call the guy and then meet him later. He propositioned me. So I called Tony—he lives downtown—and Tony said he'd come across. Then I met this guy in a speak in Fortieth Street. I told him. We called Tony again and told him to come here."

"Where were you at noon today?"

"There was a traffic jam on Sixth Avenue. Some guys were takin' pictures I was tied up under the 'El' for about ten minutes—"

"Thanks," Cardigan cut in. He turned to Kinnard. "So, that was it, eh? You dropped it from the rear platform of the 'El' train when you saw you were cornered. You droppped it in this guy's truck. When Garrity hauled you down to the street you saw the truck—the number of it and the name of the construction company. You went up to Eighth Avenue this afternoon, just before quitting time. You saw the truck, you followed the driver home. Swell, Kinnard—very swell!"

Kinnard bit his lip to silence.

Cardigan said: "You guys — you, Babe—you, Tony—better scram out of this. You going to rat on these guys, Kinnard?"

"No. To hell with them. Let 'em go."

Cardigan nodded. "That's pretty white, Kinnard."

Babe grabbed his hat. "Come on, Tony. This ain't no place for us." He heaved across the room, yanked open the door. He reared backward with a hoarse outcry, fell against Tony. Both men toppled to the floor.

Cardigan had taken out the bracelet and was looking at it. His eyes darted upward. He saw Micah standing in the doorway—small, plain Micah. There was a gun in Micah's hand, a strained look on his face, a strange gleam in his eyes.

"You will put your hands up," he said. "Not a move out of anyone."

Cardigan blinked. It was hard to believe his eyes. But the man was Micah, and there was a gun in his hand. Entering swiftly, Micah closed the door.

"Now," he panted, "we'll see. Kinnard, you have a gun. Take it out. Help me cover these men. Take the bracelet from Cardigan. Quick! I listened. I heard. We'll have to hurry, Kinnard."

Kinnard did not move. He seemed shocked, rooted where he stood, at this pale, panting apparition of a man. Goldfarb groaned. Tony and Babe remained where they had fallen. Cardigan stood holding the bracelet in one hand, the case in the other.

He said: "Micah, you're mad. Put that gun down, man. I'm Cardigan. You're—"

"Oh, yes, oh, yes," Micah sing-songed.

"I know who you are. Kinnard, will you hurry up! Don't stand there like a fool!"

Kinnard shook his head slowly. "I'm caught, Micah. There's no use. The job was a flop and I couldn't get away with it. I'll take my medicine. I'm not strong on gun work. Take my advice. Beat it."

Micah panted: "What! You're turning me down! You think I'm going to let this go? You've got to come, Kinnard. If you let yourself get arrested, you'll tell about me. One way or the other, they'll know about it—and we may as well have the bracelet. I've got to have my share. My sister—she needs more doctors—that damn firm is firing me—I need money. Don't you understand? Don't you see I've taken a step I can't undo? I've got to go through with it, I tell you! Money—doctor bills—my sister."

"I'm not going, Micah. I won't squeal on you. You better lam out of this."

Micah's voice strained: "But I have to have money! You said—you remember what you said—one third—"

"For God's sake, beat it!"

MICAH shook. The gun in his hand shook. His glazed eyes burned on Cardigan and he took a jerky step forward, held out his left hand. "The—the bracelet, Cardigan—give it to me."

Cardigan watched the gun's black muzzle come toward him. "Micah, you're out of your mind. You can't get away with this."

"Give—me—the—bracelet." The words ached out of his mouth. Anguish was scratched across his face. "I'll have to—kill—you—if you don't. Money—I need money—for my sister. Ten years with that firm—and they fire me—fire me."

"Micah—"

"Don't talk! God, don't make me kill you!"

Kinnard was leaning across the table.

His hand rose. He switched out the light.

There was the gun's roar—the stab of flame. Somewhere in the dark there was a choked cry.

Cardigan struck out. His fist collided with something that gave. He stumbled and fell on top of Micah. Micah's gun exploded a second time and glass broke. Cardigan got hold of the gun, ripped it from Micah's hand. "Lights!" he yelled.

There was stumbling in the dark. Then the droplight sprang to life. Goldfarb stepped back from it, stumbled, said: "*Ach!*" as he looked downward.

Kinnard was lying on the floor. His head was bleeding.

"Micah shot him!" Goldfarb cried.

Cardigan was holding Micah up. He dragged him across the floor and looked down at Kinnard.

"Accidents happen, huh?" Kinnard said, and grimaced.

"I—I didn't mean it!" cried Micah.

"Shut up," growled Cardigan. "Goldfarb, get a doctor. Hurt bad, Kinnard?"

"Yeah. I guess I'm going . . ."

Micah gibbered and Cardigan swung him around and shook him violently. "You fool! How did you get mixed up in this anyhow?"

"My sister—money—doctors. The firm was firing me. I did recognize Kinnard. I knew he was the man robbed me. But I began to think. I thought that if I said I wasn't sure, they'd let him go. Then I could go around to him later and tell him. I did that. I went around and told

him. I wanted one third for my silence. The pay-off was to be here tonight. So I came—and then—You see, Cardigan, I needed money—lots of it—for my sister —and there was no way. I've been honest all my life. All my life. Until now. Ten years with the firm—and—and" He covered his eyes.

Cardigan stepped away, shook his head. It was this sort of thing that often cropped up in his business—men down to bed-rock, men who turned criminals over night for a reason that no law would recognize. Cardigan had read the letters in Micah's room. He knew.

Goldfarb was saying: "I call the doctor but—but"—he was pointing—"Kinnard won't need one yet—ever."

Kinnard was staring at the ceiling. His mouth was slack.

Cardigan said: "You, Goldfarb—go downstairs to the store. Tony, Babe— you too. The cops are there now."

Nightsticks were beating on the pawnshop door. The three men went down. Micah was staring at the man he had murdered. Cardigan took a breath, crossed the room, gave Micah back the gun he had ripped from his hand. He didn't say anything. He walked down the stairs slowly, listening. Reached the store. The thunder of the gun upstairs seemed to shake the building. Cardigan saw flakes of plaster dribble from the store ceiling.

"What was that?" Goldfarb choked.

Cardigan said: "Use your head."

Marked Money

A Dane Skarle Story

by

Erle Stanley Gardner

Author of "Crooks Carnival," etc.

She was gasping, choking, trying to fight free.

Dane Skarle, sleight-of-hand expert, had quit the carnival lot cold. And why not? It was ten times as easy to snatch reward money from the hands of crooked cops than to pull rabbits from a hat. And bank notes don't have to be fed lettuce three times a day.

CHAPTER ONE

Enter—The Law

THE rooms were on the west side of the building, and the afternoon sun turned them into veritable ovens.

Dane Skarle sat on the bed in trousers and undershirt. Perspiration glistened on his forehead. A newspaper was spread out on the bed. Clippings from other newspapers were arranged in a semblance of order.

Flies droned in buzzing spirals. The shades were down, making oblongs of sickly yellow light over the windows. They kept out some of the sun, but made the air close and sultry.

The door of the connecting room opened and Vera Colma came into the room. She wore a thin sport outfit which showed her legs to advantage. There was an air of crisp determination about her, as though she had decided to settle some problem, definitely, once and for all.

Dane Skarle looked up from the newspaper. His eyes traveled up and down in a survey of her figure. He said nothing.

The girl came over to the bed, sat down beside him, looked at him, then looked away and said slowly: "Listen, Dane, I've got a swell job for us."

Dane Skarle's voice was without emotion as he said: "Doing what?"

"Our regular line, sleight-of-hand, hypnotism, card tricks, mental telepathy. I put on some color and a turban and not much else and go as an Indian Princess. You wear Hindu clothes. We get a percentage of the take and a guarantee."

She let her eyes study his face in anxious appraisal. He kept silent.

"Well?" she asked.

"No," he said.

She took a deep breath, reached out and placed a hand on his bare arm, near the shoulder. "Listen, Dane, you've got to snap out of it. You did some clever work and copped a reward at that hick town, and now you want to go around chasing rewards. It won't work."

He straightened on the bed and said: "Why won't it work?"

"Because it won't. I'm—I'm frightened. You go up against a funny class of people in that business. And every one is crooked. It's a crooked game. They all seem to want to gouge you. They've tried to frame us. They'll try that again. Maybe they'll make it stick. Forget it. Let's go to work in our regular line. We get our three squares

a day and nobody tries to rub us out. You get to mixing in this crook stuff and people try to hang things on us."

Dane Skarle spoke patiently. His voice gave the impression of restraint, boundless physical energy being held in leash. "People are like that, all over," he said, "whenever you get to playing for big stakes. In the carnival game we weren't playing for big stakes. Now we are. You can't go up against folks with big stakes on the table and not have to fight and have them fight you. It's only on Sundays that people get soft. Then they sing hymns and dress up. Go out on Monday and try to do business with 'em and they gouge."

She moved her fingers along the flesh of his shoulder. "I'm afraid," she said, softly.

"I'm not."

THE room was silent for a few moments, a silence that was broken by the droning of the flies as they circled a patch of sunlight that leaked past the side of the shade.

"How you coming with Dabney?" he asked.

Her voice was weary. "So-so. He's a pain in the neck. Small-town stuff all over. He took me to lunch."

Skarle asked, casually: "Get fresh?"

"Of course he got fresh!" she said with feeling. "These small-town guys always do. Just because a girl's been on the road in show stuff—"

"Find out anything?" he asked.

"No," she said. "I don't know what makes you think he could have had anything to do with it."

Skarle said: "Sure he could have had something to do with it."

She shrugged shapely shoulders. Skarle went on: "It was all set, just like a stage stunt. I think he's had some experience. He pulled a professional line."

"How do you figure that?" she asked,

her hazel eyes softening as they studied his profile.

He turned to her. "Why do you show your legs on the stage?" he asked.

She grinned and said: "Because they're pretty."

He shook his head, wearily. "Baloney," he remarked. "You show 'em to distract attention. When I'm doing that watch-smashing trick I say that I'll ring for an assistant. I press a fake bell. The audience figures some stage hand or other is coming in. I look at the left wing, like I thought you'd come in there.

"You come in the right. You've got on a skirt that comes halfway to your knees, black silk stockings, and you're wearing a little white frilled apron with ruffles that are all starched out. It's about the size of a postage stamp.

"You make all of the hicks gasp. Right then is when I switch the watches. There ain't an eye in the house that's on me. It's a cinch. That's why stage magicians always have girls with pretty legs. That's why you're supposed to wear a turban and not much else in this act. It distracts attention."

Vera Colma hitched around on the bed, cupped her knee in her locked fingers, grinned. "Bill Dabney ain't got that much sense. He wouldn't figure anything like that out."

"He could have," Skarle insisted, "if he'd ever been on the stage."

"He ain't got sense enough to go on the stage," Vera said. "He's small town, and he's a pain in the neck. He's got restless hands, and he smirks when he gets personal. He acts like his mind needed renovating."

Dane Skarle motioned toward the clippings from the papers. "I chased back through the files of the local rag," he said, "and I find where this guy went on in amateur theatricals. They had some sort of a home-talent bunch here that put on benefit shows. Bill Dabney was a sleight-of-hand guy once. He got some swell write-ups."

She laughed, but her laugh lacked conviction. "That was because he was a home-town guy. If it hadn't been for that they'd have thrown him in the can for obtaining money under false pretenses. He ain't got anything on the ball at all. His hands are all left thumbs."

"That don't keep him from knowing how they work sleight-of-hand," said Skarle.

She got to her feet, straightened her stockings, walked to the mirror and surveyed her face. "Well," she said, "if you won't listen to reason you won't. What you planning on——"

Heavy knuckles pounded on the door.

Dane Skarle got slowly to his feet. Vera Colma looked at him questioningly, then walked to the door which communicated with her room, paused for a moment, slipped through and closed the door, but did not latch it. The knuckles thundered on the thin panels of the outer door. A voice gruffed: "Open up here. What's the idea?"

DANE SKARLE jerked the door open. A big man walked uninvited into the room and said: "You the guy that went out to see Bob Cromton last night?"

Dane Skarle pushed the door closed. He stared at his visitor. "Who wants to know?"

"I do."

"Who're you?"

The man raised a thumb and flipped the lapel of his coat back. He disclosed a side-coat pocket filled with folded papers, backed with colored binders, giving them a legal look, a gold shield with the number "12" engraved on it.

"The law, eh?" said Skarle.

"The law," said the man and walked to the little table, pushed a water pitcher and a tray with a thick glass on it out of the way and sat down.

"Well?" he said.

"Yes," said Skarle. "I went out there."

The man had eyebrows that stretched across the bridge of his nose. They were black and shaggy. His eyes were hot and brown. The lips were thick and a mustache bristled in every direction from the upper lip. The skin was oily, and the light at the windows gave greasy highlights to the prominent features.

"O. K.," he said. "That washes you up. You're floated. You're getting out of town. There's a train at seven-twenty tonight. Take it!"

"What's the idea?" asked Skarle. "You ain't got nothing on me. I talked to this guy. That's all. Guess I got a right to go see a guy and talk with him. He didn't raise any squawk."

The officer laughed. "Yeah? And you told him you thought you could locate the gems that were missing in that stick-up, and how much of a reward would you get! Pretty slick, ain't you! You have your accomplices stage a stick-up. The swag is too hot to move, and you decide you'll cop a reward selling it back to the man you copped it from. If we let crooks like you play those sort of games, you'd have the laugh on us all the time."

Skarle planted his feet wide apart on the floor. His eyes were black and glittering. His voice was vibrant. "You know I'm not mixed up in that thing at all. I'd never even heard of Bob Cromton, or his store, or the stick-up. I just happened to be here and to be interested. I said I thought I could clean the thing up for him."

"Says you," sneered the officer.

"Says I!" rasped Skarle.

The man got down off the table, came over closer to him, lowered his voice slightly. "All right," he said. "Get a load of this. I'm Pete Girkin, and I'm on the detective force of this man's town. If there's going to be any gems recovered I get the credit, see? If there's going to be

any rewards paid, they go to me. See? Think I'm going to let a guy drift in and chisel off some easy cash on me? Nix!"

He strode toward the door.

"That's all I've got to say, guy. There's a seven-twenty train out of town. I'll be down at the depot. When you get aboard I'll give you the glad mitt and that'll be all. You stick around and see what you get."

He twisted the knob of the door, jerked it open, walked out, turned in the corridor to remark over his shoulder: "Seven-twenty."

The door slammed.

There was a moment of silence, broken by the drone of the buzzing flies. The window curtain flapped once, lazily, in the current of air caused by the slamming door. Then Vera Colma came out of her room, pushing the door which connected with Skarle's room with a caution that held something of stealth in it.

Skarle jerked his hand at her. "Scram," he said.

She stared at him.

"He ain't connected you with me," said Skarle. "He didn't say anything about you ducking out of town. Get the sketch? He don't know you're with me."

She came to him, put her hands on his shoulders.

"Dane, I'm frightened. Tell me you'll take this job. Let me close up for the Hindu magician act. Please?"

He shook his shoulders and her hands dropped. He motioned to the connecting door. "Scram!" he said.

CHAPTER TWO

Run-Around

BOB CROMTON sat at his desk. There was a luncheon-club emblem on a stand, a pile of mail, a ledger and an ashtray on the top of the desk. His eyes were weak and watery, and they blinked cautiously at the world in conservative appraisal. The spectacles which he wore had dark celluloid rims, and kept sliding down on his nose. At intervals he would push them back. As he talked, his nose wiggled and the glasses started a perpetual slipping process.

"The question is," said Dane Skarle, trying to hold the watery eyes in his gaze, "whether you want those stones back or not."

"I've got to have them back," said Cromton. His voice was like his eyes, weak and evasive.

"Well," Skarle told him, "you won't get 'em back running to your local law and blabbing everything I tell you. If those guys could have cut the mustard and got the stuff back, they'd have done it before this."

Cromton said, defensively, and with a trace of spirit: "They're working on the case."

Dane Skarle opened his mouth. "Haw, haw, haw," he said, mirthlessly, not as a laugh, but as a mouthing of the syllables.

Cromton said: "I can talk to whom I like."

"Sure," Skarle admitted. "I can get gems back for whom I like. If you'd rather talk than have the stones back, then, cripes, go on and talk."

Cromton said: "I've got to have the stones back."

Skarle said nothing. His silence was the more significant because of his eyes, eyes that sought out the watery eyes of the jeweler. From time to time those watery eyes blinked into Skarle's, then tore themselves away from the direct gaze by an effort.

Cromton scraped back his chair. "All right. I won't say anything. Listen, it's about lunch time. There's a meeting of the luncheon club today. You come as my guest."

Skarle said: "O. K."

Cromton heaved a sigh. "You haven't any hard feelings have you?" he said.

Skarle shook his head.

Cromton took a hair brush from a drawer of the desk, smoothed his colorless hair into twin parts that curled down with mathematical precision on either side of his forehead. He pushed his glasses back up on his nose, surveyed himself in a hand mirror, took the brush and smoothed the hair again.

"We open with patriotic songs," he said. "It's a wonderful inspiration. You sing, don't you?"

Skarle said: "No!" explosively, and turned his back.

Cromton finished arranging his hair. "This way," he said, and led the way down the stairs from the mezzanine floor to the jewelry store. They walked the length of the aisle, flanked by glistening counters. As they went out the front door, Vera Colma was approaching, returning from luncheon with Bill Dabney.

Dane Skarle stared at Vera with unseeing eyes. Dabney spoke to Cromton and raised his hat. He was tall and well groomed. His face was handsome and his smile was a smirk, the sort of smirk which characterizes one who considers himself irresistible to women.

"My clerk," said Cromton, and there was a touch of pride in his voice. "I don't know who the young lady was. But he's a devil with the women, a regular devil!"

Dane Skarle grunted.

THEY walked three blocks, turned into an entrance where little groups of men were chaffing each other good naturedly. Bob Cromton's face lit up. He swelled out his chest. A man thumped him on the back. Cromton expanded into a devil-may-care man-about-town. He introduced Skarle to half a dozen people, went into a room ranged with long tables. Men sang songs in chorus, ate food with gusto, indulged in some awkward horse play and listened to a speaker who recited statistics in an uninteresting manner. Then there was more singing and an adjournment.

Dane Skarle strode to the sidewalk, inhaled deeply of the fresh air. Bob Cromton's hearty manner evaporated and left him a pale, stoop-shouldered merchant, walking uncertainly along the sidewalk.

He peered at Skarle with his watery eyes, and said: "Have you got any clues, anybody that you suspect?"

Skarle laughed without humor and remarked that he suspected everybody. A light car drove by with Pete Girkin at the wheel. He didn't seem to glance at the pair, but Cromton saw him, and became abruptly silent.

He turned at the door of his store. "I won't ask you in. I've got some correspondence to get out."

His voice was lame, as though he felt the explanation unconvincing and was seeking something which would elaborate it and make it carry more weight.

Skarle reached out a hand and gripped his lapel. "O. K. I'm on my way. But I want to find out a couple of things while we're standing right here. Now this is the door that the stick-up came through?"

"No," said Cromton. "It was the back door. I told you that."

"That's right. But there was some shooting. How did that happen?"

Cromton said, wearily: "I'll tell you the whole thing over again. You've got it mixed up. The clerks were putting out the display stuff from the vault. We have cheap stuff we don't take much care of, and then we have high-class stuff that's ticketed in and out every night.

"They're instructed to rush that stuff for the vault if there's any sign of a stick-up. This man didn't wear a mask. He was a stranger to us all. We never did find out how he got in. He must have come in the night before and slept in the back of the store. When they opened the vault and started out with the display stuff, he threw down a gun and told the boys to put up their hands.

"We've got guns planted here and there in the store. In the event of a hold-up, somebody's always where he can grab a gun. This time it was Dabney, the young man we met as we went to lunch. He grabbed a gun and started to shoot. The bandit returned the fire for a shot or two, and then took to his heels.

"He had his escape figured nicely. There was a car waiting in the alley with the motor running. He jumped into that and got away. Dabney chased him clean to the door, shooting. We thought he'd hit, but I guess he hadn't."

Cromton spoke as though he'd repeated the story until it had become mechanical with him.

Dane Skarle said "But the stuff that was missing?"

"That's the strange thing. It was an assortment of particularly large gems we'd been getting shipped in from wholesalers throughout the country. We had an order to match them up for a necklace. They were the most valuable things in the store.

"No one saw the robber pick them up. He ran past the trays all right, and he had them when he went out the door. There's no question about that. They were kept in a distinctive chamois bag. Two of the boys saw the robber with that bag."

DANE SKARLE stared moodily at the sun-drenched street, the black-surfaced pavement shimmering in the heat. "Shopping around through a bunch of wholesalers, there was a good chance for someone to have been tipped off."

Cromton said: "Yes," wearily.

"How much is the reward?" asked Skarle.

"I told you, I'd pay three thousand dollars for the gems."

"And no questions asked. That right?"

Cromton shook his head. "No. I didn't say that."

Skarle jerked on the lapel of Cromton's coat, pulled him half around, stared at him with eyes that were sullen.

"Yeah," he said. "That was what I was leading up to. I just put you through the hurdles on this other stuff to see if you'd come clean. You told me you wanted the stones because they represented a big profit on an order, and that the woman who had ordered them was crazy to get the thing completed. You said, between you, there'd be three thousand dollars for the stones, and no questions asked. Now don't tell me you didn't say that."

Cromton fidgeted. "Come into my office for a few minutes. I want to explain something."

"No," said Skarle, "you've got that important correspondence to attend to. And, anyway, I've got no time to go listen to a lot of blah. The question is do you want those stones back or not?"

"Yes," said Cromton. "I've got to have them back."

"O' K. You may be able to get 'em if you use your head."

Cromton reached up and pushed Dane Skarle's hand away from his coat. "But I'm not going to jail to get them," he said.

"How's that?" Skarle asked.

"The police. They explained to me that if I compounded a felony, I'd be sent to jail."

Skarle laughed mirthlessly. "And I suppose Pete Girkin was the lad that put that idea in your head."

"I talked with Girkin," said Cromton.

"I thought so," said Skarle grimly. "If Girkin surrenders the gems to you, it's all right to pay him the reward. If anybody else does, you're likely to go to jail. That the idea?"

Cromton said: "Not exactly."

"If," pressed Skarle, "you pay the reward to Girkin, it's O. K. Is that right?"

"Yes. Oh, yes."

"But if anybody else gets it, it's compounding a felony. That right?"

Cromton said again: "Not exactly." He swallowed with an audible effort, and added: "I'd be allowed to pay the reward, I believe, but I'd have to report the entire affair, and the man that turned in the stones would be arrested and held until he could account for the manner in which he had secured them. That, I believe, was the general idea that Girkin gave me. I wanted you to know."

Dane Skarle laughed. "Yeah," he said. "I could see how eager you were. You were trying to keep from telling me. If I hadn't dragged it out of you, you'd never have peeped. You'd have let me get the stones, and then had Girkin jug me, eh?"

"Not at all!" snapped Cromton. "You've no right even to insinuate I'd do such a thing."

Skarle took the lapel of the coat again. "Did Girkin make you mark some cash to use as a reward payment?" he asked.

Cromton's watery eyes avoided Skarle. "What do you mean?" he asked.

"You know what I mean!" Skarle said. "Did he?"

Cromton said, in a very subdued tone of voice: "Yes."

Dane Skarle laughed, dropped his hand from the lapel of the coat, turned on his heel and walked away. Cromton stared after him for a moment, then raised a solicitous hand to the lapel of his coat and smoothed it carefully. He adjusted his necktie, and then pushed open the plate-glass swinging door of the jewelry store and entered.

Bill Dabney, standing behind a counter, regarded him curiously.

CHAPTER THREE

Hot Plant

DANE SKARLE turned the key in the lock of his door and pushed it open. Everything was just as it had been the previous afternoon, just as it would be every afternoon during the late summer. The sun was penetrating the jaundiced shades to give the room a sickly yellow light. The air was stuffy and flies were buzzing aimlessly.

Skarle closed the door behind him, turned the lock.

Vera Colma poked her head from the adjoining room. Her face was white and strained. "Where the devil have you been?" she asked. "I thought you'd never come back!"

Dane Skarle hurled his hat on the bed. "Been listening to a bum speech," he said, "from a guy that was making a living out of making bum speeches for some charity or other. Cromton turned yellow on me and was afraid to spill the dope until I yanked it out of him. . . . What's the matter?"

She put her hand down the front of her sport dress and pulled out some white tissue paper. She unwrapped the tissue and disclosed three unset stones and a bit of platinum setting from which the stones had been gouged.

He stared at them. "Where'd you get them? Did Dabney—"

She came closer to him and lowered her voice. "No. Not Dabney. Somebody came into your room. I heard the click of the key in the lock. I thought it was you, and I came in. There was a man bending over the dresser. One of the drawers was open. I thought I'd seen him before. I think he was the wise dick that barged in here yesterday. I'm not sure. I ducked out and slipped the door closed, quietly."

Skarle frowned. "Why didn't you ask him what he was doing?" he wanted to know.

"I don't know. I was afraid—and I'd been lying down. I didn't have too many clothes on. I was afraid he'd grab me as some sort of a criminal."

Skarle said, "O. K. That's sense. What did you do?"

"Waited until he got out and then I went to the dresser. I had a hard time finding it. He'd pulled one of the drawers entirely out and fastened this little package on the back with wax. See, you can see where the wax was on the paper."

Skarle said: "Did you leave any wax on the drawer?"

She grinned at him. "Give me credit for some sense, Dane."

He took the gems and turned them over and over in his hand. He went to the dresser, pulled out the drawers, looked at the backs of them, turned to her, and said: "You sure he didn't plant any more stuff?"

She made a gesture with her shoulders. "How can I be? I couldn't see through the closed door. You'd told me to be sure they didn't connect us as being together, so I was afraid to leave the door open."

"How long was he here?"

"Just a minute or two."

"Then that's all of it," said Skarle. "That bozo wouldn't waste hot stuff sprinkling it around here."

SHE walked over to him, slid under the crook of his arm, held her face up close to his. "Listen, Dane, they may spring that any minute. If it's a frame and that stuff is hot you've got to get rid of it."

He nodded. "Still got cold feet?" he asked her.

She pulled herself away from him, stared at him with level eyes. "Dane Skarle, I'm not a piker, and you know it. And I don't nag. I told you I was afraid and wanted to get out of it. We're going up against the guys that have the power. I was afraid they'd frame us and put us in the pen. I didn't want to waste my youth staring at four stone walls and a barred window. You said to stay with it, so I'm staying. The thing's finished as far as I'm concerned. See? I'm not talking about it again. You're making the play and I'm backing it. But I'm just telling you that we've got to work fast."

He patted her shoulder. "Good kid," he said.

A PEREMPTORY knock sounded on the panels of the door. She caught her breath in a quick gasp. Dane Skarle's eyes narrowed. "Listen, kid," he whispered, "slip into your room, and keep under cover. Better lock the connecting door. I don't think anybody's connected us, yet. But keep your ear close to the panels. I may want a witness to what happens."

She slipped through the connecting door, paused for a moment to grin at him, then pulled the door closed. As the bolt clicked, Dane Skarle opened the outer door of the room. Pete Girkin was standing on the threshold. He barged into the room.

"Now what?" asked Dane.

Girkin grinned. "Come on in, Sid," he called.

A man who had been flattened out against the wall in the corridor walked into the room. He was thin and stoop-shouldered. His face sagged into folds of leathery skin. The eyes were big and glazed as with a film. He kept his mouth partly open, and big teeth, protruding from the upper jaw, caught the light.

"Sid Hare," said Girkin, easily.

"Who's he, and what do you want?" demanded Skarle.

"This the guy?" asked Girkin of the stoop-shouldered man.

The glassy eyes revolved in their sockets as they swung from Girkin to Dane Skarle. The mouth twitched. Sid Hare was breathing through that mouth, and the sound of his breath was plainly audible in the afternoon silence of the room.

Girkin spoke, easily, forcefully. "Of course," he said, "you can't be absolutely certain. The guy that did the job had a mask on, and it wasn't any too good a light. He moved fast, and you was excited. But you can tell me whether or not he's got about the same build; whether or not it might have been this guy."

Sid Hare said: "It could have been him all right. You'd know that from the description. It was a man about this build. He had a mask on over his face."

Girkin grinned evilly at Skarle. "O. K., guy, that ties you up with a stick-up where some jewelry was stolen. I figured you for a gem crook the minute I seen you fooling around trying to work some hot stuff back on Cromton. This identification ties you up with another crime."

Skarle fastened moody, purposeful eyes on Hare. "You're identifying me as a man who robbed you?" he asked. "Just speak right up if you are, because then I want to get a lawyer over here and have him hear what you say. Then I'll see how much I can get out of you by way of damages—"

Hare said: "No, no! I'm not doing anything of the sort. I may never have seen you before. Your voice doesn't sound like the voice of the man who held me up. He wore a mask. He was about the same build as you, but lots of men have about that build."

Girkin pushed Hare back and to one side, strode into such a position that he was between Hare and Skarle. "So that's your line, is it?" he asked Skarle.

"That," said Skarle, "is my line."

Girkin sneered. "See where it gets you. Get over there, and don't do any more talking. I'm going to look around."

"Got a search warrant?" asked Skarle.

Girkin planted his feet, thrust forward his jaw. His lips quivered at the corners. "I've got all the warrant I need. Was you going to figure on stopping me?"

Skarle said: "You can't search this dump without a warrant."

"The hell I can't," said Girkin.

"I'm calling on you as a witness," said Skarle to Hare.

Hare blinked his glassy eyes, looked at Girkin. "Maybe I'd better wait out in the hall, Pete."

"Nonsense. You stick right around

here. That's the way all of these cheap crooks talk. Talk's cheap. A guy can't buy anything with talk. You don't need to be afraid of what this guy'll do."

He moved over to the bed and pulled back the pillow, lifted the mattress, peered under the bed. He walked to the dresser, yanked out the drawers, looked in them. He walked to the closet, opened the door, ran his hands up and down the clothes which were on hangers.

Dane Skarle laughed. "Is that a search?" he asked.

Girkin's face was twisted into an evil leer. "That, guy," he said, "is a search. Take it and like it."

He jerked a suit off the hanger, ran his fingers through the pockets, held the garments upside down and shook them. He dropped them in a careless heap on the floor.

He walked back to the dresser, pulled it out from the wall, and looked at the back of it. "Some slick crooks," he said, "stick stuff on the backs of the dressers with wax."

"My, my, ain't you clever!" mocked Skarle.

He turned to Hare. "You're a witness, Mr. Hare, that this man is proceeding to search my room, despite the fact that I have objected, and despite the fact that he has no warrant."

Hare turned his back and looked out of the window. "I'm not a witness to anything," he declared.

Girkin said to him: "The hell you're not. Turn around here and watch me. S'pose I should find some of that hot stuff that came from the stick-up, and this guy should claim I planted it! You're the one that's been riding us about not getting results. Now you back up my play, or you'll hear from it."

Hare fastened his glassy eyes on Girkin. "Really, Pete, I don't see—"

Girkin jerked the drawer of the dresser open, savagely. He pulled it free of the dresser and looked on the back of it.

"Another slick trick of these crooks—" he began, and came to an abrupt stop. His eyes were fastened on the back of the drawer. He blinked them several times, then slowly slid the drawer back into place.

"O. K.," he said. "I guess this guy ain't got anything."

Skarle grinned. "That all the searching you going to do?"

"That's all of it—now," said Girkin meaningly. He was grinning. "You haven't got any jewelry, have you; any platinum or diamonds or anything like that?"

"No," said Skarle.

Girkin's grin was meaning, significant. "That's all I wanted you to say," he remarked, then turned to the flat-chested man with the glassy eyes. "Come on, Sid. We're finished."

They walked to the outer door. Girkin held it open. Sid Hare went through the door as though he would have liked to start running as soon as his feet hit the corridor. Girkin paused to shoot one grinning glance over his shoulder. Then he slammed the door shut.

Skarle turned the key in the lock.

DANE SKARLE bored into the cake of soap with his knife. The soap whittlings fell into the washbowl in little showers. Vera Colma stood at his shoulder, watching. Skarle enlarged the cavity he had made in the soap. When he had the cavity large enough to suit him, he inserted the stones, the platinum setting. He had a soap plug ready to fit into the hole he had made. He pushed this plug into place, took a hot curling iron which Vera handed him and seared the soap together so that it would not appear the cake had been tampered with.

Vera watched him with eyes that seemed oblivious of what was taking place. "Why didn't he blow up when he found you'd pulled the stuff out of the place where he'd cached it, Dane?"

Dane Skarle said: "Don't ask me to follow the mental processes of that crook. He planted the stuff. If he'd found it there, there might have ben a squawk that I'd been framed. As soon as I took the stuff and started doing things with it, I was sunk if he ever caught me."

Vera didn't say anything.

"It's getting hot. We've got to have a showdown," said Skarle. "I want you to keep that dinner date with Dabney. Somewhere along the line I'll make a play. You watch for it and back it."

Her voice was low, vibrant with some emotion. "Dane," she said, "I'd do anything for you, but I won't play stool pigeon. I won't get a man's confidence and betray it."

He whirled on her. His eyes met hers with a sullen fire of smoldering emotion that made it seem his gaze had the shock of physical impact. "You going to run out on me?"

"No. I'll play along. I'm just telling you what I won't do in advance, so there won't be any misunderstandings."

"Well, then, what won't you do?"

"I won't play stool pigeon."

"Thought you didn't like this guy."

"I don't. He's a pain in the neck, only more so. But I won't lead any man on to give me his confidences, and then betray him. If you make me go to the point where he confides in me, I'll keep that confidence, no matter what it means."

He watched her with eyes that were half closed, with lips that trembled in the start of a smile. "And yet you don't like him?"

"I hate him! But that doesn't keep me from shooting square."

He grunted, grinned, put an arm around her and patted her shoulder. "You're a good little kid," he told her. "Nobody's asking you to do any stooling. I just want you to stall this guy at dinner and back my play."

She took the fingers of his hand in hers, stroked them gently, one by one. "You won't take any chances, Dane?"

"I've got to take some chances. I won't take any I don't think I can get away with. This hick dick is following me around trying to pin hot stuff on me and force an identification that'll give me a record on some other crime. Then he'll pull this Cromton stuff on me, and get Cromton to say I was negotiating for a return of the stones. After that it'll just be too bad."

"But how you going to keep from being framed, Dane?"

He bent and kissed her eyelids, then pushed her away. "Never mind that, kid. That's my business. Scram."

She watched him longingly.

"Gee, Dane, I'd—"

"Scram," he said.

She opened the connecting door and slipped through it, pulling the door softly shut behind her.

CHAPTER FOUR

Bait For a Trap

DANE SKARLE dressed in front of the mirror with scrupulous care, adjusted collar and tie. There was another knock at the door. He went to it.

Pete Girkin grinned at him. Behind Pete were two uniformed officers.

"This time," said Pete, "I got a warrant to search the place, and I got a warrant to search you!"

"Ain't you," sneered Dane Skarle, "the slick guy with the ball-bearing brain!"

Girkin pushed into the room. "Never mind that," he said. "You can make all the wise cracks you want to after we get done. Come on, boys. Let's take this dump to pieces. I know what I want is here!"

The men filed into the room after the detective. They searched the place with microscopic thoroughness. They searched Skarle, going through every stitch of his clothes. Girkin's face darkened with rage as the futility of the search became apparent. It was more than an hour and a half after they had started the search of the room that the men gave it up.

Girkin left the room, his eyes blazing with rage. The uniformed officers seemed to have lost interest in the entire affair. They made the search with thoroughness, listened to Girkin's suggestions and followed them mechanically.

Dane Skarle closed the door on them, locked the door, went to the bathroom, cut the cake of soap open and took out the gems he had concealed. He dropped them carelessly into his pocket, put on his hat, went to the door, opened it, and walked down the corridor.

Girkin and the two officers were standing across the street as Skarle walked out of the place. Girkin moved over. His eyes were narrow and glinting. "Suppose you got 'em on you now, eh?"

Dane met his eyes. "Move on, guy. Don't think I'm a dub. You had a search warrant. You made your search under that warrant. That uses it up. You've got to get another warrant if you're going to do any more searching."

Girkin said: "You sure of that?"

Dane remarked: "That's what my lawyer said. He seemed to be sure of it."

Girkin sneered and observed: "I never knew an innocent guy before that had to have a lawyer at his elbow every minute."

Dane Skarle kept his lips twisted into a smile, but his eyes were cold and hard. "There's lots you never knew before. And never will!"

He walked away.

Girkin made no effort to follow. He called after Skarle: "You ain't done with me yet, guy."

Skarle raised his voice so that he was certain the two officers could hear him: "Yes I am. You had a search made, both of me and the room. Nothing was there. Now if you find something there, I've got these two officers to testify that it was planted."

He didn't make any further comment, but continued to walk until he came to Cromton's store. He waited across the street until Bill Dabney came out. He followed Dabney to an apartment house, then to a hotel. Dabney waited in the lobby. After ten minutes he was joined by Vera Colma.

THEY went to a speakeasy, then to a dinner where there was some dancing and no liquor. Dane Skarle had a table from which he could watch them. Vera Colma seemed tired. She smiled infrequently. Dabney danced with her twice. The third time he asked her she shook her head. He kept his hands on the table, moving them over to rest on Vera's hands. Once or twice he raised them to her arm and pawed the bare flesh with the tips of his fingers. Vera pulled her arms free on such occasions.

Dane Skarle waited until Dabney started pawing again. Then he got up and walked across to their table, barging purposefully across the floor. Vera looked up and saw him coming. There was a trace of panic in her eyes, but she kept them steady, questioning.

She gave no sign of ever having seen him before.

As Skarle paused before the table, looking down at her, Bill Dabney asserted his rights as escort. "She ain't dancing with strangers," said Dabney. "On your way! On your way!"

Skarle didn't even turn his eyes toward Dabney. He stared at Vera, and said: "So you're pulling the stall of not knowing me, eh?"

He could see that she was trying to figure his play, and he twisted the corner of his lips in a signal that meant, according to the code they had used in their stage act: "I'm going to ad lib from here. Keep your eyes open, and follow my lead."

Vera Colma spoke in a thin, frightened voice, and said: "Who are you?" And, as she spoke, scraped back her chair and arose.

Bill Dabney got to his feet. "Hey, you—"

Skarle turned on him. "That'll be about all out of you, young fellow. You probably don't know it, but you're dining with one of the slickest gem thieves that's ever operated anywhere in the state!"

Bill Dabney's jaw sagged slightly.

Dane Skarle pulled up a chair, sat down. "I won't make a scene," he said. "You can just pretend that I'm a mutual friend who dropped over for a chat. Sit down, you two."

Vera Colma sat down. Bill Dabney waited for a moment and then sat down. His manner was sullen, but startled. Dane Skarle reached his hand down under the table cloth, leaned forward until his palm rested on Vera's lap. He dropped the gems and platinum setting that the detective had planted in his room. As he did so, he winked both eyes twice, a spaced blink that was also a code signal, and meant: "Slip these things over to him."

Then he straightened, leaned back in his chair and lit a match. "I've got a hot tip, Stella, that you were in on the Sorenson job, and that you've got some of the stuff on you right now."

Vera said: "That's a lie!"

As she spoke, she leaned forward. Dane Skarle could see the play of the muscles in her shoulder as she kept groping under the table, trying to touch Dabney.

Leaning back, touching the match to the cigarette he held in his lips, letting the first puffs of smoke seep out, Dane watched Dabney's face. He could see the puzzled expression when Vera touched his leg, the sudden consternation as his hand dropped, contacted hers, and received the touch of the diamonds.

Vera slowly straightened, turned toward him and gave a little cough, which meant: "It's finished O. K.," and said: "Can't you dicks ever give a jane a chance? You've hounded me from one place to another. I'm going straight and have been for six months."

Dane Skarle removed the cigarette, and said, smokily: "Tell it to the marines."

BILL DABNEY'S hands were moving under the table. Dane Skarle couldn't tell just how they were moving, but he could see from the manner in which the shoulders of the coat twitched that Dabney was doing something.

"What do you want?" asked Vera of Dane Skarle.

"I want the lowdown on that Sorenson job," he said, "and I want your share of the sparklers. You've got 'em on you."

"A lie!" she said.

He sighed wearily. "Then I'll have to take you to headquarters and book you. The matron'll search you there, and, what I mean, she'll make a good job. I know how clever you are at ditching hot stuff."

She laughed in his face, and said: "Baloney!"

Dane scowled. "That ain't helping you any, sister."

"The hell it ain't," she said. "You got a warrant on that Sorenson job? You got a search warrant for me?"

He shook his head and said: "I don't need any. You're going to come with me, and like it!"

She flung her head back so that the table lights made a long, graceful line of her sweeping throat, and laughed. It was an amused, patronizing laugh.

"Be your age," she said. "Just because you're in a hick town, you don't need to act like a hick. I thought you were a smart guy."

"I am," grunted Skarle.

She continued to laugh throatily.

Dane Skarle let his forehead knit. He

scraped back his chair. "O. K.," he said. "I wanted to make it easy for you. You wouldn't give me any sort of cooperation. Now you'll take it the way it comes. Get up and come along with me, or I'll put the bracelets on and drag you out."

Dabney scraped back his chair. "Maybe I'll have something to say about that," he said.

Skarle laughed nastily. "Yes?" he said. "It wouldn't take much to jail you as an accomplice. Maybe I'd better look you over, too."

Vera Colma caught Dane's eye, then made a gesture of surrender.

"Oh, shucks, Bill, what's the use? He's just a dumb dick that has to be shown. I'll go to the jail and let the matron search everything I got. Then he won't have anything to hold me on, and it'll all be finished. We stand here and argue with this boob, and he'll be talking until midnight. What's more, he's got no more sense than to drag me out of here. He's that dumb."

Skarle nodded. "You're damned tootin'!" he growled.

Bill Dabney paid the check. His face was strangely white. He kept scowling as though trying to concentrate on something. But Dane Skarle kept up a running fire of conversation so that Dabney wouldn't have a chance to think things over.

"You've got to come as far as the cloakroom and give up the check that'll get the girl's wraps," said Skarle. "Then you can duck—if you don't make any more wise cracks. And don't get over close to the broad. I ain't going to have her slipping you any hot stuff."

Dabney said, huskily: "What's eating you? Think I want to get dragged into this mess?"

"I didn't know," remarked Skarle. "You acted as though you did."

"Well, I don't."

"O. K., then. Keep out of it!"

Dane Skarle called a taxicab. He handed the girl in. "Police headquarters," he said. Vera Colma smiled wistfully at Bill Dabney. "Good night, Bill."

Dabney raised his hat, said nothing. The cab lurched into motion. Dane Skarle leaned forward and tapped the glass. "Never mind going to headquarters right now. Drive to the corner, swing around it, and then crowd right in to the curb."

The taxi driver stared at him in a swift, wide-eyed glance of surprise, then muttered: "O. K., boss."

The cab lurched around the corner. There was a parking space near a fire plug. The brakes gripped as the cab swung into the vacant parking place. Skarle jerked the door open. "Wait here," he said to Vera.

SKARLE walked back around the corner, flattened himself against the wall of a building, hugging the shadows. He saw Dabney walking slowly toward him, along the street. A cruising cab gave him a horn and Dabney nodded. Skarle sprinted back to his own cab.

"Follow the checker that's coming around the corner," he said to the driver. "Don't let it out of your sight, no matter what happens. But don't let him know he's being followed. There's—"

The checker rounded the corner and the rest of the sentence was bit off as Skarle's cab jerked out from the curb. Skarle leaned forward, peering at the back of the checker. He could see the back of Dabney's head. There didn't seem to be any suspicion whatever on the part of the jewelry-store employee that he might be followed. He didn't once look back through the glass window.

Dane Skarle settled back against the cushions. Vera Colma snuggled up close to him, asked: "What was the big idea, Dane?"

"Wait," he told her. "We'll see if it works. He took the stuff all right?"

"Yes. He took it. Did you see the surprise on his face?"

"I'll say."

"But, Dane, that doesn't show that he's a crook. Lots of men would have done as much to keep the girl from getting into a jam with the law. You take a man and shove some hot jewelry into his hand when another man is browbeating the girl he's dining with, and——"

He gave a gentle pressure to her hand. "It's all right, kid, I know. And I know what I'm doing. This gets rid of the hot stuff that was wished off on me, and it's bait for a trap."

"What sort of a trap, Dane?"

"Well," said Skarle, leaning forward, his eyes fastened on the tail-light of the cab ahead, "he thinks that stuff is hot, see?"

"Yes. Sure. Of course he does."

"O. K., Vera, he's naturally going to get rid of it. He's fallen for you, so he won't just chuck it away. He's going to hide it some place where it'll be safe. He hasn't had any time to think, and he won't have time to do much thinking. He'll rush to some place that he's previously thought of. See the point? If he's figured out some really safe hiding place in advance, that's where he'll put this stuff.

"Now, if he's the chap that was back of this stick-up business at the store, he'll have had some safe hiding place picked for the swag he copped then. He'll naturally put this bunch of stuff in the same place."

Vera Colma nodded. "That's a cinch," she said, "but he may not be the one that's mixed up in that store job, and, in any event, he'll have the stuff put away somewhere in his apartment. We can't see where he puts this stuff."

Dane Skarle nodded. His eyes were narrow slits. "Sure," he said, "but as soon as he's had a chance to put it away, you show up and knock on the door. He comes to see who it is. You grin at him, and tell

him that you got to headquarters, panned me for being an outside dick that had tried to give you the rush act without a warrant, got me put on the carpet, and you got free, that you want your stones."

She nodded. "Then what?" she wanted to know.

"Then if he's a crook you can tell it. You pretend you're a crook at first. If he falls, all right. If he don't fall, hand him a line that these stones were given you by a friend to keep, that you know they're all right, but that if they'd found them on you, what with your record and all, it would have meant at the very least a term in jail, and you didn't want that. Tell him you used to be a crook, but that you've started straight."

She frowned, gripped Dane by the arm with savage fingers that bit into his arm through the coat. "Damn it, Dane, I won't cross a man. If he fights, I'll fight. But if he tries to play the gentleman and kicks through with any confidence, I won't betray that confidence."

Dane Skarle met her eyes. "Not to me?"

"Not to you," she said. "I'm not used to pulling a vamp line to get a man off his guard, and I don't like it. If he shoots square with me, I'm going to shoot square with him."

"Even if it means turning me down, Vera?"

Moisture brimmed her eyes, but they remained steady. "Yes," she said.

HE SHRUGGED his shoulders. "He won't shoot square with you," he said. "He's a crook, that's why. He's crooked all through. He betrayed the man that employed him. Dabney gave a duplicate key to the back entrance to the tool who used the gun. Then when Dabney opened the safe he slipped out the chamois bag that had those matched stones in it. He put that bag where a man could grab it.

"If he hadn't done that, do you think a

crook could have busted into a store, engaged in a snap gun fight and still copped the one bit of swag that was the most valuable?"

"I don't know," she said.

"Well, I know," he told her. "It just wasn't on the cards. It had to be an inside job. That is, the brains were on the inside."

The checker cab swung around a corner and pulled in to the curb, opposite the apartment house where Skarle had trailed Dabney earlier in the evening.

"Shall I stop?" asked the driver of Skarle's cab.

"Keep going," snapped Skarle. "Swing in to the curb after you round the corner, and then stop. Get down on the floor, Vera."

They swept past the checker. Bill Dabney was paying off the driver. He didn't even look up as the other cab whizzed past. Skarle nudged Vera, and said: "O. K. You can get up. He ain't suspicious. He didn't figure on being tailed."

The cab swung around the corner, stopped. Skarle hopped out and thrust a bill into the hands of the driver. He grabbed Vera by the arm, escorted her down the sidewalk. He walked on the opposite side of the street, across from the apartment house. They could see the front of the building, looming some six stories.

A S THEY walked along a light came on in a corner apartment on the third floor. The window shades were down, but there was a certain amount of light which seeped through them, giving the windows a soft appearance of mellow light.

Dane Skarle said: "I'll bet that's his apartment," and turned back.

Vera Colma said nothing. She was clinging to Dane's arm. Her eyes were fastened straight ahead. They walked rapidly. Dane Skarle peered at the direc-tory on the apartment house after they had crossed the street. He nodded. "That's his apartment sure as shooting. You go up, Vera. Give him a minute or two, but not too long. Better listen in front of his door. As long as you can hear him moving around, you won't knock. Wait until he quits moving and then knock."

"Remember," she warned, "if he shoots square with me, I'll shoot square with him. Even—even against you, Dane. I can't help it. That's just the way I'm built."

He nodded, absently. "Maybe we better give him a few more minutes. Now listen, Vera, you can manage to lean up against one of those front windows. When you're doing that you can press your hand against the curtain, tight, and I can see it.

"You do that once, and it means that he's a crook, but you haven't located the hiding place of the swag. Do it twice and it means you've found out where he's got the stuff. If he should happen to be on the square with you—"

Vera Colma interrupted: "Listen, Dane, I've double-teamed around with you. I'm a sleight-of-hand assistant. I didn't want to go in for this reward chasing. I told you what I'd do and what I wouldn't do. I can't help it. It's the way I'm built. If he shoots square with me, you won't see any signal."

"No matter what happens?" he asked her.

"No matter what happens," she said.

He took her arm, gave her a push. "O. K., then, Vera, go on up."

She walked into the apartment house without a single backward glance. Dane Skarle walked back across the street to a place from which he could see the lighted windows of the apartment on the third floor.

CHAPTER FIVE

Double Cross

DANE SKARLE looked at his strap watch. It had been five minutes since Vera Colma walked through the door of the apartment house. He lit a cigarette, inhaled feverishly and deeply. He waited until the cigarette was half consumed, then flipped it into the gutter, looked at the strap watch again. There had been no signal.

He fell to pacing the sidewalk, taking swift, short strides, jerking himself around abruptly into a reverse. His eyes never left the faint yellow oblongs which marked the windows of the apartment he was watching. His strap watch showed him that Vera Colma had been gone fourteen minutes.

Dane Skarle snapped himself around, crossed the street. The apartment house had a directory with bells opposite the names of the tenants. Dane Skarle wasted no time ringing the bell opposite the name of Bill Dabney, but pressed first one button, then another, choosing the buttons at random. On the third try he received a response. The electric door release buzzed. Skarle pushed on the knob and walked in.

A woman stood at a half-open door midway in the corridor. She stared at Skarle, said: "I don't know you!"

"Don't stand there staring at me, then," snapped Skarle, and took the stairs. He went at once to the apartment where he had seen the lights in the windows. He tried the door. It was locked. His face a grim mask, he tapped with his knuckles. Motion sounded from the interior of the apartment. A key clicked. The door opened a crack. Dane Skarle sank his shoulder against the door and it went open, Bill Dabney staggering back under the force of the impact.

Skarle kicked the door closed, twisted the lock without taking his eyes from Dabney.

"What do you want?" asked Dabney.

Dane's voice was husky. "I thought I wanted a reward," he said. "I gambled the regard of a damned square shooter on it, and lost. I don't intend to lose. Where is she?"

Bill Dabney stood with blinking eyes. His face was white, but remained composed. He had been piling things into suitcases. There was one packed and strapped on the floor, one on the bed that was half filled with garments. A light aeroplane trunk was standing on its end, closed and locked. Bath water was running in the bathroom.

Dabney said: "You're crazy. There's nobody here."

"You had dinner with her," said Skarle.

Dabney's face lit with recognition. "Oh," he said, "that jane! The one you took to the station to search, eh? O. K., brother, I'm going to come clean with you. I guess she was a crook all right. When you braced her about being a crook she slipped something to me under the table. I couldn't see what it was. I wasn't strong for you. You'd busted in on my dinner party and you didn't act sociable to me. So I didn't say anything. I stuck the stuff in my pocket without noticing what it was.

"I guess it was mechanical for a guy to sort of protect a frail he's out with that way. Anyhow, I put it in my pocket and started home. Then I got to thinking. I pulled out the stuff. It was something that didn't look so good, gems and stuff. So I called a cop and told him a woman had brushed past me on the street and slipped it into my pocket as she went past. He took my name and address and the stuff.

"I figured I wouldn't say anything to you. But you're here, and that's the straight goods. I haven't seen the broad again, and don't want to. She slipped me that stuff, and I fell for her line. But I'm finished."

He ceased speaking, stared at Skarle with wide-open, frank eyes.

"She didn't come here?" asked Skarle.

"Not here. If she had, I'd have turned her over to the law. She got me in one jam. That's enough."

Dane Skarle said: "You're not stringing me?"

"No. Honest to God! I'm giving it to you on the square. She got me in bad. I know that. I was figuring on lighting out because of it. I couldn't afford to get mixed into a mess. That's on the square, guy. Take it or leave it."

DANE SKARLE swung his right. It caught Dabney on the side of the jaw. Dabney went sprawling back. His knees hit the edge of the bed, spilled him over backward on top of the suitcase, sent him on his back kicking and clawing. Skarle said: "Damn you, come through or I'll kill you."

Dabney twisted, rolled off the other side of the bed. His hand shot to his hip pocket. Skarle went over the bed in a long leap, tackled Dabney about the waist. Dabney got out the gun. Skarle clamped his hands around the wrist. Dabney slowly twisted the wrist so that the gun was pointed at Skarle. Skarle flung around with his body. His knee kicked Dabney in the pit of the stomach. Dabney weakened; Skarle twisted the gun from his hand, caught the wrist and twisted it. Dabney screamed: "Don't! I won't fight. You're breaking my arm!"

Skarle released the tension. He crawled free of the bed and to his feet. Dabney crouched as though doubled with pain. From that crouching position, he suddenly shot out a wicked right. Skarle blocked it, crossed his own right. It caught Dabney on the button, and Dabney went backward, quivered for a moment. His muscles drew

up, then relaxed, and he straightened out on the floor.

Skarle walked to the closet and flung the door open. He went to the bathroom, opened the door. Vera Colma was lying in the bathtub, bound hand and foot. The water was turned on in both faucets. She was gagged. The water level had crept up until it was over her mouth and little wavelets were touching her nostrils. She was gasping, choking, trying to fight free, strangling for air. Her eyes were wide with panic.

Skarle made a leap, caught her head, raised it. He shut off the water, reached to his pocket, got out a knife. He cut the gag, then the strips of rope which held her hands, arms and legs. She had been making noises back of the gag which had been inaudible with the water running. She continued those noises mechanically as he cut the gag out. Then she spat out the wadded cloth, looked at Skarle.

The panic slipped from her eyes. She forced a white-lipped smile.

"You came damn near not getting here," she said.

Skarle patted her shoulder. She stood by the side of the bathtub, her clothes dripping water. She raised her hands and started divesting herself of the wet clothing.

"See if you can get me some clothes," she said, "and a drink. Get the drink first. I need it!"

Skarle went back into the apartment. Dabney lay on the floor as Skarle had left him. The suitcase which had been on the bed had been spilled to the floor, and a miscellaneous assortment of wearing apparel had cascaded into a pile.

Skarle searched the pile for a flask, found none. He went into the kitchenette, opened two cupboards, found a square bottle of gin in the second cupboard. He took it to the bathroom.

"Coming up!" he said.

Vera Colma stretched out a bare arm, took the bottle, tilted it to her lips.

"Clothes," she said, and coughed.

Dane Skarle took clean underwear, shirt, socks, tie and a suit of clothes from the pile of clothing that was on the floor, and from the aeroplane wardrobe trunk, which he opened. He took them in to Vera.

SHE emerged from the bathroom, hair wet, stringing down on the side of her face. The clothes were too big for her, but they were not so big as to be grotesque on her. She stared down at the unconscious form of Bill Dabney.

"Damn him, he was going to drown me. Couldn't you hear me, Dane?"

"Not through the door and with the water running," he said. "How did it happen?"

"He was evidently wise. I came in and said I'd returned for the stuff I'd given him. He went out in the kitchenette. I followed him. He had it in a flour bin. Just as he had his coat off and his arm in up to the shoulder, he turned and caught me peeking through the door. He made a rush. I should have screamed or flung something through the window. But I thought I could alibi myself out of it. He never gave me a chance. He socked me a beauty on the chin and I went groggy. Then he did what you saw to me."

Dane Skarle cursed under his breath.

"Where's that gin, Dane?" she asked.

He went over to the bathroom, found the gin bottle, brought it to her. "What'd he do with the stuff?" he asked her.

She gulped gin, took the bottle from her lips and shook her head. "You can search me. I suppose it's in his suitcase, or on him somewhere."

Dane looked in the suitcase which had been closed. There was nothing there except clothes and toilet articles. He ran his hands over Dabney's clothing. Dabney stirred, gasped, cursed, rolled over on his side and retched. Skarle ripped open the shirt.

"I think he's got a chamois belt against the skin," he said.

Dabney kicked futilely, groaned and retched again. Skarle ripped open the garments and pulled out a chamois belt. He opened the pockets and nodded. "This is the stuff, Vera," he said.

She sighed. "Well, that's that! It's not been worth it. I'd rather have worn a turban and a couple of coats of color and done things on the stage."

He grinned at her. "No variety in that. Let's go."

"How about the stuff that Girkin planted?" she asked.

"That's right," said Dane. "No sense in leaving that for him to make trouble with."

He made another search, found the gems in a pocket. He transferred them to his own pocket. "Now," he said, "we'll tie him up so he'll be here nice and pretty when the police come."

"You're not going to notify them now?" asked Vera.

"Not a chance. Cromton stands up and chants high-sounding sentiments at the luncheon club, but he'd cross us in a second if he had a chance. I want to get the reward cinched first."

"O. K.," she said. "If you're going to tie him up, stick him in the bathtub and turn on the water. I want to see how he takes it."

Bill Dabney twisted, half screamed: "No, no. I wasn't going to do anything except frighten her!"

Skarle grabbed his coat collar, jerked him around the foot of the bed. "O. K.," he said, "I'm going to scare you!"

"What you going to do?" asked Dabney.

"You wouldn't be so frightened if you knew," said Vera.

Skarle said, grimly: "Don't think he wouldn't. He might be more frightened!"

He picked up the wet ropes which had been used to tie Vera Colma, and twisted them expertly around Dabney. "I learned this trick on the stage," he said. "Try and get loose and you'll tighten everything, including the rope that's going around your neck. Start any kind of a struggle and you'll strangle yourself."

He knotted a slip knot around Dabney's neck, led the rope down to the man's wrists, and continued the same rope to the ankles. He doubled the knees and pulled the ankles up along the back, so that any tension on the rope caused by a motion of the legs would have the effect of tightening the slip knot around the neck. Then he fashioned a gag which he crammed into Dabney's mouth, tied the gag in place.

"He can still make noise," said Vera. "I know I could, and he had my whole throat crammed with rags."

Skarle nodded, wordlessly, dragged Dabney to the closet, put him in there on the floor, took the mattress from the bed and piled it in on top of him.

"He'll smother!" said Vera.

"Not if I get the reward matter straightened up and get the police here in time," said Skarle.

"What if you don't?" she asked.

He closed one eye at her, and said: "Then that'll be his hard luck."

DABNEY made muffled noises of protest from behind the gag. Dane Skarle closed the closet door. The noises were audible but not sufficiently loud to attract attention. Skarle took the girl and led her through the door.

"I look a sight!" she said.

"What do we care," Skarle observed. "We're going to pick up a nice fat reward."

He led her out of the apartment. They caught a cab. Dane had it stop at a telephone station and called Cromton's residence. The jeweler came to the telephone.

"Got that reward money in cash?" asked Skarle.

Cromton's voice was eager. "You—you've got the stuff? Tell me have you got the stuff?"

Skarle said: "You're shooting square with me?"

"Yes, yes! Have you got it? Tell me—"

"There's no one can overhear you?"

"No one. Have you got—"

"I will have," said Skarle, "by the time you get down to the store. Make it snappy. I figure we'll get there about the some time. Bring the money. You'll get the stones."

"The police—" began Cromton.

"Leave that to me," said Skarle.

He hung up, returned to the cab, and gave the address of Cromton's jewelry store. He grinned at Vera Colma, patted the back of her hand. "Well, baby, it was worth a fight, wasn't it? Gee, you've got cold hands!"

"That damned bath," she said, "and I didn't bring the gin."

He grinned at her again, started chafing her hand. The cab rolled smoothly along the streets.

They slowed to a stop before Cromton's store. The jeweler was there ahead of them, standing in the entranceway.

"You didn't let anyone know?" asked Skarle as he paid off the cab.

"No one. Not a soul!"

They went up the stairs, into Cromton's office.

"Let's see it," said Cromton.

"Let's make sure about the reward," said Skarle.

Cromton hesitated. Suspicion showed in his watery eyes. "It's here. In cash. You can't stick me up, though. If you haven't got the stuff—"

Dane Skarle muttered an impatient:

"Hell!" He opened his vest and shirt, pulled off the money belt, flung it on the mahogany table top.

SKARLE said nothing, but sat and watched the jeweler. Cromton's fingers opened the chamois-skin pockets, one at a time. He checked the contents. Skarle reached his right hand into his coat pocket, and pulled out the stones which he had found planted in his room at the rooming house. He tossed these, together with the platinum setting on the table, and said: "You might as well have these, too. They're stones the crook had on him."

Cromton stared at the stones, gasped: "Why this is my stuff. It was missing. It wasn't as important as the stones for the necklace, because those were matched. But this is all my stuff, too. Who did it? Do I know him?"

Dane said: "Sure you know him. It's Bill Dabney, that slick clerk you're so stuck on."

Cromton sat back with sagging jaw. "It can't be! Why I'd trust him with my life! He's as honest as the day is long!"

Skarle said: "Well, maybe the days are getting shorter now we've quit daylight saving. How'd you figure I got this stuff if I didn't get it from the thief? Dabney wouldn't have been packing it around for his health, would he?"

Cromton let his breath whoosh out from his lungs in an audible indication of his surprise. He opened a drawer in his desk and disclosed a small cash box. He unlocked that box and took out sheafs of money. He passed these over to Dane Skarle.

Skarle stared at them. "What're these little marks in the corners?" he asked.

Cromton poked his glasses back up on his nose and leaned forward. "What marks?" he asked.

Skarle pointed to the little marks which appeared in the corners of the bills. Cromton said: "Why those are the marks that Girkin put there. I told you about those."

Dane Skarle laughed, a harsh, metallic laugh. "So, even after I called your hand about Girkin marking the money, you didn't get any unmarked money. You went ahead and figured on paying me off with this marked money. That right?"

Cromton's watery eyes blinked several times, rapidly. "Yes," he said.

Skarle pushed the money back. "Take this dough that's marked. Only the money that Girkin gave you is marked. You know how much it is. You take it and give me your check for the difference."

Cromton said, slowly: "I've heard enough of your arbitrary commands. That's the reward money. You're lucky to get a cent of it. I may have trouble over it the way it is. Are you going to take it or shall I keep it?"

"Like that, eh?" sneered Skarle.

Cromton nodded. His eyes could not meet those of Dane Skarle, but he said: "Just like that!"

Skarle hesitated a moment. Then he reached out and pocketed the money. His face was not pretty. The eyes were sullen, smoldering with resentment. He glared at Cromton, and Cromton continued to avoid his eyes.

There was a low-pitched sound, a rumbling jar which communicated itself through the building. Cromton cocked his head to one side and listened. Then he got to his feet.

"Somebody banging on the outer door," he said. "Probably the watchman who's seen the lights and wants to know who's in here. I'll go and explain so he won't call the police."

He walked down the stairs. They heard him at the door, then heard voices.

Vera Colma said: "But, Dane, if the money's marked—"

He shook his head, impatiently. "It's a legitimate reward. You're a witness to that. I'm going to call the police."

He moved toward the telephone, picked up the receiver.

A voice behind him gruffed: "Drop that telephone and get 'em up! Get 'em up high!"

CHAPTER SIX

Big Stakes

DANE SKARLE peered over his shoulder as he heard Vera's gasp. Pete Girkin stood framed in the doorway, his hat pulled down low on his forehead, a gun in his right hand. Bob Cromton stood behind him, peering with watery, anxious eyes over Girkin's shoulder.

Girkin moved forward, purposefully. His eyes were glittering.

Dane Skarle read that expression rightly. He dropped the telephone and elevated his hands. Girkin came forward, slammed the receiver back into place, let his left hand pat Skarle's garments.

Girkin's hand went into the pockets, came out with the sheaf of money. He looked at it, at the marks on the corners of the bills. He grinned.

"You and your lady accomplice are under arrest for robbery," he said. "Anything you say'll be used against you at the trial."

He whirled to Cromton. "This the man that surrendered the stolen jewelry to you?"

"Yes," said Cromton.

"This the money you gave him?"

"Yes."

"Why didn't you call me, like I told you to? I've a mind to jug you as an accessory, and for compounding a felony."

Cromton swallowed, tried to speak. His voice gave only a squeaky semblance of sound.

Dane Skarle said: "Girkin, you're crazy. I recovered these stones from the real thief, and I'm entitled to a reward."

"That's the truth!" blazed Vera Colma. "He was calling the police when you made him put down the telephone."

Girkin laughed. "You mean he picked up the telephone when he heard me coming down the corridor outside of the door here. There never was any crook except you two, and you know it."

Dane Skarle said, wearily: "Listen. I knew this was an inside job. I figured Bill Dabney, a clerk here, for the guy that did it. I got him dead to rights and found the stones on him. I came here to surrender the stones and get the reward that had been agreed on. I left Dabney for the police. He's tied up so he can't escape."

Girkin yawned, obviously. "Yeah," he said. "It's a good story, only you can't make it stick."

Vera Colma snapped: "It'll stick if you go and find Dabney all tied up, with proof of the guilt, won't it."

Girkin turned to her, let his eyes travel appreciately up and down her form.

"Yes," he said. "It'll do if *we* go and find him tied up."

"Well," said Dane, "let's get the police and go."

"You've got the police," said Girkin, "and we're going. Hold out your hands, you two!"

Skarle said: "You can't handcuff me."

Girkin lunged forward. Steel glittered in his hand. "Try and stop me," he said, "and I'll give you the works for resisting an officer!" His tone carried conviction. Dane Skarle surrendered his wrist. The handcuff clicked around it, around Vera Colma's wrist.

"Come on," said Girkin.

He led them from the store. He had a car outside. The motor was running. He loaded them in to it. An officer in uniform came from the shadows and moved forward. "O. K." said Girkin. "I'm taking this pair of gem crooks to headquarters."

Dane Skarle called to the officer: "And, for some reason, he'd like to find an excuse to use that gun of his. I'm surrendering to you. This guy's just a lousy dick. I want you to go along and see that we get to headquarters!".

The uniformed officer scowled. "What's it all about?" he asked.

Girkin slammed the car door, took the officer's arm, started to lead him away. "Remember," called Dane Skarle, "that I asked you to come."

The officer shook Girkin's hand free and said: "Can the chatter. I'm coming."

HE climbed in front, settled on the cushions, slammed the door. Cromton got in with Dane Skarle and Vera Colma.

"Now this guy, Dabney," Skarle began, talking for the effect the words might have on the uniformed officer, "was trying to make a getaway—"

Girkin whirled. "Shut up. I'm running this show. You claimed you'd left Dabney tied up and were trying to get the police. We're going there. If what you said is true, that's all there is to it. If it ain't, you're finished. So shut up!"

Skarle dropped back against the cushions and said, "Go ahead then. Run the show your way."

Dane smiled, shook his head. Soon the car lurched around a corner, swung into the curb in front of the apartment house where they had trailed Dabney. There was a light on in the apartment. The shades showed a trickle of sickly illumination which seeped through them. Girkin got to the pavement, jerked the door open.

"Come on out," he said. "Don't try any funny stuff."

They all went to the door of the apartment. Girkin pressed a button. The electric door release buzzed instantly. They went into the elevator, up to Dabney's apartment. Girkin raised his hand to pound on the door panels when the door opened.

Bill Dabney, attired in pajamas and slippers, a dressing gown thrown over his shoulders, stared at them blankly.

Girkin pushed him back, went into the apartment. The uniformed officer pushed the others ahead of him, brought up the rear.

The apartment was in perfect order. The mattress was on the bed, the bed made. The clothes were on hangers in the closet. There was no sign of the suitcases or of the aeroplane trunk. The bed had not so much as an indentation upon the counterpane.

Girkin leered at Skarle. "This is the thief, eh?"

Dane Skarle said: "We found him packing up. We got the stones, and left him tied up—"

Dabney interrupted: "Why what a damned lie. I never saw this man before in my life. I've seen the woman. I think she's some sort of a blackmailer. She tried to frame me a couple of times. I never knew who the man in the combination was."

"We're going to headquarters," said Skarle. "I demand that we go to see some one in authority."

Girkin laughed sneeringly. "That's one thing you said that I'm listenin' to. You're going to headquarters. And you're goin' into a cell."

Dane said to the officer: "And you bring Dabney along. This man is the thief who robbed the store of the gems. We got them from him. We left him tied. He got loose and decided to bluff the thing through and accuse us of being the thieves, because we'd taken the gems from him."

Girkin laughed. "What a yarn!"

Skarle said to the officer: "Never mind what he says. You're the officer in charge here. He's a detective. I'm telling you that Dabney is the man you want. Let him slip through your fingers, and you'll be finished."

The officer stared at Dabney. "Get your clothes on," he said. "You're a witness, anyway."

Dane Skarle said: "And take us to someone in the police department. We don't want to do business with the detective bureau. We want to talk with a man who's got some authority and some sense."

Girkin's face was dark. "You're goin' in cells," he said. "You can talk with a judge, after you hire a lawyer. You're caught dead to rights with the stolen stuff, and with the marked money you got for peddling it."

He grabbed Vera Colma's handbag, snapped it open. She stared at him with white face. His stubby fingers rummaged through the contents. He found the key to her room. To the key was affixed a round disk on which was stamped the name of the rooming house, the number of the room. Girkin looked at it, suddenly laughed.

"So that's it!" he said. "You've got the adjoining room! And you played back and forth through the connecting door, eh? Gee, I was dumb. I should have looked for an accomplice!"

His eyes glittered with satisfaction. He slipped the key back into the purse, the purse into his pocket. "This," he said, "cinches the case. You can go before anybody you damn please!"

DABNEY got his clothes on. They filed down to the car, packed themselves into it. Skarle and Vera Colma were handcuffed to each other. The others crowded them into the smallest possible space. Dabney chatted with Cromton. "I think," he said, "that this is the guy who shot it out with me. I think I can identify him."

Girkin growled. "Wait'll you see where he claims he was. Sometimes they pull a fast one by having an accomplice with an iron-clad alibi peddle the hot stuff."

The car pulled in to police headquarters. The uniformed officer ushered them into the presence of a sergeant. Dane Skarle heard Girkin state the case. He spoke to the sergeant. "You've heard what Girkin has to say. I admit I surrendered the gems and got the marked money. But there's another angle. This man Dabney double-crossed me. Take him into a separate room and let me tell my story. Then let him tell his."

The sergeant frowned. Girkin said: "That's not necessary. This man, Dabney—"

The uniformed officer coughed, looked at the sergeant. The sergeant said: "O. K. Take him into that office."

Girkin took Dabney's arm. "This way," he said.

Dane Skarle spoke so fast the words seemed to tread on each other's heels. He waited only until Girkin and Dabney had left the room.

"Girkin's in on this," he said. "He tried to plant some stones in my room. The girl caught him. We ditched the stones. They were part of the stuff that was stolen from Cromton. I wanted to find out where Dabney had the stuff hidden, so the girl posed as a crook and I pretended to be an officer. We slipped him the stones. He recognized them and was for making a getaway. He telephoned Girkin. He must have done it before we tied him up. That's how Girkin knew enough to come to see Cromton just when he did. He went to Dabney's place. Dabney was tied up. Girkin turned him loose and framed things so we'd take the rap."

The sergeant stared at Dane Skarle. "You're making a wild accusation," he said. "Have you any proof at all?"

Skarle said: "Yes. Girkin drove his car directly to Dabney's apartment house without any one telling him where it was."

The uniformed officer nodded assent. "He did that," he agreed.

Skarle continued to speak rapidly. "Listen, when Girkin comes back let this officer go in and collar Dabney. Let him tell Dabney that Girkin made a slip and has confessed. Put it on thick and—"

He stopped. Girkin came striding out of the other office.

"Well," said the sergeant, "let's have the real facts now. Girkin, you're first. What happened?"

The uniformed officer slipped out of the room. Girkin began a recital of the facts of the case, the robbery, his suspicions of Skarle. When he had finished, the sergeant said to Skarle: "What have you to say? How did you come by this jewelry?"

Skarle said: "Some of it I got from Dabney. Some of it Girkin tried to plant in my room."

Girkin whirled on him. "That," he said, "is a damned lie!"

Skarle swung his left fist. Girkin gave a bellow, leapt forward. The sergeant came around the desk and yelled: "None of that! None of that!"

The door of the office where Dabney had been taken came open. Dabney came out, his arm grasped by the uniformed officer. His face was sickly. The officer said: "Girkin, it's my duty to arrest you as an accomplice and accessory in the robbery of Cromton's Jewelry Store!"

DANE SKARLE leaned back against the green plush of the Pullman cushions and put slippered feet on the opposite seat. Vera Colma, standing in front of the mirror in the drawing room, her lithe body swaying with the motion of the train, patted her hair and rubbed powder into her skin.

She surveyed the final result, turned from the mirror, walked over to Dane Skarle. She sat down beside him, put her hand on his arm. "Dane, won't you wire that we'll accept that magician booking?"

He grinned at her, shook his head. His left hand moved up to touch the fingers of her hand that rested on his sleeve. His eyes gave that suggestion of restless force, being held in leash.

"They'll frame us," she said. "Girkin almost framed it on us."

Skarle shook his head. "Not after I found out that those gems he planted were from the Cromton job," he said. "Not after he drove to Dabney's place without any one telling him the way."

She stared at him. "Then you knew we'd find Dabney loose when we got to his apartment?"

He nodded.

She sighed. Dane Skarle reached into his pocket and drew out a sheaf of bills. In the upper corners of these bills, traced with a fine-pointed pen were hairlike marks. He grinned at her.

"Big stakes," he said. "That's what we're playing for nowdays."

She shuddered.

He stared out of the window at the flashing landscape. His eyes were dark, inscrutable. There was a suggestion of dominant force in them, a force that had been held in leash too long and was struggling to free itself.

He said nothing.

The doctor dropped to one knee beside the dead man.

The Three Horrible Heads

by
Richard J. Credicott

There they lay—each in its own glass case—three horribly shriveled leering human heads. And Fletcher recognized the faces, even in their mummied state. Knew it was only a matter of moments before his own would make a fourth in the grisly collection.

CHAPTER ONE

Death Strikes Twice

IT WAS fifteen minutes to seven in the morning when Kokura, James Van Styne's diminutive Philippino servant, discovered that the lock on the apartment door had been broken from the outside.

He gazed wide-eyed at the damage, then trotted to the door of his master's bedroom and rapped sharply. When he received no reply to repeated knocks, he opened the door and put his head inside.

The next instant he was running hysterically down the corridor, screaming so loudly that the house detective, roused by a telephone call from a tenant, lost no time in getting there.

"Dead, sair!" gasped Kokura. "All blood, sair—blood everywhere! And his head—"

The house detective hastily silenced the terrified boy and dragged him back to the apartment. He took a single look into Van Styne's bedroom and promptly notified the management, who in turn called the police.

The police investigation began slowly and rapidly gathered momentum. Two precinct detectives arrived within fifteen minutes. Ten minutes later came the usual swarm of men from detective headquarters — plainclothes officers, fingerprint experts, photographers, followed shortly by Dr. Durand, medical examiner, and Inspector Thomas Sullivan.

And at exactly seven-thirty in the morning the prolonged ringing of his bedstand telephone roused Anthony Fletcher from sleep.

"This is Sullivan," came the voice over the wire. "Sorry to get you up so early, but a murder case has just broken and we need you."

Fletcher swore under his breath. "Look here," he pleaded sleepily, "won't this keep for a few hours? I was up all night, working on the Jellico case for the commissioner. Just got to bed two hours ago—"

"This case won't keep," said Sullivan. "It's hot—red hot. James Van Styne, the big Wall Street broker and millionaire, was murdered last night. We found him in bed, his head cut clean off."

Fletcher sat up and began to pay attention.

"And," went on the police inspector, his voice rising, "the head's gone! We can't find it!"

"So," said Fletcher. He lit a cigarette and blew a cloud of smoke at the ceiling. "It sounds interesting, Sullivan. I knew Van Styne. He lives at the Lusonia, doesn't he? I'll be right over."

ANTHONY FLETCHER was a physician by training, specializing in psychology and pathology. He was head of the department of criminology at the university and the author of a number of well-known books on the subject. He held a commission in the police department, lectured at the police academy, and was frequently called upon for help when some crime baffled the central-office detectives.

He was of medium height and build, with crisply black hair. His eyes were gray and piercing. He would have been called handsome had his forehead not been so high.

It was Fletcher's contention that all crimes could be solved. He utilized all the resources of modern science. But, more than that, he utilized that mysterious new science, psychology, to untangle trails not open to the test-tube and microscope. He believed that the skilled psychologist should map out the campaign for the solution of a crime, just as an architect makes the plans for a building which others will construct.

A taxi bore him to the Lusonia. It was one of the older apartment hotels just off the Avenue, of faded magnificence, famed for its quiet exclusiveness. It was patronized by those who valued spaciousness above modern cramped smartness.

A uniformed officer met him at the door, saluted, and took him up in the elevator to Van Styne's apartment on the third floor. The detectives had been shunted into the corridor in expectation of his arrival, and Sullivan and Dr. Durand had the place to themselves.

"I haven't disturbed the body," said Dr. Durand. He was a stolid and energetic little man, very competent, and delighted to work with Fletcher. "I knew you'd want to see it just as we found it."

Fletcher nodded briefly and accompanied them into the bedroom. It was large and gloomily furnished with heavy oak furniture and thick rugs. Drapes had been drawn from the high windows and the morning sunlight streamed across the bed.

It revealed a gruesome sight. A man— or what was left of a man—lay in a pool of clotted blood. He was short and fat, with round protuberant stomach, clothed in brilliant scarlet pajamas.

And the gory pillow, where his head should have been, was ghastly—for upon it lay only the short stump of a neck.

"Done while he was asleep," said Dr. Durand in his precise fashion. "The head was cut off with a single blow. No other wounds that I can find. If you look close-ly you can see where the knife slashed down through the pillow. The man who did it must have been abnormally strong."

"Or have used a weapon suited to such purposes," said Fletcher. "A machete, for instance; or perhaps a scimitar or bolo. Have you determined the time of death?"

"Around two o'clock in the morning, I should say."

"There's no trace of the head?"

"It's gone," answered Sullivan, shud-dering as he turned his eyes from the corpse. He was a big, sandy-haired Irish-man, and an excellent officer. "We've searched this apartment from top to bot-tom, and it isn't here. Not a trace of it! What do you make of that?"

"Nothing, just yet," said Fletcher dryly.

He completed an examination of the room and asked how the murderer had gained entrance. Sullivan showed him the broken lock on the door.

"Looks to have been done with a jim-my," he said. "How the murderer got in —unless he lives in the hotel—I don't know. But they've got a rotten system here; anybody can walk in or out, and they don't check up on 'em. We haven't been able to find anybody that saw anyone

suspicious. Want to see Van Styne's ser-vant?"

KOKURA had recovered from his hys-teria, though his eyes were red. Some-what reassured by Fletcher's friendly atti-tude, he answered his questions willingly.

"Meestair Van Styne come home meb-be ten las' night," he said. "He had small package. Take it into libr'y and read til mebbe twelve, then go to bed. And this morning—"

"A package?" growled Sullivan. "You didn't say anything about that before."

"Your policemens shout and I did not remember, sair," replied the boy gravely.

Sullivan reddened. Fletcher, having witnessed Sullivan's men questioning sus-pects before this, smiled and suggested that they take a look at the library.

It proved to be more of a trophy room than library. The walls were hung with the heads of animals. On racks and in cases were primitive bows and arrows, clubs, swords, and more modern hunting rifles. Over the fireplace was a huge ana-conda head, mounted with gaping jaws.

"Your master was a big-game hun-ter?" asked Fletcher.

"Yes, sair," said Kokura proudly. "He hunt in Africa, South America. I go with him, help him."

Fletcher's gaze swept about the room, photographing every object and storing it away in his memory. It was his theory that the psychologist, by studying the en-vironment with which a man surrounded himself, could pierce through to the very mainsprings of his character.

His attention was suddenly arrested by a strange group of objects on the mantel. There were half a dozen of them, little doll-like heads no bigger than a large orange. Their faces were grimacing, dis-torted, hideous; grotesque travesties on the human features. Had it not been for their long, tangled, black hair they might have been taken for the stuffed heads of monkeys.

He balanced one of them on the palm of his hand. He knew it to be a human head, such as is preserved by the little-known Jivaro Indian tribes on the upper reaches of the Amazon.

"Meestair Van Styne buy those on river, in South America," Kokura volunteered. "They real heads, shrunk like raisin."

As Fletcher replaced it on the mantel, Sullivan gave an exclamation. His hand came out of a wastebasket with a small cardboard box and a wadding of paper. He unfolded the paper and smoothed it out on a desk. On it was pasted a small red cartouche, resembling an imperial seal in design.

"That package he had," announced Kokura.

"So," grunted Sullivan. "And now what the devil was in it? Couldn't have been very big; not more than four or five inches square. And that's a funny-looking seal."

"It's a Russian coat of arms," said Fletcher. "I've seen it before. Prince Alexis uses it. He claims to be of the Russian nobility, though the Russian royalists will have nothing to do with him. He has a sort of showroom and art gallery on Fifth Avenue and deals in modern painting and sculpture, most of it worthless. He's made himself the center of the modernistic art world in New York, and more than a few wealthy old ladies consider him the last word in such things."

"Prince Alexis!" exclaimed Kokura, with an expression of distaste."

"You know him?" queried Sullivan.

"Oh, yes, sair. He go to South America with Meestair Van Styne."

"That sounds promising, Fletcher," said Sullivan. "I think this package and what was in it will bear looking into. It might

have been something valuable, something the murderer wanted—"

He broke off as the desk phone rang. It was a call for him. When he hung up, his square face was flushed with excitement.

"That was the commissioner. There's been another of these murders. Man found with his head cut off, no sign of the head. And that man was a watchman in this Prince Alexis' art gallery!"

CHAPTER TWO

The Jivaro Head

PRINCE ALEXIS' establishment was a modernistic structure of granite, three stories in height. To the right of the show window was a tall portal of burnished metal. The thick glass of the door bore in small aluminum letters the simple inscription *alexis*.

Sullivan seized Fletcher's arm as they were about to enter. "My God, look at that!" he cried. "More of those crazy heads."

The window presented a strange exhibit for a private art gallery. Ranged in a semicircle were a dozen shrunken Jivaro heads. Concealed lighting made them stand out starkly against the black velvet background, emphasizing their weird ugliness.

In the center of the exhibit was a figure which at first glance appeared to be a negro dwarf. It was scarcely thirty inches in height, naked except for a loin cloth. It was the shrunken body of a full-grown man, preserved with consummate art. It gave the disquieting impression of a twisted, mishapen gnome emerged from the bowels of the earth. Its little pinched face, its broad flat nostrils, its leering slit of a mouth, were like nothing human, or rather something subhuman created by the gods in a malevolent mood.

"Is—is it real?" asked Sullivan hoarsely.

"It's real enough," said Fletcher. "It's uncommon to find the entire body shrunken, though there are several specimens in one of the museums here."

"Ugh! It gives me the creeps."

They entered and found a group of clerks and policemen. The clerk who had found the watchman's body was still white and shaken from the experience.

"Bensen, the night watchman, should have been here to open up for me this morning," he said. "I had to use my own key and, when he didn't appear, I became worried and started a search. And I found him—on the third floor, horribly mutilated—" He stopped and licked his lips.

"Is this Prince Alexis here?" demanded Sullivan.

"No, sir. But we've telephoned him and he should arrive any minute."

The clerk took them to the third floor in the elevator. It opened into a long corridor, thickly carpeted, and decorated with odd bits of sculpture.

In the center, near closed double doors, two detectives stood by a dark huddle on the floor. Dr. Durand commenced his routine examination briskly, rattling off his findings as if dictating a letter.

"This man was killed in exactly the same manner as Van Styne. His head was cut off with a single blow by some sharp instrument. Probably he was lying in this very position when it was done. At least, the slash in the rug beneath the neck tends to prove that. No other marks upon the body. I should say, purely as a guess, that he was struck on the head and knocked unconscious before the decapitation; though, since the head is gone, we can't verify that."

"And the time of death?" asked Fletcher.

"Around one o'clock. Possibly a bit later."

"That is, before Van Styne was murdered?"

"Unquestionably."

"You think the same man did it?" asked Sullivan.

"It begins to look like it," said Fletcher, and turned to the detectives. "Did you search for the head?"

"Not us," one of them answered. "We looked around a little but didn't find it. When we phoned into headquarters, we got orders to hold everything for you. But—" and he pointed dramatically at the double doors—"if you want to see something, take a look in there!"

The clerk who had brought them up coughed discreetly. "It contains the collection of Doctor Hartzell," he said. "Perhaps you noticed the specimens in the window as you entered."

"Doctor Franz Hartzell?" asked Fletcher. "The authority on head hunting?"

"The same, sir. He and Prince Alexis are close friends. When Doctor Hartzell returned from South America last week, the prince suggested that he might use this gallery for an exhibition."

"I've read Doctor Hartzell's book *Head Hunters of the Ages*," said Fletcher. "He's the one authority on that branch of anthropology. Let's take a look at this collection, Sullivan."

Followed by Dr. Durand, they entered the door at which the detective had pointed. The gallery was long and narrow, paralleling the corridor. It was without windows, roofed with skylights which tempered the brilliancy of the morning sunlight to a soft glow.

A ROW of tables ranged the walls. Upon them was perhaps as weird and ghastly a collection as had ever been assembled. It was composed entirely of heads and skulls, hundreds of them, gathered from every corner of the world, wherever the grizzly practice of head hunting has been known.

There were Dyak heads from Borneo, staring at them with their unnaturally distended eyes of whitened wood. Bamboo poles from Assam, topped with bleached white skulls. Heads taken in the Balkan Wars of 1912-1913, with the long locks of hair by which they were carried. Skull racks from New Guinea. Heads from the Amazon, Nigeria, Fakiristan, the Philippines, Formosa, Malaya, Indo-China. And another complete shrunken figure similar to the one which had been in the window.

"Good Lord!" blurted Sullivan. "Why would any sane man want to collect these things?"

"Scientific investigation," said Fletcher. "It is impossible to understand the men of other ages, or even many of the primitive races of today, without an understanding of head hunting. It is practiced, even today, in many parts of the world, and goes back to paleolithic times, thousands of years ago. The general theory is that the soul of man resides in the head, and that the taker of a head brings to himself, and thus to his family and tribe, the strength and virtues and fertility of the man slain—"

"Stop it," groaned Sullivan. "I don't want to hear it. It's got my head swimming."

Fletcher's gray eyes were bright with interest and he would not be stopped.

"Yes, there must be some sort of connection," he said. "Here we have three men—Van Styne, Doctor Hartzell and Prince Alexis—all interested in the same dark subject. Van Styne was murdered and his head taken. The watchman taking care of Doctor Hartzell's collection met the same fate. Surely a remarkable set of circumstances to explain away as coincidence!

"The common interest of these three men in head hunting must have some sort of bearing upon these crimes. With that as our starting point, we must find the focusing point, the nexus of this strange chain of events."

At that moment a detective announced that Prince Alexis and Dr. Hartzell were waiting for them downstairs. Sullivan, visibly relieved that the investigation was taking a concrete turn, ordered them sent up.

"You talk to 'em, though," he told Fletcher. "You know what you're talking about—and I don't. Anyway, the commissioner put you in charge of this."

PRINCE ALEXIS was a distinguished figure in impeccable morning dress, set off by a glittering gold decoration on his breast. His body was tall and powerful, though he walked with a slight limp.

Looking at his thin aristocratic features and his dark beard and mustache, cut in the fashion of the last Romanoff czar, Fletcher told himself that here was a man to reckon with. The blood of Cossacks or the boyars ran through his veins. He was accustomed to command, to exact obedience, to bend people to his will—particularly women, if the stories of him were true. He wore an air of hauteur and arrogance that antagonized Fletcher.

"So," he said tonelessly, looking down at the body; and shrugged and turned away.

Dr. Franz Hartzell, however, dropped on one knee beside the dead man. He remained immobile for a moment, then rose slowly to his feet.

Once he had been tall and large-framed. But advancing age, or perhaps some tropical disease, had crooked his spine and dried the flesh from his body. The skin of his face was like wrinkled parchment stretched over a bony framework. His high domed head was bald, except for a tonsure of straggling white hair.

"You found him—like this?" he asked, gesturing toward the dead man without looking up.

"We did," said Fletcher, and introduced himself, mentioning that he had read the scientist's book.

Dr. Hartzell seemed scarcely to have heard him, so deeply was he immersed in thought. "Very strange," he muttered, half to himself. And then, becoming conscious of the eyes watching him, he glanced up.

Fletcher got a shock when he saw the scientist's eyes. He had seen such eyes before, in men whose brilliant intelligences had carried them to the brink of insanity. They were set deep in cavernous sockets, their dark fire almost hidden by lowered lids. For a moment he thought he detected a strange expression in them, one of terror or fear, but it vanished instantly and he could not be sure.

"Prince Alexis phoned me of this—this terrible thing," the scientist explained. "He thought that, under the circumstances, I should know of it."

"I'm glad you came," said Fletcher. "I may have a few questions to ask you later.

FLETCHER was convinced that Dr. Hartzell knew something, or had some well-founded suspicion, but that could wait. He turned upon Prince Alexis, who stood leaning upon his cane, wrapped in uncompromising silence.

"I am hopeful that you can help us," he said. "You knew this watchman and his duties. Can you suggest any motive for his murder?"

"It is utterly incomprehensible to me," replied the prince coldly.

"You have things of value here? Anything that might attract the attention of thieves?"

"That is true. Much of the statuary and paintings are priceless. But my clerks inform me that nothing has been taken. They did not, of course, check Doctor Hartzell's exhibition."

"I think it would be worth while to do so," said Fletcher. "Doctor Hartzell, would you mind checking over your specimens and telling us whether any is missing. This crime is so lacking in clues that we can't afford to pass up anything."

The scientist agreed and entered the gallery. He walked the length of it and stopped suddenly before a table. "They're gone!" he cried hollowly. "Four of my heads have disappeared."

"Heads?" queried Sullivan.

"Shrunken Jivaro heads," explained Dr. Hartzell and he gave the description of them which Sullivan asked. "Though why they should be taken," he added, "I cannot imagine. They have no great value, save from a collector's standpoint."

"Nor from any other standpoint?" asked Fletcher, eyeing the scientist closely.

Doctor Hartzell stared at him queerly. "I don't grasp your meaning," he said.

"No matter," replied Fletcher carelessly. "You will, perhaps, a bit later. Did you know James Van Styne?"

"Slightly."

"And you, Prince Alexis?"

The Russian nodded.

"You traveled with him in South America?"

Prince Alexis stared hard at Fletcher. His eyes grew cold and his cane tapped softly on the floor. "You seem to have been investigating me," he said dryly. "Yes, Van Styne and I were in South America together. We are both members of the Tropical Explorers' Club. May I inquire why you ask?"

"I ask," said Fletcher, "because Van Styne was also found dead. He had been murdered. His head was cut from his shoulders and is gone."

The two men reacted to this startling information in different ways. Prince Alexis dropped his cane and stooped to recover it. If his face showed confusion, it was composed when he straightened to face them. Dr. Hartzell caught his breath in an audible gasp; then his mouth shut like a steel trap and his eyelids veiled his eyes.

Fletcher went on to give them the salient details.

"It is impossible to believe," he concluded, "that these two crimes are not the work of the same hand. In both, the method of murder was the same. But the link that binds them together is stronger than that."

He paused a moment. Prince Alexis, his bearded face inscrutable, lit a monogrammed cigarette and Dr. Hartzell rubbed his chin with a skinny hand.

"Van Styne's servant informs us," continued Fletcher, "that his master returned about ten o'clock last night. He carried a small package. That package bore your seal, Prince Alexis. We found the package, empty, in the wastebasket. Whatever it contained apparently has vanished."

"And I am to explain," sneered the Russian, with unaccountable hostility. "Luckily for me it is very simple. Van Styne was, as I am, interested in head hunting. At his suggestion I brought him here last night to show him Doctor Hartzell's collection. He expressed a desire to purchase one of the specimens and, as Doctor Hartzell had given me certain of them to offer for sale, I sold him one. I personally wrapped it in a package and gave it to him."

"And that specimen?"

Prince Alexis smiled icily. "It was a shrunken Jivaro head. Not an Indian's, but a negro's."

Fletcher nodded to himself. It was as he had expected. It made the mystery more puzzling, because the shrunken heads in Van Styne's library had all been those of Indians.

The murderer had taken the head which Van Styne had brought home with him.

CHAPTER THREE

The Thief That Limped

WITH this disclosure the investigation ran up against a blank wall. They had charted the appalling course of the murderer, but had not the slightest clue to his identity.

As for the motive—

"It's insane," declared Sullivan, when they discussed it later in the day. "It's the work of a madman. This murderer is a head hunter himself. So far he's taken seven heads—two live and five dead ones. He may not stop there. And what does he want 'em for?"

Fletcher could not answer this question, nor many others which he put to himself. Bizarre conjectures presented themselves to his mind. Heads were occasionally used in magical rites. Could this be the work of followers of some new *voodoo* or *obeah?*

The explanation, while ingenious, was too fanciful to satisfy him. And it did not fit the facts.

The watchman's murder could be dismissed from consideration. The murderer had patently come to Prince Alexis' gallery for the shrunken Jivaro heads. Since no locks had been tampered with, Bensen must have admitted him. This did not mean necessarily that the watchman knew or recognized the murderer. He might have been forced to unlock the door by the menace of a weapon through the glass, which would not stop a bullet. It seemed reasonable to suppose that the watchman had been killed to prevent a later identification, and not for any personal motive. The cutting off of his head might have been incidental, or the result of a mad lust for heads.

As for Van Styne's murder, that was more difficult to explain. Had the murderer particularly wanted the shrunken Negro head? If so, how had he learned that the broker had purchased it that very evening? There was the possibility, of course, that the watchman, who had known of the transaction, had told him. But why, having once gained entrance to the apartment and found the Negro head, had he taken Van Styne's life?

Fletcher was convinced that Prince Alexis and Doctor Hartzell knew more than they had told or had well-grounded suspicions. Several hours questioning, however, failed to glean any additional information from them. The Russian preserved his attitude of hostility and said nothing; and while the scientist was persuaded to talk at length on the theory and practice of head hunting, he also said nothing.

The utter mystery of the two crimes both baffled and challenged Fletcher. This was a type of murder so different from the ordinary run that routine police methods did not suffice to deal with it. It fascinated him, absorbed his time to the exclusion of everything else.

As was to be expected, the newspapers greeted the murders with whoops of joy. Nothing so spectacular or fraught with morbid drama had occurred in months, and they made the most of the "Head Hunter," as they quickly termed the unknown murderer.

They developed many theories, only two of which merited any attention.

The first was the theory which Fletcher had considered and discarded. That the murders and the thefts were the work of a cult of voodooists, perhaps of Haitian origin. They required the heads for their worship of Damballa, the fearsome snake god, to propitiate his fury.

The second theory was equally sensational. It supposed that Jivaro Indians had come to New York to recover the heads of relatives and friends treacherously slain from ambush. The two murders had been revenge for the possession of the heads.

The Gallery Alexis became suddenly popular, and crowds thronged it throughout the day. Prince Alexis cannily took advantage of this and charged admission. Enormous prices were offered for specimens from the collection. The publishers of Dr. Hartzell's book found it necessary to rush a new edition through the presses.

As for Dr. Hartzell, he appeared first bewildered, then pleased with the publicity he received as the one authority upon the subject of head hunting. He wrote articles for the newspapers, most of them couched in language too technical for laymen, and delivered several lectures.

The always morbid imagination of the public had gone mad.

ON THE third night the Head Hunter struck again.

It was not until the next noon that a stevedore discovered the headless body hidden behind the piles of an ancient wharf. The dead man was never positively identified, though he was thought to be a homeless tramp who had drifted into the city.

The police, quite unable to connect this logically with the other murders, tried to pass it off as an unrelated crime. The newspapers would not have it, and gradually came to agreement upon one theory.

These murders were the work of a high priest, a *papaloi*, of a cult of voodooists. He required the freshly killed head of a man—the "goat without horns"—for his terrible and unspeakable ceremonies. He had struck three times, and could be expected to strike again and again, until the police ran him to earth and put a halt to his satanic activities.

Their prophesy seemed to be justified, for the headless death struck twice the following night.

The first victim was found in an alleyway in the early hours of the morning. The man was a clerk in a drugstore, and had evidently been on his way home, after working late, when the killer leaped upon him and dragged him into the alleyway.

The second victim was discovered, several hours later, by a policeman making his first morning round through Central Park. The body was almost hidden under a clump of bushes, and it was not until he had dragged it out that he saw it was headless.

Papers in the pockets identified the man as Charles L. Greenwald, senior partner of the law firm of Greenwald, Roberts and Harrison. He had left his home at eleven the preceeding night for a short walk through the park, as was often his custom. From the state of *rigor mortis* which had set in, it was established that he had been slain at about midnight, perhaps a half hour before the clerk had been attacked.

Greenwald's murder brought a development which at first promised to bear fruit. It was rumored that the lawyer had been associated with Van Styne in certain financial transactions, not strictly within the letter of the law. But so secret had these been that not even Greenwald's partners knew their nature, nor were there any papers bearing upon them remaining.

"It's becoming more and more hopeless," Sullivan told Fletcher wearily. "I'm almost ready to believe this voodoo theory, crazy as it is. At least it offers something to work on."

"It's not entirely beyond the realm of reason," admitted Fletcher. "There are powerful voodoo cults in Harlem, even in the heart of New York. It's rather the fashion now, though I think few would go to such lengths."

His face was thinner and his eyes bespoke lack of sleep. For more than a week he had been driving himself relentlessly. The call of mystery and adventure and danger was in his blood, and until he had solved these crimes and seen the murderer taken into custody he could not rest.

Sullivan suddenly leaned forward and pointed his cigar at Fletcher. "Look here," he said, "why don't you have another try at this Prince Alexis and Doctor Hartzell? You've admitted you think they're hiding something, or at least know more than they've told. And I'm convinced of it, though I can't get anything out of 'em. Damn it, when I talk to 'em, they just sneer at me in their superior way!"

His square face crimsoned and his eyes glittered.

"You know what I think?" he continued. "They've guessed who this—this Head Hunter is, because he's somebody they know and who is interested in head hunting. And they're afraid—afraid that if they talk he'll get them!"

"It's possible." Fletcher glanced at the wall clock then reached for his hat and gloves. "I've got an appointment with Doctor Hartzell at eight o'clock, and it's nearly that now. Prince Alexis is out of town, but I hope to reach him in the morning. If anything developes, let me know."

HE GAVE himself over to serious thought as a taxicab bore him up the crowded, noisy lane of Fifth Avenue. During the afternoon several theories had begun to crystallize out of his subconscious mind. He had a hunch that one of them would prove the right one.

Dr. Hartzell's home was in the Fifties, not far off the Avenue. It was a narrow stone structure with a bleak, gloomy exterior. Its heavily curtained windows showed no lights.

He had scarcely touched his finger to the bell when the door swung open. A voice with a foreign accent roughly bade him enter. Fletcher glanced sharply at the man, saw a short stocky figure, straight black hair, a reddish complexion. He judged him to be an Indian, probably of South American extraction.

Without another word he was shown into a long narrow room, illuminated by a single desk lamp at one end. It had a musty, ancient odor. The walls were lined with bookshelves and glass cases. In the deep shadows he caught sight of tomtoms, barbaric costumes, unfamiliar weapons, savage idols.

Dr. Hartzell was hunched behind the desk. The light from the lamp streamed upon his high domed head, his pointed nose, his bony chin. He pushed away the books in front of him and greeted Fletcher without rising, motioning him to a chair.

Fletcher lit a cigarette and inquired whether the scientist had heard of the two murders discovered that morning. Upon learning that he had not, he outlined them.

"Incredible!" murmured Dr. Hartzell. "It is unbelieveable that such things can happen in a modern city. If this were one of the outposts of civilization, one might —But you have not told me your errand."

Fletcher crushed out his cigarette and drew his chair closer to the desk. "I want your help, Doctor Hartzell," he said.

"My help! How could I help you?"

"By being frank with me. Whenever I have talked with you, you have had an air of holding something back. Prince Alexis has had somewhat the same attitude. What you know or suspect may not seem of any importance to you, but these murders have become so serious that we can't afford to pass up any clue, however unpromising it may appear."

Dr. Hartzell cupped his chin in his long fingers. For seconds before he spoke he stared into the shadows.

"Of course I cannot speak for Prince Alexis," he said at length. "Of late he has been distant toward me and we have scarcely exchanged two words, so I don't know what theory he holds. But, I did notice something peculiar, something that puzzled me. Yet it seemed so silly, so utterly preposterous that it could have any bearing upon these murders, that I did not mention it.

"Briefly, it is this: I brought back with me from Ecuador six shrunken heads which I had secured from a certain tribe of Jivaros. I had reason to believe that those heads had been taken in a raid but a week before I got there, but that did not concern me.

"Four of those heads I put on exhibition at the Gallery Alexis. It was those four which were stolen. A fifth was among those I gave to Prince Alexis for sale. It was the Negro's head which he sold to Van Styne. Interpret that as you wish. I think it only a coincidence— though a rather remarkable one."

FLETCHER was disappointed, though interested. He remembered the newspaper theory of vengeful Jivaro Indians coming to New York to recover the heads of slaughtered relatives. He mentioned it to Dr. Hartzell.

"Sensational nonsense!" snapped the scientist. "Jivaros try to retaliate against their enemies, but it is impossible to imagine such ignorant, poverty-stricken savages finding their way to New York—"

"That accounts for five of the heads," said Fletcher. "What became of the sixth?"

"I have it here. Care to see it?"

Fletcher nodded and Dr. Hartzell disappeared into the hall. He was gone for some minutes and Fletcher fell into a revery. This development was unexpected, but it did not conflict with the theories he had formed. Rather, it lent additional color to one of them.

He was roused suddenly by a loud shriek. It was the despairing cry of a man in mortal terror.

IT TOOK Fletcher but an instant to slip out his automatic, gain the hall. There he paused, uncertain from which direction the cry had come. The darkness of the hall, his unfamiliarity with the house, confused him.

Then the cry was repeated and he saw that it came from a door at the rear which showed a ribbon of light at its base. He heard the crash of bodies and muffled oaths.

Shouting, he ran the length of the hall and flung open the door. It gave into a small room, brightly lighted. Against the wall was a stack of small cases, some of them open.

Dr. Hartzell lay on the floor, twitching convulsively. A thin ribbon of red ran from a gash in his forehead.

And close by his head was a heavy, broad-bladed knife, of the type known as machetes in tropical America. Its point was embedded deeply in the flooring, so that it stood out at an angle from the floor.

"He went—out the window!" gasped the scientist.

Fletcher saw at a glance that Dr. Hartzell was not severely injured. It was more important now to capture his assailant

than to stanch his wound. He leaped to the open window at the rear and scrambled through it, fell cat-footed to brick pavement below. It took a moment for his eyes to accommodate themselves to the darkness; then he saw that he was in an alleyway.

At the same instant he heard feet and saw a shadowy figure shuffling away. It broke into a hobbling run, as though one leg were crippled. He caught sight of a face turned toward him, the features almost hidden behind a thick black beard and the downturned brim of a hat.

He shouted a warning to the man and ran toward him. But when he reached the spot at which he had seen him he was gone, swallowed up in the darkness. There were a dozen hiding places and, without a flashlight, he was almost helpless.

After five minutes' futile search Fletcher returned to Dr. Hartzell's home. The scientist was sitting up on the floor, wincing a little as his Indian servant wound a bandage about his head.

"He got away from me," Fletcher said briefly. "What happened?"

"I—I scarcely know," answered the scientist. "I heard the window go up and started to turn around. Then something hit me on the head and I fell down. I saw a man standing over me. He swung a machete at my neck, but I squirmed aside and it struck the floor. I got to my feet again and tried to fight, but he knocked me down again. Then I heard you shouting and the man disappeared through the window."

"Did you recognize him?"

"No. But he must have been this fiend the papers call the—the Head Hunter! He had a black beard. And I think—he walked with a limp."

A picture of Prince Alexis flashed across Fletcher's mind. The Russian was black-bearded and had a limp. But it was hard to reconcile the impeccable proprietor of the art gallery with the skulking figure he had lost in the alley. And yet Dr. Hartzell had hinted at strained relations with Alexis—

Fletcher examined the machete, hoping to find a trace of fingerprints. The wooden handle bore none and the blade was brightly polished.

"By the way," he asked, "did you find the sixth head you were going to show me?"

"I had it in my hand when I was attacked," said Dr. Hartzell. "I must have dropped it." He looked about the floor and his eyes slowly widened with horror. "Why—why it's gone!"

CHAPTER FOUR

The Shrunken Man

IT WAS AN hour past midnight. There was no moon, no stars, and a thick fog upon Fifth Avenue set each street light apart from its fellows, leaving a pool of darkness between them.

A man detached himself from the shadows, moving stealthily across the face of the buildings. He was clothed in black and had a hat pulled down over his eyes so that his face was invisible.

When he reached the show window of the Gallery Alexis, he paused a moment to peer through the glass. The lights had been turned off several hours before and its grisly exhibit was only a shadowy blur.

The man raised his arm. Clasped in his fist was an object the size of a paving brick. He brought it down once, twice, three times against the plate glass, and it broke with a loud report, sprinkling fragments of glass about him.

At the same instant, touched off by hidden wires, an alarm bell overhead set up a raucous clamor. The man glanced up, startled; then quickly thrust his arm through the large aperture he had made. He brought it out with a bulky object and began to run down the street with a hobbling gait.

Before he reached the corner a whistle shrilled. Above the clangor of the alarm echoed the pounding feet of a patrolman. The man tried to increase his speed, but stumbled and fell. The object he had taken from the window whirled from his hands and rolled into the gutter.

There was no time to recover it, for the patrolman had burst out of the fog and was swooping down on him. The man scrambled to his feet and ran, dodging down a side street, where the mist curled about his figure and hid him from pursuit.

When the squad cars arrived, the patrolman was relieved of his duty and sent to detective headquarters. Inspector Sullivan and Anthony Fletcher had only that minute returned from Dr. Hartzell's home. Their investigation had been thorough but without profit. The bearded man seen by Fletcher had left no fingerprints, no clues, nothing by which he might be identified.

They listened to the story of the policeman, then inspected the object which the window breaker had dropped.

It was the shrunken figure of the human body which had been the central exhibit in the window of the Gallery Alexis. Beneath the glaring droplight in Sullivan's office it seemed even more hideous and repulsive. Its broad lips leered at them with gnomish mockery, as though daring them to probe its secret.

"Good Lord!" Sullivan cried in awe. "Won't there be any end to this? It's the devil himself that's doing these things. Look here, O'Connor," he addressed the patrolman, "can't you give us any sort of description of this man?"

"No more than I did, sir," replied the officer. "It was that dark and foggy I

never got a good look at him. He had on
dark clothes and ran with a limp. And I
think he had a beard."

"It's the same man who attacked
Doctor Hartzell," said Sullivan. "The
one you saw, Fletcher. The Head Hunter. At last we're getting close to him."

Fletcher wondered. After his own en-
counter with the bearded limper he had
played with the idea that Prince Alexis
might conceivably be the marauder. But
this new development seemed to preclude
any such possibility. Why in the world
would the proprietor of the gallery break
his own window for the purpose of rob-
bing something to which he had easy ac-
cess every day? There didn't seem to be
any answer to that.

Fletcher was subjecting the shrunken
figure to a minute examination. He prod-
ded its face, scratched the skin with his
fingernail, broke off a strand of hair and
held it to the light. An exclamation
broke from him.

"Found something?" inquired Sullivan.

"I don't know . . . I believe I'll ask
Doctor Durand to look this over. It's
just possible—"

"He may be here now," said Sullivan
eagerly. "He was going to drop in as
soon as he finished a case on Pell Street."
He lifted a desk phone and barked a question, then hung up with a grunt. "He's
downstairs and is coming right up."

The medical examiner entered and nodded to them. He gave only an indifferent
glance at the tiny body on the desk. "The
Head Hunter again," he guessed.

"It may be," said Fletcher. "I'd like
you to do a personal favor for me, doctor.
Take this little mummy to your laboratory and give it a thorough examination."

"What do you want to know?"

"Everything. How long the man has
been dead. His race, his age, his probable
description."

Dr. Durand agreed and departed with
the shrunken figure tucked carelessly
under one arm. Sullivan eyed Fletcher
curiously.

"You've got something on your mind,"
he declared. "I don't suppose there's any
use in asking what it is."

Fletcher smiled as he rose to leave.
"Not just yet. We'll wait and see what
Doctor Durand has to report."

He returned wearily to his apartment
and tumbled into bed. A night's rest was
what he needed to clear his brain. Tomorrow he intended to attack the problem from a fresh angle, and his hunch
that the case was near to conclusion was
stronger than ever.

HOW LONG he had been asleep he
did not know. A soft, rasping noise
reached his consciousness and galvanized
him to immediate wakefulness.

He did not move, but lay rigid, his
eyes sweeping the darkness. If anyone
were there, he was invisible. Then he
saw that one of the windows, which he
had opened but a few inches, was all the
way up. He remembered the narrow stone
coping which ran about the building just
beneath his windows. It was wide enough
for a man to stand on, to inch his way
from the fire escape to his bedroom windows.

He heard a soft, scuffling sound. Feet
moving stealthily over the carpet toward
him.

Fletcher's pulse raced. The Head Hunter? Was he to be murdered as Van
Styne had been, his head cut from his
body, carried away . . .

His hand slid under his pillow, felt
the cold hard outlines of his automatic.
Its flat bulk nestled reassuringly in the
hollow of his hand. One finger found
the safety catch, snapped it off.

The click it made was distinctly audible
in the dead silence. Perhaps it was that

which saved Fletcher's life. The intruder waited no longer, but made a leap to the bed and brought a huge knife down on the pillow in a swishing arc. But his aim had been hasty and Fletcher was able to scramble out of the way, slipping from the bed and falling to the floor.

His automatic barked at the vague shadow which pursued him around the foot of the bed. In the almost total darkness he missed. The next instant the weapon leapt from his fingers as the leg of a chair struck his wrist with paralyzing force.

He gritted his teeth and made a lunging spring from the floor. His fist sank deep into a stomach and air whistled through set lips. But that did not stop the full-armed swing of the chair crashing down upon his head.

Fletcher tottered and slumped to the floor. He was still conscious, but his muscles and vocal cords would not respond to the messages sent to them.

He had no doubt that his assailant was the Head Hunter. And he expected nothing but the swish of a knife through the air, the feel of its blade biting into his neck . . .

The he heard a door slam. It was the outer door of his apartment. Dazedly he realized that the Head Hunter, unaware of his helplessness, or fearing that the occupants of neighboring apartments had been aroused by the shot, had fled.

It seemed to take minutes for him to crawl to his feet and snap on the light. He recovered his automatic and staggered through his apartment into the hall. Doors were opening, heads were peering out, and he heard a woman shrieking for the police.

But the Head Hunter had vanished. An open fire-escape door showed the direction of his flight. It was too late to pursue him.

Fletcher returned to his bedroom. Upon his bed was a machete, similar in design to the one he had found sticking in the floor of Dr. Hartzell's store room. As had been the case with the other, it bore no fingerprints.

IT WAS late the next morning when Fletcher entered Dr. Durand's private laboratory. He found the little medical examiner, wrapped like a mummy in the habiliments of his profession, fussing over a microscope. He removed his mask and rubber gown and showed Fletcher into his tiny office.

"I found something," he said, when he had a cigar going. "Don't know whether it's what you expected, Fletcher. That mummy is the body of a white man."

"You're certain?"

"No doubt about it. I examined the skin, the hair, the nails, the wax in the ears. I wanted no mistakes and made every possible microscopical and chemical test. The hair is that of a Caucasian, not an Indian's or Negro's. The skin is white, though it has been dyed black. The wax in the ears still bore a trace of the dust and smoke of cities."

"How long has he been dead?"

"Less than a year, probably not as long as six months. Do you want to check my tests? I have everything in readiness."

"No need of that," said Fletcher. "Can you give me a description of the man?"

"Very little. Without a skeleton to take measurements from it's nearly impossible. I should say he was a German or Pole, of medium height, probably between fifty and sixty years of age. He had black hair. A plastic surgeon might be able to do something about reconstructing the face; I don't know. Tell me—what does it mean?"

"That remains to be seen," said Fletcher thoughtfully. "I've an idea it may prove important—in a roundabout fashion. You've informed Inspector Sullivan of your findings? . . . No matter; I'm going to see him in a few minutes."

Sullivan, however, was not expected in his office for several hours. While Fletcher was chatting with the lieutenant in charge a call came for him from Prince Alexis.

"I would like to see you as soon as possible," the Russian said. "You could come to my gallery, perhaps? I am ready to tell you who—who the Head Hunter is."

When Fletcher arrived at the gallery, Prince Alexis was limping impatiently about his office. His bearded face was haggard and he was puffing nervously at a long cigarette.

"Mr. Fletcher," he began, "I suppose you have resented my attitude of indifference and—well, call it hostility. But if you know of my unfortunate experiences with your New York police, I think you understand. I come to you because you are—a gentleman."

Fletcher nodded. He knew that the Russian had been unjustly suspected of being connected with diamond smugglers, and had been subjected to a year's surveillance which must have been galling to him—enough to embitter him against the police.

"James Van Styne was a very dear friend," continued Prince Alexis. "When he was murdered I swore to myself that he would be avenged. Just how, I did not know. I suppose that even then I had a suspicion of the truth. But it was so vague, so uncertain, so utterly lacking in proof, that I did not care to mention it.

"Now I have that proof, though I did not come upon it until a few hours ago. When I returned to the city early this morning and learned what had happened —the attack upon Doctor Hartzell and the robbery of my show window—my terrible suspicions became a certainty and I made a quiet investigation."

PRINCE ALEXIS paused to light a fresh cigarette. His hands trembled a little as he held a match to it.

"I think I can make you understand more easily," he went on, "if I preface my theory with an explanation. Doctor Hartzell is a strange man, a genius in his field. I consider him mentally unbalanced—but then, isn't it said that all geniuses are touched with insanity? I have known him for years and do not pretend to understand him. He has an overwhelming passion for scientific investigation that has carried him into places no other man has dared to go, that has impelled him to do things normal men would not do.

"But that, as I said, is the preface to my theory. You have heard of Emil and Paul Jorgens?"

"The famous explorers?" said Fletcher. "The two men who are reputed to know South America better than anyone else?"

"The same. But perhaps you do not know that they and Doctor Hartzell are implacable enemies. How it started I do not know—nor would they tell. At any rate the two brothers headed an expedition into the jungles of Ecuador about a year ago. They never came out nor was any word heard from them.

"It may have been a coincidence that Doctor Hartzell entered that territory at the same time. I do know that Doctor Hartzell came out—and Emil and Paul Jorgens did not. There was a rumor at the Tropical Explorers' Club—not generally credited—that the Jorgens did not come out because they were dead. And that they were dead because Doctor Hartzell, in his mad hatred of them, had natives ambush and slaughter them.

"It sounds mad—but then, as I have explained, I think Doctor Hartzell a little mad. I myself did not believe the rumor until I learned this morning that the shrunken figure had been taken from my window. And then a ghastly thought leaped into my mind. It was incredible, unthinkable, unbelieveable. Nevertheless I found a picture of the Jorgens brothers and compared it with my mental picture of the shrunken figure which was taken.

"And, Mr. Fletcher," concluded Prince Alexis, "that figure was, I am convinced the shrunken body of Paul Jorgens!"

Fletcher nodded, not greatly surprised. He had been prepared for just such a revelation. "You have that picture?" he asked.

The Russian gave it to him. It showed two men standing on the prow of a boat, a jungle in the background. They were of a stocky Polish type. The hair on Fletcher's neck rose as he looked at the shorter man on the left.

There was an unmistakable resemblance between him and the gnomish figure Dr. Durand had proclaimed to be a white man.

"They are the same," he said, and went on to tell of Dr. Durand's examination.

"It's the last proof we need!" cried Prince Alexis. "And I will tell you something else. Doctor Hartzell, in his zeal for scientific knowledge, has actually participated in head hunts with the natives and helped them prepare the heads. Perhaps it was he who prepared Paul Jorgens' body."

FLETCHER winced. He'd seen many forms of murder, but nothing to match this. Certainly it was gruesomely unique not only to kill one's enemy, but also to shrink his hide to the size of a large doll, to make it into a grotesque and hideous travesty of the living man . . . He asked a question, anticipating the answer.

"And Emil Jorgens?"

"Emil Jorgens escaped! Somehow he made his way through the jungle to the coast. He is now in New York. One of the members of the Tropical Explorers' Club saw him, though he disappeared into a crowd before he could speak to him. He said the man was wasted away to a shadow, bearded, and apparently crippled, for he walked with a limp."

Fletcher thought once more of the figure he had seen shuffling away from Dr. Hartzell's home. And the policeman's meager description of the man who had broken the window of the Gallery Alexis.

He looked at the picture again. Yes, he was certain now that he could recognize in Emil Jorgens the man he had seen in the alleyway.

"Emil Jorgens is the Head Hunter," continued Prince Alexis. "His experiences have snapped his mind. He has reverted to the savagery of the people he studied. He is aping their methods in dealing with enemies. He has a purpose, but has wandered far from it, killing almost indiscriminately. Last night seems to have been the first time he kept to it, and he almost succeeded both in murdering Doctor Hartzell and recovering the body of his brother."

"If Jorgens is in New York," said Fletcher, "depend upon it that the police can find him."

Prince Alexis suddenly scowled and stroked his beard. "I suppose this seems like disloyalty to a friend," he added. "But I know you can never prove that Doctor Hartzell brought about Paul Jorgens' death. I tell this to you only so that you can safeguard Doctor Hartzell's life. He is in danger as long as Jorgens remains uncaptured."

Fletcher smiled grimly. "And so the police must protect a murderer from revenge," he said. "It will be done, Prince Alexis."

CHAPTER FIVE

The Devil's Laboratory

THE interview concluded, Fletcher called detective headquarters and learned that Sullivan had not yet returned. Not wanting to wait for him, he proceeded at once to Dr. Hartzell's home.

It seemed deserted and it was only after he had rung the bell some half-dozen times that the door opened. The scientist confronted him sourly; then permitted himself a smile as he recognized his visitor and invited him into his study.

"I thought it must be the reporters again," he explained. "They've been making my life miserable this morning. Have there been any fresh developments?"

Fletcher looked narrowly at Dr. Hartzell as he spoke. The man was extremely nervous. His deep-set eyes jerked constantly from one side to the other, as though he dreaded some horror which might be lurking in the shadows.

"You've heard of the attempted robbery at the Gallery Alexis?" asked Fletcher.

Dr. Hartzell nodded.

"That robbery," continued Fletcher, "brought to light a rather astonishing fact. The shrunken figure with which the thief tried to make off was the body of a white man."

The scientist's fingers clenched upon the edge of his desk like bony claws. "Impossible!" he burst out.

"Doctor Durand has proved it in his laboratory. And we have identified the body, so we know its race. The man was Paul Jorgens."

Dr. Hartzell whispered the name after him. His eyes blazed with hatred. He opened his lips to speak, then closed them tightly.

"I have learned the entire story," went on Fletcher, "though much of it is guess-work. It is said that you instigated Paul Jorgens' murder. That you yourself prepared his body—"

"You're insane!" rasped the scientist, coming to his feet. "I secured that body from a tribe of natives in Ecuador. I did not inquire where it came from—nor did I care. If it should be Jorgens' body, as you say, I was ignorant of that."

"That may be. But did you know that Emil Jorgens is now in New York?"

"Emil Jorgens—in—New York?" Dr. Hartzell fell back into his chair. His domed forehead beaded with sweat. He wiped his lips with the back of his hand.

"No doubt about it," said Fletcher. "He has been seen and recognized by a man who knew him well. His description tallies with that of the man who attempted to carry off the shrunken figure—the body of his brother."

The scientist abruptly leaped to his feet and strode the length of the room. "I can't believe it," he muttered. "When he crawled away and escaped into the jungle, he was badly wounded—" He broke off, becoming conscious that he was speaking aloud.

Fletcher was watching him like a hawk, missing nothing of the other's agitation. He had a purpose behind this interrogation other than merely warning him of the danger. He wanted to drive the man beyond the limits of his mental endurance.

"It was Emil Jorgens whom I saw last night, fleeing from this house," he pursued relentlessly.

"Come back to kill me," said Dr. Hartzell. "Come back for revenge."

He continued to pace about the room, muttering to himself. He seemed to have become oblivious to Fletcher's presence. Fletcher made no comment and waited patiently for the breakdown he was sure would come.

There was a small glass case standing

on the table against the wall which he had not noticed before, and he let his eyes rove over it. It contained a shrunken head, which instantly arrested his attention. It was dyed a darker hue, he thought, than the others he had seen, and did not seem to have the same facial contours, which he recalled in those at the Gallery Alexis.

But it was not that which riveted his gaze upon it. It was its remarkable resemblance, distorted and shrunken as it was, to some face filed away in his memory.

HE stared at it, forgetting for the moment the striding figure behind him. Forgetting everything in his intense concentration. Every lineament of that hideous little face was familiar to him; yet he could not place it, rack his memory as he might.

At last, convinced that his imagination was tricking him, he began to turn away. And as his eyes swung obliquely from it; as he saw it from the corner of his eye, his memory clicked.

It was the head of James Van Styne!

It had, in miniature, the same bulbous nose, the same sagging jowls, the same squinting eyes and bushy eyebrows. Though less than five inches in diameter, the craftsman who had shaped it had preserved the human character of it with diabolical art.

As he gazed at it with dawning horror, a step sounded behind him. Under the hypnosis of his discovery, he was slow to act. Hands came about his chest and locked, pinning his arms to his sides. The hot, fetid breath of Dr. Hartzell's Indian servant fell upon his neck as he was held helpless.

Dr. Hartzell was laughing when his captor swung him around.

"So! You have caught on at last, my friend! Then you know that I am the Head Hunter!"

After the first attempt to struggle from the encircling arms, Fletcher stood quiet. He was in the power of a madman and he would need all his wits if he were to stand any chance of escape. He regarded the scientist with level eyes.

"I have suspected it since yesterday— perhaps even before that," he said. "I knew that only a brain such as yours could conceive and execute such monstrous things. Tonight I had hoped to goad you to the point of admitting it, or giving me some proof. But, until I found Van Styne's head, I could not prove it."

Dr. Hartzell threw back his head and laughed. His voice had taken on a fiendish rasping quality. The light striking up against his face made it look a death's head, parchment skin stretched tightly over its bony frame.

"You guessed too late," he mocked. "Yes I—I am he whom the papers call the Head Hunter."

A change had come over him. Gone was the reserved scientist, gone was the terror-stricken man, to be replaced by the homicidal maniac, mad with the lust for blood.

"You are the first to learn my secret— I should have kept that head upstairs with the others—but it doesn't matter. You will be the last. The secret dies with you. And your head, with Van Styne's and all the rest, will go to swell my collection."

He got a rope and with the aid of his servant bound Fletcher's wrists behind him. They took him to an upstairs room almost bare of furniture. Against the wall was a gas range and several kettles. Beside it was a small table, on which was an outlay of knives, bottles, several buckets of what appeared to be sand—and three more horrible heads, each in its own glass case.

Fletcher guessed that they were the

heads of Dr. Hartzell's latest victims. One of them he thought he recognized from a picture he had seen of Greenwald, the unfortunate lawyer, who had been found in the park, and now his own head was to be added to the three in view—He riveted his gaze on the monstrous group and a cold sweat broke out on his forehead.

"My equipment," Dr. Hartzell was explaining. "I am the greatest head preserver in the world. Greater even than the Jivaro masters of the art—under whom I studied until I surpassed them. My servant was a Jivaro sub-chief; but he preferred to follow me, the greatest exponent of their sacred art."

He slipped off his coat and donned a rubber apron which enveloped him from chin to feet. Meanwhile his Jivaro servant had lighted the gas stove and was putting kettles and pots on the flames, filling them with sand and water.

Behind his back, Fletcher tensed his wrists against his bonds. They gave ever so slightly, enough so he could twist two fingers up and begin working on the knots. The scientist had not thought to remove his automatic from its holster; and if he could get his hands free long enough to get at it, he might be able to turn the tables.

"Van Styne's head was a masterpiece, a work of art," he said, sparring for time. "Will you tell me what your technique is?"

"If you read my book, you should know," answered Dr. Hartzell proudly. "Of course I employ certain refinements which are my own secret. Be assured that your head will be shrunken very carefully. I will prize it highly. You saw Van Styne's head; it is perfect, without a blemish."

"Why did you kill him?"

DR. HARTZELL was testing the blade of a knife on the edge of his thumb. The question touched off his murderous rage and he swung around with a snarl.

"I killed him because I hated him! When I left for South America, I entrusted my fortune to Van Styne and Greenwald for investment. And they stole it, lost it, robbed me of almost every penny!"

The mysterious connection between Van Styne and Greenwald!

"And the others?" asked Fletcher.

"I killed the others because I wanted heads. Except the night watchman at the Gallery Alexis. I knew the stupid police might suspect me, so I robbed my own collection to turn suspicion from me. The watchman had admitted me and knew me, so he had to be silenced."

Fletcher thought he understood everything now. Dr. Hartzell, already partially unbalanced, had become completely insane when he learned that his fortune was gone. Rightly or wrongly blaming Van Styne and Greenwald for the loss of his wealth, he had avenged himself upon them. Then, carried off by his mania, or perhaps by the fame he had attained as the one authority upon the subject which was engaging everybody's attention, he had been unable to stop.

The ropes about Fletcher's wrist gave a little more. He had one of the knots untied, and he thought that with a few seconds' more time he could slip his hands out.

He froze as he saw Dr. Hartzell looking at him piercingly. But the scientist was thinking of something else, and his lips curled in an insane leer.

"Perhaps I shall not take your head after all," he said. "No, I believe that I shall consign you to a better fate. I will preserve your entire body, make it into a beautiful little doll, as I did with Paul Jorgens. Your head, your body, your limbs will be shrunken together until you are like a little monkey. Would you like that?"

Fletcher shrugged. And he took advantage of the shrug to give his wrists a powerful wrench, putting all the power of his shoulders into it. The knots, partially untied, slipped enough so that his hands were almost free.

The scientist muttered to himself and turned away. On the very instant his back was turned, Fletcher hunched his shoulders again and jerked his wrists free from the ropes. His hand snaked toward his shoulder holster.

But he had miscalculated in one important respect. His fingers, numb and half paralyzed from the constriction of the bonds, were awkward and he almost dropped his gun as he drew it out.

And Dr. Hartzell must have been expecting just some such move. With a shriek he leaped across the room, caught the gun's muzzle in his left hand and twisted it away from him.

The Jivaro Indian struck him with a crash and he fell on his back to the floor, almost carrying Dr. Hartzell down with him. The automatic whirled from his fingers and dropped into a corner. The scientist cursed gutturally and brought the knife he still carried down in an arc for Fletcher's heart. Fletcher caught his wrist in the nick of time, held it so that the point of the knife was suspended several inches over his chest.

But he could not hold it there for long. The Indian was choking him and his vision blurred. The scientist's mad face hung over him like some monster's, jaws slathering as he tried to push the knife downward.

FLETCHER was fast losing strength. He felt the point of the knife prick his ribs, but he could not push it back, try as he might. A moment more . . . .

Then a shriek rang through the room. Dr. Hartzell cried out in alarm and leaped away, taking the knife with him. For an instant the Indian loosened his strangling hold upon Fletcher's throat. Fletcher gasped air into his tortured lungs, then put everything into a single effort. He kicked upward with his legs, turning a backward somersault. His toes caught the Indian in the chest, drove him away like a battering-ram.

Fletcher came to his feet like a cat. He sprang upon the Indian just rising from the floor and met him with short-armed jabs that battered his face, his stomach, and ended with a knockout blow to the jaw.

As he straightened up, something rolled gently against his ankle. He looked down, then jerked his foot away. It was a human head, eyes open wide, blood still spurting from the neck.

Dr. Hartzell's head!

The scientist's body lay close to the door. Crouched over it was an emaciated, bearded figure dressed in ragged black clothes. From one hand dangled a machete, its long polished blade crimson.

The man was laughing insanely, his head thrown back, his long beard sticking straight out. His body shook as peal upon peal of merriment poured from his wrinkled throat.

"J o r g e n s ! Emil Jorgens!" said Fletcher.

The man's laughter broke off short. His gaze swung toward Fletcher. The blade slipped from his hand and clanged upon the floor. He took a few steps backward and stopped with his back against the wall.

"What . . . where am I?" he faltered.

His face slowly relaxed. He put his hands to his head and clenched it.

"My head . . . it hurts. Something hit it." Then the light of madness faded from his eyes, leaving them dazed and frightened.

Fletcher retrieved his automatic and snapped handcuffs on the Jivaro Indian. He was not anxious to stay in this den of murder. He took Emil Jorgens' arm and guided him down to the study, where he put in a call to the police.

"But I don't understand!" cried Jorgens. "I was in the jungle with my brother—then I find myself here."

"Don't excite yourself," said Fletcher. "You've had a bad shock, but you'll come out of it all right. It'll all come back to you after a bit."

He found a bottle of liquor in the desk and poured out a drink. Jorgens gulped it eagerly.

"I remember it—like a dream," he said. "Doctor Hartzell killed my brother and wounded me, but I managed to crawl off into the jungle. Then there were months and years of starving. The rest isn't clear . . . . . Did I come to New York? Was it I who was hunting for Doctor Hartzell to kill him? Last night I looked through a window and saw him. It was in the back of this house. He drove a knife into the floor and screamed—"

"A false attack upon himself," murmured Fletcher. "To divert my suspicion from him."

"And then I found my brother's body in a window. It was hideous! Shrunken up—like the Indians do. I tried to take it, but a policeman chased me. I knew Doctor Hartzell did that, so today I came to kill him. I got in through a back window and found a machete. And then I saw him attacking you—and I went mad. I killed him. And I'm a murderer."

Fletcher gripped his shoulder.

"Not a murderer," he said. "You have rid the city of a monster. You were an instrument of justice."

Smart Like a Fox

by

Joseph Mulvaney

The D. A. thought he had the case sewed up but he'd forgotten one thing. That money talks—even in a court of law!

THE aged and able attorney for the defense was summing up in the case of The People of the State of New York vs. Terence Harrigan.

"Gentlemen," he was saying, "you have heard the eloquent district attorney promise to pin the crime of bribe-taking on the defendant facing you—Patrolman Terence Harrigan, a young officer of the law, with a spotless record—and you have heard the fashion in which he has tried to fulfill that promise. You listened to the testimony of that unspeakable felon, 'Mulberry' Mitchell, who sought to swear away the liberty of a policeman, his enemy, as all police protectors are enemies of lawbreakers.

"Surely, you noted the expression on Mitchell's face as he described how in the presence of witnesses three weeks ago, he drew that thousand-dollar bill from the Trader's and Drover's Bank to pay the price of protection for his gambling den. You heard him tell, and his glib associates parroted his story, of marking that bill in the presence of our prosecutor—our new prosecutor named on a reform ticket and determined to reform this town to the satisfaction of the yelling yellow press, no matter how many honest men he ruins in his reformation!

"You saw the type of humanity those undercover operators were! He must have seined the sewers to land such rats! Oh yes, they swore they saw the money drawn, marked, and passed to this policeman. Others of their ilk testified to finding it—this Federal Reserve banknote, fresh from the mint.

"There it is, gentlemen! Look at it closely! Take it into the jury room when you deliberate this charge of bribe-taking, extortion, graft! The justice of this court will permit you, I am sure, to examine any exhibit, even this precious certificate—so take it with you, tainted with the touch of Judas as it is, and—"

From the rear of the crowded court came commotion. An excited youth with a long, legal-looking envelope, broke past the attendants. Even the rappings of the gavel on the bench did not halt him. Oscar Graves Fox, known to the metropolitan bar as Old Gray Fox, checked his summation and confronted the intruder angrily.

He was dramatic as he stood there—lean, sharp-muzzled, bright-eyed, bushy black brows and thick hair shot through with gray, and clad in gray, as was his habit, from scarf to spats. The aquiline prosecutor stared. Mulberry Mitchell and his swarthy associates registered curiosity. The judge's face was ominously dark. The jury appeared mystified. But the messenger undaunted forced his way to his master, presented the envelope.

O. G. Fox tore the envelope, extracted a folded paper and with head thrust forward peered at the written lines. Then

117

waving the paper, he exclaimed: "May it please the court—I have word from my office that a very important witness has just arrived and is hurrying here. May I ask a brief recess until he arrives? Fifteen minutes will suffice. After I have examined him, the prosecution may cross-examine and I will resume my summing up."

OBVIOUSLY perplexed, the district attorney consented. The judge called a recess.

In ten minutes another messenger arrived with an envelope for Fox. He was about to open it when a stranger entered, bearing a traveling bag and wearing an appearance of haste. He conferred swiftly with the lawyer at the counsel table and when the judge reappeared to resume the proceedings, the stranger stepped to the witness stand and was sworn.

"Your name, please?"

"Ledyard K. Hatch."

"Address?"

"Washington, D. C."

O. G. Fox then took the witness. Leaning over the counsel table, he picked up the thousand-dollar bill in evidence and inquired silkily: "By whom are you employed, Mr. Hatch?"

"By the United States Government."

"In what department?"

"Department of the Treasury."

At that, Mulberry Mitchell and his companions manifested sudden personal interest. This scholarly-seeming, black-bearded stranger was a prohibition agent, then? Their eyes set on him and stayed there as did the eyes of the prosecutor, and from the bench the judge displayed renewed interest in a case that had been hopelessly drab with a defendant hopelessly guilty.

"How long have you been employed there?"

"Twenty-two years."

"What is your present position?"

"Special technical assistant to the Secretary of the Treasury."

"Define your duties briefly, please."

"I exercise supervision over engraving and printing of currency."

"Are you an expert engraver?"

"I have been for fifteen years."

"And a printer, too?"

"Yes, for ten years."

"Are you familiar with the colors used in currency, and the paper?"

"I am."

Fox thrust the certificate into his hand.

"I hand you State's Exhibit A, marked for identification—please examine it and tell the jury if you know what it is."

Adjusting his spectacles with a professional gesture, the witness glanced at the bill, turned it over, felt the paper carefully. Still studying the exhibit, he drew from his pocket a case containing another pair of glasses with tiny oblong lenses that set on the very tip of his nose.

"Come, come now," rallied O. G. Fox, gently. "You do not mean to tell us that you never saw a bill of that kind before, when you work in the treasury?"

The tattoo of the gavel on the bench stilled the outburst of mirth, but for several seconds longer the witness did not even shift his glance. Then he replied, unruffled: "No, I never saw one just like this before."

"Then you do not know what it is?"

"Oh, yes, I know what it is."

"Please state exactly what it is."

"It is a piece of engraved paper bearing the numerals and sign $1,000 and the words 'United States of America'—"

"Then it is a certificate pledging the credit of the United States to the payment of a thousand dollars to the bearer?"

"Oh, no, it is not."

"Then please," urged O. G. Fox, "tell us exactly what that exhibit is."

Calmly and slowly the witness responded: "In plain and simple terms, this is a counterfeit of a thousand-dollar United States gold certificate and nothing else."

SWIFTLY, amid the hubbub about him, the witness flicked a fountain pen from his pocket and in an instant had scrawled heavy red writing across the face of the exhibit. The prosecutor's voice shrilled.

"If Your Honor please—before this extraordinary proceeding goes further, I demand that the witness state what he did with that certificate just now, and why, and that he return it to the court at once."

"No objection!" exclaimed O. G. Fox, raising a hand, and the witness, passing the paper to the judge, explained: "Instinctively, I wrote on that paper the Latin words, *Damntum Est,* meaning 'It is damned or condemned.' It is an ancient rule among the men that protect American currency never to let a counterfeit out of their hands unbranded. That bill is a skilfully executed, dangerous counterfeit, the first of its denomination I have ever seen."

While the judge pondered the paper before him, Fox continued the examination. "Can you tell exactly why you know it to be a counterfeit?"

"I can. For one thing, there are silk threads in the paper indicating that it was printed on Government paper no longer used. The paper for the new currency contains silk threads but they are chopped up finely. The portrait of Grover Cleveland lacks depth, is flat. The ornate design 'One Thousand' is less intricately wrought than the genuine—there is no doubt that it is fraudulent."

"When did you see me before you entered this court today?"

"Never that I recall."

"What prompted your visit to the city?"

"The Secretary of the Treasury di-rected me to appear here in court, if possible, because he said that an attorney, Oscar Graves Fox, had informed him that a new counterfeit bill was in circulation and called for the highest technical skill to detect it."

O. G. Fox nodded and waved an arm in friendliest fashion, inviting the prosecutor to cross-examine.

The district attorney, with bared teeth and bloodless face, begged: "With the court's permission, I shall waive cross examination and ask permission to call to the stand in rebuttal, Irving Chambers, cashier of the Traders and Drovers Bank, who is in court."

The judge nodded, his eyes on the exhibit. The cashier was sworn and led into testimony by the prosecutor.

"Did you on the third day of September last past, deliver a piece of paper currency to one John Mitchell, known locally as Mulberry Mitchell?"

"I did."

"Would you recognize that certificate if shown you?"

"I might."

"If Your Honor will please—"

Roused from his scrutiny, the judge thrust the exhibit into the witness' hand, rising from the bench and ignoring the court attendant's aid. The cashier studied it as the District Attorney asked: "Is that exhibit, marked 'State Exhibit A,' the certificate you delivered?"

"It is not."

"Are you sure?"

"Certainly, this is a counterfeit, and—"

Too late, the prosecutor's voice halted him as Oscar Graves Fox broke in: "And I move you, sir, that that exhibit be impounded by the court and that the persons of John Mitchell, Theodore Horgan, William Hastings *et al* be seized and held in custody by the sheriff pending the drafting of warrants on the complaint sworn to by my client charging conspiracy. And, sir, I further move you that the indictment charging bribe-taking against this defendant be dismissed forthwith, on the ground that he accepted and received no valuable consideration but a piece of fraudulent, worthless paper from the complainants in this action."

"Bang-bang-bang-bang!" resounded the gavel. With glassy eyes, the district attorney shook his head and dropped his arms lifelessly. He was licked and knew it. All motions were granted and the defendant released in custody of counsel.

IN STRUTTING triumph, O. G. Fox led the burly policeman from court.

Mutely, Harrigan turned toward his liberator: "I can't thank you enough, counsellor—"

"Keep your thanks," retorted Fox, tartly. "I had satisfaction enough breaking the back of that snivelling hypocrite of a district attorney."

"I'll never forget it—but I'll never know how you did it."

"I'll tell you because you can't repeat it without going to jail. All I did was to substitute a counterfeit while they were staring at the final surprise witness."

"Geez!" commented the cop, in amazement, "that took nerve. But counsellor,

how could anyone do it? Wasn't that grand marked in evidence, didn't they have serial numbers, the clerk's signature and all that?"

"Of course," commented O. G. Fox, "and didn't I know the numbers weeks ago and didn't I know that clerk's signature and writing of old? Hadn't I been studying that bill from the time you were arrested weeks ago—for I had the right to look at it as often as I liked to prepare my defense.

"All I needed was a reasonably good copy and I got it from 'Scratcher' Schmidt, whom I saved from a long stretch last year.

"Now you ride home in the subway and go down to headquarters tomorrow. You'll be reinstated with back pay in full. I'm hurrying on important business. You can stop in to see me if anything goes wrong.

"I have my fee, one grand, in my inside pocket and I'm taking it to a place where those marks of identification can be bleached right off and the grand salted away until it's forgotten.

"Now get the hell out of here, you dirty crook!" exclaimed the Old Gray Fox.

STATEMENT OF THE OWNERSHIP, MANAGEMENT, CIRCULATION, ETC., REQUIRED BY THE ACT OF CONGRESS OF AUGUST 24, 1912,

Of DIME DETECTIVE MAGAZINE, published monthly at Chicago, Illinois, for December, 1932.

State of New York,
County of New York, ss.

Before me, a notary public in and for the State and county aforesaid, personally appeared Harold S. Goldsmith, who, having been duly sworn according to law, deposes and says that he is the Business Manager of DIME DETECTIVE MAGAZINE and that the following is, to the best of his knowledge and belief, a true statement of the ownership, management (and if a daily paper, the circulation), etc., of the aforesaid publication for the date shown in the above caption, required by the Act of August 24, 1912, embodied in section 411, Postal Laws and Regulations, printed on the reverse of this form, to wit:

1. That the names and addresses of the publisher, editor, managing editor, and business managers are: Publisher, Popular Publications, Inc., 205 East 42nd St., New York City, N. Y.; Editor, Harry Steeger, 205 East 42nd St., New York City, N. Y.; Business Manager, Harold S. Goldsmith, 205 East 42nd St., New York, N. Y.

2. That the owner is: (If owned by a corporation, its name and address must be stated and also immediately thereunder the names and addresses of stockholders owning or holding one per cent or more of total amount of stock. If not owned by a corporation, the names and addresses of the individual owners must be given. If owned by a firm, company, or other unincorporated concern, its name and address, as well as those of each individual member, must be given.)

Popular Publications, Inc., 205 East 42nd St., New York City, N. Y.; Harry Steeger, 205 East 42nd St., New York, N. Y.; Harold S. Goldsmith, 205 East 42nd St., New York, N. Y.

3. That the known bondholders, mortgagees, and other security holders owning or holding 1 per cent or more of total amount of bonds, mortgages, or other securities are: (If there are none, so state.) None.

4. That the two paragraphs next above, giving the names of the owners, stockholders, and security holders, if any, contain not only the list of stockholders and security holders as they appear upon the books of the company but also, in cases where the stockholder or security holder appears upon the books of the company as trustee or in any other fiduciary relation, the name of the person or corporation for whom such trustee is acting, is given; also that the said two paragraphs contain statements embracing affiant's full knowledge and belief as to the circumstances and conditions under which stockholders and security holders who do not appear upon the books of the company as trustees, hold stock and securities in a capacity other than that of a bona fide owner; and this affiant has no reason to believe that any other person, association, or corporation has any interest direct or indirect in the said stock, bonds, or other securities than as so stated by him.

5. That the average number of copies of each issue of this publication sold or distributed, through the mails or otherwise, to paid subscribers during the six months preceding the date shown above is....(This information is required from daily publications only.)

HAROLD S. GOLDSMITH.

Sworn to and subscribed before me this first day of October, 1932.
[SEAL.]

EVELYN P. BAER.
(My commission expires February 16, 1934.

Nobody Knows

• ● •

THERE are plenty of problems hanging fire today to which nobody knows the answers. Predictions and prophecies and guesses are flying thick and fast about everything from politics to what the market's going to do.

But nobody really knows!

And that's why, amid all the uncertainty and doubt, DIME DETECTIVE MAGAZINE feels justifiably proud to consider itself among the few sure things —the few safe bets —that are left to bank on.

We may have had a pretty good idea what would happen at the polls November 8th — but that was about all we had. However, if elections had come a week later on the 15th we could have given out some definite advance information about the day. Not political information but just as exciting in its own way. For the 15th of the month is the new date on which DIME DETECTIVE appears on the newsstands. And predictions, prophecies and guesswork have come to be unnecessary quantities where that great detective-mystery magazine is concerned.

We could have said with certainty—and so could you, if you've become acquainted with DIME DETECTIVE and watched the announcements—that the appearance of the new issue guaranteed page after page of the fastest-moving detective fiction that could be found. It would have meant a safe bet—and safe bets are worth taking these days!

And now just a word about a writer who helped to make this issue the sure-fire thing it is. Mr. Credicott says: "I came to light in St. Paul, 26 years ago and live in Freeport, Il., famous in the past for the Lincoln-Douglas debate, and somewhat infamous (just now) as the scene of Tiffany Thayer's newest novel *Three Sheet.*

"I started to write poetry and fairy tales at the age of ten. The poetry is terrible (and still is). Nothing was more natural than to turn from fairy tales to detective stories.

"In the course of time I spent two years each at both the Illinois and Wisconsin universities. The education didn't take; there were so many interesting books to read I had no time for study."

"Since then I've been writing."

More power to you, Mr. Credicott. Don't stop!

Richard Credicott

"CLOVER"
THE FAMOUS 35 YEAR OLD FLAVOR FORMULA
GIN OR RYE

$1 MAKES 20 QUARTS

(NON-ALCOHOLIC)

NOW you can obtain the very same concentrated RYE or GIN essence that has been used for thirty-five years by hotels and establishments who "Know"! One cellophane sealed, one-ounce package will flavor 5 gallons or 20 delicious quarts. It is absolutely pure, highly concentrated and the results are perfect with that real old "aged in the wood" flavor.

THE DROPPER DOES THE TRICK!

The dropper furnished with each bottle removes all guesswork as to proper proportions, and enables you to make any amount from a pint to 5 gallons, for instant use. Forty drops make one quart. Obtainable at the better drug or food stores or use the coupon below. Satisfaction guaranteed or money refund.

WILLIAM BETSCH COMPANY
"Established 35 Years"
Desk P12, 222 Greenwich St., New York City.
Gentlemen: Enclosed find $1.00 for which send me, postage prepaid, one bottle of the Clover flavor I have checked
☐ RYE ☐ GIN
(Or $2.00 for one bottle of each flavor).

Name ....
Address ....
City............................... State..............

LONESOME?

Let me arrange a romantic correspondence for you. Find yourself a sweetheart thru America's foremost select social correspondence club. A friendship letter society for lonely ladies and gentlemen. Members everywhere; CONFIDENTIAL introductions by letter; efficient, dignified and continuous service. I have made thousands of lonely people happy—why not you? Write for FREE sealed particulars.
EVAN MOORE   BOX 908   JACKSONVILLE, FLORIDA

GIVEN

Simply send name and address

BOTH GIVEN Boys' and Men's six-jewel lever movement Wrist Watch with metal link bracelet or 22 cal. Hamilton Repeater Rifle with magazine holding from 12 to 15 cartridges. Merely give away FREE beautifully colored art pictures with our famous WHITE CLOVERINE SALVE which you sell at 25c per box (giving picture free) and remit as per plan in catalog. Liberal Cash Commissions. Our 37th year. Be first. Offer limited. Write quick for order of salve. Wilson Chem. Co., Dept. 91-K   Tyrone, Pa.

SEND NO MONEY WRITE NOW

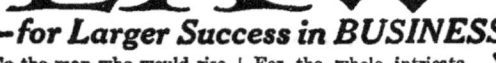

LAW
—for Larger Success in BUSINESS

To the man who would rise to a commanding position in business, a sound and practical knowledge of Law is exceedingly valuable. Among the larger business enterprises, the law-trained man is often preferred for the higher executive positions. Many great corporations—the C. & N. W. Ry., for example, the International Paper Co., the Packard Motor Co., the Mutual Life Insurance Co., the Standard Oil Co. of N. J., the Anaconda Copper Mining Co., the Consolidated Gas Co. of N. Y.—are headed by men of legal training. In the smaller corporations or in one's own business, a knowledge of law spells larger success.

For the whole intricate structure of business is based on LAW. "In looking over the field," writes a prominent Eastern manufacturer, "I find that nearly all the positions commanding a salary of $10,000 or more are filled by men who have studied law." Fit yourself at home, in your spare time, for larger success in business. Full law course leading to degree of LL.B., or shorter Business Law course. LaSalle will guide you step by step. We furnish all text material, including 14-volume Law Library. Low cost, easy terms. Get our valuable 64-page "Law Guide" and "Evidence" books free. Send for them now.

LASALLE EXTENSION UNIVERSITY, Dept. 1281-L   CHICAGO
The World's Largest Business Training Institution

HOW DO YOU "STACK UP" WHEN THE BOYS BEGIN TO ROUGH IT?

I will double your strength... I will add

3 INCHES TO YOUR CHEST   2 INCHES TO YOUR BICEPS

... or it won't cost you one cent!   Signed: GEORGE F. JOWETT

YES SIR! Three inches of muscle added to your chest and 2 inches to each bicep . . or it won't cost you one cent! And I don't mean "cream-puff" muscles either . . you will have real, genuine, sinewy, weight-lifting muscles that will soon make you the "Champ" of your crowd! You will revel in a new feeling of power . . you will have greater courage . . . you will have the will and ability to conquer the world . . . a real he-man's physique that will make your men friends respect you, and women admire you!

I'll teach you all the strong man stunts . . . from wrist turning . . . to hand wrestling . . . I will show you how to tear a pack of cards or a telephone book in half with ease . . . I will also teach you the Four "Key" Bar Bell Lifts!

All I ask is for you to give me a chance to prove it! Take my full course . . If I do not do all I say . . three inches added to your chest . . . 2 inches to each bicep . . . then it won't cost you a penny, and you will be the sole judge of whether or not I have made good!

MY PUPILS HAVE BECOME NATIONAL AND INTERNATIONAL WEIGHT-LIFTING CHAMPIONS

Nothing can take the place of WEIGHT RESISTANCE in the development of a strong body! My system does not depend upon the mere "flexing" of muscles . . . I use disc dumbbells that can be graduated in weight for the reason that no other method can give you strong, supple weight-lifting muscles! By graduating the weight of these dumbbells, from time to time, in a scientific manner, I will quickly develop your muscles and broaden your chest so that the heaviest weight will seem almost as light as a feather to you.

Your Employer Wants a Strong, Healthy, Dependable Man

When you apply for a position, assuming that you have the mental requirements for the job, the first thing that enters your employer's mind is, "has this man a strong, healthy body to do the work I am going to ask him to do—will he be on the job every day?"

Can You Protect Your Women-Folk From Annoyers?

When the "drugstore cowboys" pass remarks as you pass by with your sweetheart or sister, what is your reaction? Are you one of the fellows who is zed up quickly as one to whom they do not hesitate to make remarks? Or can you give them a fearless look, making them realize that you are not a man to be trifled with, and that you can defend yourself if necessary?

How Many Times Can You Chin Yourself?

How often have you been in a gym and envied the fellows who could "chin" themselves 20, 30 or even 40 times? How often have you wished that you could do this or that stunt and do it with ease? I will show you how and it won't be long before the best records of your crowd will be held by you!

Try any one of my test courses NOW . . .

Send for "Moulding a Mighty Arm" A Complete Course for ONLY 25c

It will be a revelation to you. You can't make a mistake. The guaranty of the strongest armed man in the world stands behind this course. I give you all the secrets of strength illustrated and explained as you like them. In 30 days you can get an unbreakable grip of steel and a Herculean arm. Mail your order now while you can still get this course at my introductory price of only 25c.

I will not limit you to the arm. I can develop any part or all of your body. Try any one of my test courses listed at 25c. Or, try all six of them for only $1.00.

Rush the Coupon Today

Mail your order now and I will include a FREE COPY of "NERVES OF STEEL, MUSCLE LIKE IRON." It is a priceless book to the strength fan and muscle builder. Full of pictures of marvelously bodied men who tell you decisively how you can build symmetry and strength the equal of theirs. Reach Out —Grasp This Special Offer.

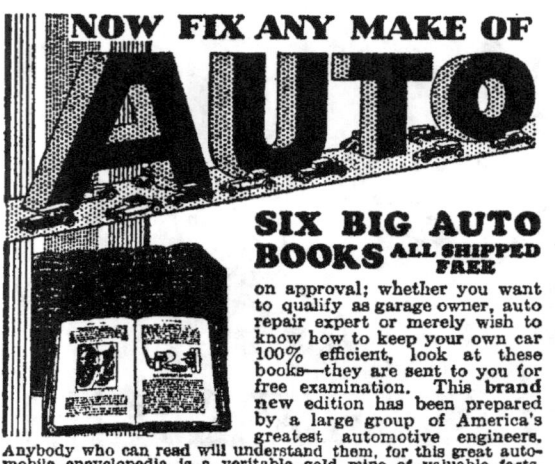

NOW FIX ANY MAKE OF AUTO

SIX BIG AUTO BOOKS ALL SHIPPED FREE

on approval; whether you want to qualify as garage owner, auto repair expert or merely wish to know how to keep your own car 100% efficient, look at these books—they are sent to you for free examination. This brand new edition has been prepared by a large group of America's greatest automotive engineers. Anybody who can read will understand them, for this great automobile encyclopedia is a veritable gold mine of valuable facts. Take advantage of this offer now; send in the coupon for FREE examination. You don't pay us a penny, you don't obligate yourself to pay anything unless you decide to keep the books. Just tell us you want to see them and the full set of 6 great volumes, just off the press, will be sent to you! Read them, look them over and prove to your own satisfaction that one fact alone, which you will find in them, may save you an expensive repair, or help you to a better job.

| Aviation Motors |
| Free Wheeling |
| Synchro-Mesh |
| Outboard Motors |
| Motorcycles |
| Tractors |
| All Fully Covered |

Very Latest Edition

Imagine books which are so new that every page is right up to date—wiring diagrams, construction details, service problems—are all right up to the minute. Nowhere else can you get as complete and up-to-date information. Over a million dollars of resources have enabled us to give you the most authoritative books on the subject ever published. Everybody interested in automobiles in any way will welcome these books published by the world's largest publishers of Technical Cyclopedias (est. 1897) with agencies all over the world.

Can You Fix It?

Can you take out "play" in differential? Can you kill the "shimmy" in steering? Can you reset TIMING? Can you put your finger on engine trouble without guessing or tinkering? Can you pull the starter off and fix it? Can you adjust and repair transmission, engine, rear axle, bearings?

These Books Tell How

and tell you how to do any and every auto job right, the first time.

6 Big Volumes

Nearly 3,000 pages, over 2,000 illustrations, wiring diagrams, equipment charts, etc. De Luxe edition with gold-stamped flexible binding. Sent FREE for 10 days' use. If not wanted return express collect. If kept, send only $2.00 after 10 days, then $3.00 a month until the special advertising price, $24.80, is paid.

A Year's Consulting Membership FREE!

Privilege of consulting engineers of million-dollar American Technical Society on any automotive problem for one year without charge, if you mail coupon immediately.

EXTRA STRONG IMPROVED MODEL COPPER BOILER

Catalog Free

SAVE 20% NOW!

Most Practical Boiler & Cooker

Made with large 5-inch Improved Cap and Spout. Safe, practical and simple. Nothing to get out of order, most substantial and durable on the market. Will last a lifetime, gives real service and satisfaction.

Easily Cleaned

Cap removed in a second; no burning of hands. An ideal low pressure boiler and pasteurizer for home and farm.

SOLID CAST NO SCREW TOP

HEAVY COPPER

5 Gallon	$6.50
7	8.85
10	11.90
15	14.20
20	18.50
25	22.50
30	27.50

Save 20% by ordering direct from factory. No article of such high quality and utility ever sold at such a seasonably low prices. Prices quoted are cash with order or one-fourth cash, balance C. O. D. Send check or money order. Prompt shipment made in plain strong box. The only boiler worth having. Large Catalog Free.

HOME MANUFACTURING CO.
Dept. 528
18 E. Kinzie St.
Chicago, Illinois

A Baby In Your Home

Scientists now state that "Complete unity in life depends on sex harmony" and that the lack of it is the one greatest cause for unhappy marriages. Also that every woman "has the capacity for sex expression" but too often she is undeveloped or suffering with general female disorders, which rob her of her normal desires. During an experience of more than 35 years specializing in the treatment of diseases peculiar to women, I developed a simple home treatment which has brought new hope, health and happiness to many thousands. Many who had been childless for years became proud and happy Mothers. Husbands have written me the most glowing letters of gratitude and now I want every woman who is run-down or suffering from female disorders to learn about this splendid treatment, and how she may use it in the privacy of her own home.

Get This Knowledge FREE

In my two books "Full Development" and "A Baby In Your Home," I intimately discuss many important subjects relating to the female sex that are vitally interesting to every woman. They tell how you too may combat your troubles as thousands of others have and often again enjoy the desires and activities of Nature's most wonderful creation—a normal, fully developed vigorous woman. I will gladly send both books postpaid free. Write today. DR. H. WILL ELDERS, Suite 467N. 7th and Felix Streets, St. Joseph, Mo.

126

www.ingramcontent.com/pod-product-compliance
Lightning Source LLC
Chambersburg PA
CBHW080911020726
47502CB00008B/2423